MALICE AND REMORSE

ZACHARY M. GARD

iUniverse, Inc.
Bloomington

Malice and Remorse

iUniverse books may be ordered through booksellers or by contacting:

iUniverse
1663 Liberty Drive
Bloomington, IN 47403
www.iuniverse.com
1-800-Authors (1-800-288-4677)

ISBN: 978-1-4620-0688-5 (sc)
ISBN: 978-1-4620-0678-6 (hc)
ISBN: 978-1-4620-0689-2 (ebk)

Library of Congress Control Number: 2011904272

Printed in the United States of America

iUniverse rev. date: 05/13/2011

Love: the greatest mystery of the heart, soul, and mind; it will make you do things you never would have done previously. Many people spend their entire lives wondering if it exists and attempting to find out. Most come to the conclusion, after several broken relationships, that it is, in fact, nonexistent. However, this is because no great mystery can be easily revealed. If it were, then what would make this occasion, this state of mind, so great and magnificent? Or is it magnificent at all? Is something magnificent if it can cause us to feel crazed—crazy enough to kill?

Prologue

A Rude Awakening

Mr. Sanderson, a man in his mid-thirties, walked along on the curb that separated the city street and the green grass yard of his house. He was a tall man, well over six feet in height, and slightly overweight. He still had a full head of brown hair and a thick mustache to match. Jack Gardner, a child who could not have been more than ten years old, accompanied him. Jack was a very small child, smaller than most his age. Jack was a friend of the family. They were both carrying fishing poles, having just returned unexpectedly early from what was supposed to have been a pleasant fishing trip with a father, his son, and a young friend of the family. They had to postpone the trip as the weather had suddenly gone bad.

Dragging many yards behind was Craig Sanderson. Although they were the same age, Craig appeared to be much older than Jack. He was at least a foot taller and was more mature looking. He moderately resembled his father, who had now walked much farther ahead of his son. The two boys had been forced to hang out with each often over the last several years, despite the fact that they didn't get along. This tension was likely brought on by jealousy from Craig. Mr. Sanderson often paid more attention to Jack than to Craig. It was for this reason that he was dragging far behind the other two and had now decided to take a seat on the curb along the sidewalk while the other two went on towards the house without him.

The house was a solid red brick house, just like many others found in the outskirts of Manhattan, in New York City. The house was two stories but nothing overly elegant. A wooden banister hung out from the edge of the house on the second story. A short cement driveway led to a double-car garage that was just to the right of the house while still connected. Surrounding the house were large oak trees, many of which hung over the roof of the house. The sun, which had been very bright just an hour ago, had now disappeared behind thick clouds, and the sky looked like it was nearing rain. The trees swayed in the light breeze.

As Mr. Sanderson walked closer to his house and up the driveway, he noticed something unusual. A fancy car, one that he had never seen before, was sitting in the middle of the driveway. "Did your mom get a new car?" he asked Jack.

"No," Jack replied.

"Strange," Mr. Sanderson responded as he walked inside the garage, which was open. He walked past his own not-quite-so impressive car to the door that connected the garage to the inside of the house. The door opened into a hardwood-floor hallway. The two of them walked slowly down the hallway, neither of them knowing what to expect. It wasn't usual for his family to have visitors. He was not scared, but he took precautions nevertheless.

They passed a small room on the left, which was the family dining room. It had a large wooden table placed in the center that almost took up the entire room. Chairs were tightly squeezed between the white walls and the table, making it look as though there wasn't enough room for someone to sit at the table.

As they continued to move through the house, a staircase led down to the basement straight ahead and the kitchen was to the right. Mr. Sanderson turned into the kitchen and Jack followed closely behind, not unlike a puppy on a leash. On the other side of the kitchen was a door that led to the main part of the house. For the most part the kitchen was pretty standard. There was a refrigerator, oven, microwave, stovetop, and everything else one would expect to see in a kitchen. The only things that stood out from the ordinary were two very unique knives that Jack had become transfixed upon. They were not in drawers or in a knife rack like normal knives, but rather hanging on the walls horizontally, much like one would expect swords to be displayed.

Mr. Sanderson continued on and walked out of the kitchen, but Jack continued to stare at the knives. They were the same size, both about a foot in length. They had thick black handles with ridges spiraling down them. The large blade started out very thick toward the base and stayed just as thick until the very end where a perfect triangle of metal was formed, creating a sharp point. Along both sides of the knives, the blades had deep ridges, each ridge forming its own point so that five deep, sharp points were on each side. Jack stood under these knives as he looked up to them. They were just out of reach, but he was sure he could climb onto the counter to get a better look at them if he wanted.

Jack's attention was drawn away from the knives as fear grasped his every emotion. A loud scream of rage had come from Mr. Sanderson, and Jack ran over to see what the commotion was about. He ran out of the kitchen and looked to his left where he saw the back of Mr. Sanderson standing in a doorway to a bedroom.

"What the hell is this?" Mr. Sanderson shrieked. Jack heard a woman speak but could not understand what she had said. He walked over to where the man was standing to see what was going on in the room. He peeked around Mr. Sanderson and saw Mrs. Sanderson, an attractive woman with jet-black hair, balled up in the corner of the bedroom with the bed sheets covering her naked body. Still sitting on the bed, now putting on his clothes, was a man that only Mrs. Sanderson knew. He was calmly putting on his clothes as if nothing was wrong. Jack could tell he was the type of rich bastard who thought he was better than the world. On the other hand, Mrs. Sanderson continued to cry and apologize.

"I'm gonna kill both of you!" Mr. Sanderson screamed in such rage that his wife let out a squeal of fright.

"Please calm down! Think about what you're doing!" Mrs. Sanderson pleaded with a mixture of shrieks that were interrupted by her hysterical cries.

"I'm going to get my knife, and then the two of you can live happily ever after in the ground!" Mr. Sanderson turned around quickly, running directly into Jack, who was still behind him. The boy went tumbling down, straight into a glass table, shattering it in the process. Mr. Sanderson also tripped, bringing him down to the ground. At this moment, the stranger jumped from the bed onto Mr. Sanderson, and a brawl broke out between them.

Jack immediately got to his feet and ran into the kitchen. Blood was now dripping down his face, and a piece of glass stuck under his left eye. He climbed on top of the counter and grabbed both knives, hiding them in a cabinet under the sink where they would not be seen for quite some time. He called the police and quickly ran outside where it was now pouring rain.

Everyone wound up unharmed physically that day due to Jack's action, except for a very distinct scar under his left eye from the glass. Jack would never forget the look in Mr. Sanderson's eyes when he found out the sacred laws of marriage had been broken, and the woman he had dedicated his life to had betrayed him in a way that could never be forgiven. The look—a mix between hatred and heartbreak—would stick with Jack the rest of his life, and he vowed he would never go through the same thing. For he knew, from a single glimpse of Mr. Sanderson's eyes, that Mr. Sanderson was going to kill the new couple; there was no uncertainty about it.

Craig Sanderson had remained outside in the rain during the whole ordeal. He was now completely soaked, and water dripped down his face. He couldn't believe his dad had left him out in the rain that whole time, without showing any concern for his only son. Craig was completely oblivious to the terrible events that had just gone on in the house and would not find out about the infidelity of his mother, at least not for a very long time.

The officer turned the page.

Chapter 1

The Trial Begins

"All rise! The honorable Judge Chadsworth Black presiding! The court is now in session," the bailiff bellowed throughout the courtroom. It was a cold, dark, windy day and Jack Gardner looked out of the side window in despair, staring at the complacent clouds as they appeared to be motionless. The clouds seemed to be transfixed in a single location, and they appeared destined for rain.

Jack sat still in the courtroom audience benches, thinking about that day, that one dreadful day three months ago when his Melanie had been taken from him so brutally. As Jack stared out the side window of the courtroom, he pictured his deceased wife, her golden blonde hair, and her green eyes. She was a decently pretty girl. She was usually friendly and outgoing, but she just as quickly felt she was being attacked by the world. She had been taken advantage of by many guys in her past, which changed her life significantly. She was always on her guard and wasn't quick to let anyone close to her heart. Jack truly had been the first man with whom she was able to let her guard down. With every other guy, she was a pessimistic girl who believed the world was out to get her—believed the world was cold at heart. Her murder showed how very right she was.

"Mr. Craig Sanderson, you are being charged by the state of New York with the crime of first-degree murder," said Judge Black, a tall, light-skinned, good-looking male who appeared to be fairly young for a judge. The voice of the judge brought Jack back to reality. As Jack looked around the courtroom, he noticed that he was not the only one staring at Craig with hatred. It seemed everyone in the courtroom had his or her eyes fixed directly on him with the same look. Even as Judge Black spoke, he stared at Craig with a certain look of disdain. Jack glanced at some of the witnesses and audience members sitting around him and wondered what they must be thinking ... *It wasn't enough to just murder that poor girl, but this bastard disgraced and humiliated her ... He used his authority to take away all means of dignity that she had ... What kind of a man would do such a terrible thing?* Well, it didn't matter what they thought because Jack knew that justice would be served.

Jack observed the courtroom some more as the judge spoke. The walls and ceiling were painted a perfect white, while the floor was a carpeted gray. A solid mahogany fence separated the audience and witnesses from the area where the actual proceeding was taking place. The audience seats were benches, much like pews inside a church. Two sides of rows of benches were separated by the aisle running from the entrance down the middle of the room. The entrance was large wooden doors that swung outward. To the left, inside the fence, were twelve comfortable seats, sectioned off by a wooden fence rectangle, which were designated for the jurors. In the middle of the section was the judge stand, which was equipped with a large black leather chair. On the right of the stand was an American flag, and on the left was the New York state flag. To the right of the stand was also a smaller stand for the witnesses to testify from.

Although Jack dreaded having to sit in the courtroom, he couldn't wait for Craig to finally get what he deserved. Jack and Craig had known each other most of their lives. They had gone to school together from the time they were in kindergarten. They knew each other, but they were never exactly friends. They had been forced to hang out together occasionally because their parents were, at a time, close friends. However, Jack and Craig never talked despite their parents' efforts to make them best friends. Then unexpectedly, they became friends their sophomore year in college and from then on had become inseparable. Neither of them could remember how they had become friends, but never before had two friends become so close so quickly. They did everything together although they were nothing alike.

Appearance-wise, Jack was about five feet, ten inches with a medium build, dark brown hair, and light eyes. It was hard to tell exactly what color his eyes were or how to explain them. If forced to place a color upon them, most people would say they were somewhat of an emerald green. He also had a very distinct scar under his left eye. He enjoyed having this scar because he felt it made him stand out from the crowd.

Craig was much taller. He was about six feet, four inches tall with much lighter brown hair and brown eyes. He had nice facial features and was considered very attractive by the female species. In fact, so was Jack. They often were in competition for the most desirable girls in college. However, eventually they both came to desire only one.

Personality-wise, they were complete opposites as well. Craig was the kid who was always getting into trouble. All of his life he had been getting into messes, and now it was Jack who balanced him out. Ever since they had become friends, Jack was always there for him, to take the blame if necessary. Everyone knew Jack to be a stand-up guy. He eventually grew to be a well-respected and successful lawyer, while Craig struggled through college to find his place in life.

* * * * * * * * * *

"How's that economics class coming along for you, Craig?" Jack asked while the two walked along the college campus toward their home just blocks away. All around them were full, green trees as they walked along the gravel paths leading through the school.

"Eh, I don't know, man. I've been busy lately," Craig replied.

"Have you been going to class?"

"I try, Jack. I've just had a lot of things going on in my life lately."

"There's no excuse!" Jack snapped. "You have to go to class, and you have to try harder."

"I know, I know."

"These are the most important days of your life," Jack continued to lecture. "The knowledge you get now will determine your job and the rest of your life." Jack hated to sound like a parent, but it was necessary. When Craig was a preteen, his parents had gone through a nasty divorce. Both parents decided they wanted to live nowhere near each other, so joint custody was impossible. Craig was forced to choose between his mother and his father. A decision like this could tear a child up. How could he possibly choose between his parents? At that age, or any age, choosing a parent is like saying you love one more than the other. After the divorce, nothing was the same for Craig. He stopped caring about his life. He stopped listening to his parents, or parent as it were. He had chosen to live with his mom, who had stayed in New York. He chose her mainly because he wanted to remain close to home, as his father was moving to California. This probably wasn't a smart decision on Craig's part, seeing as his mom was an unfit parent to say the least. His dad was the opposite of her, not completely in a positive way, however. He was extremely strict, and often too hard on Craig. But at least he cared about him; at least he would have been there to raise him. His mother didn't know how to raise a child. She was too busy with the two things she loved most in her life: her new boyfriend and whatever bottle of liquor she could get her hands on. Craig didn't know why they had gotten a divorce. All he knew was that his dad moved to California in order to stay as far away from his ex-wife as possible.

It took Craig a long time, but at the age of twenty he seemed to be over the divorce and had put all of his trust in one person: Jack Gardner. Now, five years later, Jack stared at his former best friend with complete disdain. Craig had known how much Jack was in love with Melanie. After all, they had gotten married only weeks before she was murdered. He stared at Craig now, locked up in shackles in an orange jumpsuit, just as he deserved. Jack wished he could make Craig feel the way he did. He wished it were possible to strip away everything that Craig had. Well, maybe, perhaps it was.

* * * * * * * * * *

"Will the prosecution make its opening statement?" Judge Black said.

Cynthia Miller, a medium-height woman with long blonde hair pulled back into a tight bun, stood up from the prosecution stand and walked over to face the jury. She was a very attractive woman and held herself extremely professional. She wore glasses on her face, making her look even more professional and intelligent. She wore pinstriped pants and a matching blazer.

"Ladies and gentlemen of the jury," she began. "This case is quite simple. The defendant is being charged with first-degree murder, meaning simply that the murder, in this case of Melanie Stole Gardner, was premeditated. The defendant had planned the murder before the act occurred. He was completely knowledgeable about what he was doing and was quite aware of the damage he was causing. The murder was completed with malice and pure hatred. The evidence you will hear throughout the trial, as well as the witnesses you will hear testify, will prove far beyond a reasonable doubt that the defendant is guilty."

Ms. Miller continued on for a while, pacing back and forth in front of the jury as she talked, and they listened attentively. Jack, on the other hand, was uninterested. After all, he knew the whole story; he had been there when it had happened. The last thing he wanted to do was relive the terror that occurred that day. The only reason he even attended the trial was because he was subpoenaed by the court as a witness. "This man not only killed an innocent young woman, but degraded her in the worst way possible," Ms. Miller continued. "He raped that young woman, brutally and forcefully. The way he did it was so horrific that one must come to the conclusion that this killer has no heart at all. For you, the jury, to let this man go free would be a crime in itself, not only to the victim but to everyone who was affected by this heinous act of violence."

The attorney returned to her stand and sipped from a glass of water. She showed no expression—she was too professional for that. However, it was clear she was pleased with herself. Clearly she had experience attempting to convict the accused. But it wasn't an easy task to be an attorney. After all, the details of a case must be presented in enough precision to inform the jury but not in so much detail that the jurors got lost. Also prosecutors constantly wrestled with the very difficult moral issue of convicting someone who could be innocent. It took a certain type of person to plunge forward and take the risk of an innocent man receiving life in prison or the death penalty.

"Very well," the judge said. "Would the defense make its opening statement?"

"Yes, your honor," said the attorney representing the defendant.

After rising, it was clear that the attorney was fairly tall, a couple inches over six feet. He had medium-length, wavy brown hair that seemed to stick up all over the place. He appeared to be in his late twenties, and he didn't appear to be as professional-looking as the other attorney. His wavy hair looked unkempt, and his tie was a bit off-center. Truth of the matter was that he had been assigned by the state to represent Craig Sanderson because Craig could not afford an attorney. Naturally, when the state was paying for the attorneys, there was the chance that they were either incompetent or unmotivated. You couldn't necessarily blame the attorneys. They were going to be paid the same amount whether they won or lost the case, so where was the motivation in that? But the moral issue remained. It came down to whether an attorney could sleep at night if an innocent client was sentenced to prison or death because of a lack of effort on their part.

The defense attorney, Joseph West, was not someone to lie down on the job. However, at first, this case seemed to be far too simple. Joseph West had been certain that his client was guilty of the crime he was charged with. In fact, everyone knew it. All of the evidence pointed directly at

Craig, and West felt that no matter what he did, his client would not have the option of going to prison. No, instead he would receive the death penalty. It was for this reason that West had originally not cared about the case. He could still remember the first time he had met Craig Sanderson.

A month before the trial, he had gone to Rikers Island Prison on a scheduled date in order to talk to his client. Rikers Island, located on an island in the East River between Queens and the Bronx, was one of New York City's largest jail facilities and was used to hold prisoners awaiting trial or transfer to another facility. West wanted to confer with Craig and determine what their defense would be.

"Hi, Craig, I'm your attorney, Joseph West," Joseph said from behind the protective glass separating the two. Prison officials wouldn't allow an accused murderer and rapist like Craig to come in contact with anyone without the proper restraints and protection.

"I didn't kill anyone," Craig mumbled in a low voice.

"All right, just hold on, and let's go slow. I didn't accuse you of anything."

"But do you believe me?" Craig questioned.

"Well, Craig ... I haven't heard your side of the story yet," West replied.

Craig cracked a devious looking smile and gave a little chuckle. "I knew you wouldn't believe me."

"Yeah, well, whether I believe you or not, I have to defend you. It's what I get paid to do."

"No, no, no. That's no good," Craig said while shaking his head. "You can't defend someone unless you truly believe them. I might not know a lot, but I know that much."

"All right," said Mr. West. "Why don't you tell me your side of the story, and I'll agree to keep an open mind?"

"Fine," said Craig. "First of all, let me start out by saying that I would never have hurt Melanie in any way." However, Craig Sanderson did currently look like the criminal type. His head was now shaven, no longer showing the attractive brown hair he once had. He looked much older now, with a scruffy beard that looked like he hadn't shaven for a week. He definitely looked as though he was the killer type, never giving a smile. "Melanie was a close friend of mine, very close. Not to mention her husband, Jack, was like a brother to me. I would never even think about causing him grief."

"Unfortunately, that's a typical response," replied West. "Why don't you just tell me where you were on the night of October the twenty-fourth?"

"That's the thing, I was at the airport," Craig answered.

"What were you doing at the airport?"

"What do you think I was doing? I had a flight."

"And I suppose it's just coincidence that you were flying on the same day she was murdered?" West interrogated.

"Yeah, I suppose so. I had to go to my mom's funeral in Denver."

"I thought your mom lived here in New York?" West asked curiously.

"She did," Craig said. "But, she and her husband moved to Denver about a year ago."

"I see, and what happened to your mother?"

"What do you mean, what happened?"

"How did your mother die?"

"I'm not sure, all right," Craig said, getting more irritated. "My mom died from a stab wound in the heart."

"So they assume it was murder? " West questioned. "Were there any suspects?"

"The only suspect was her husband, David, but he was found dead in the same room as my mom."

"How did he die?"

"Look, I really don't want to talk about it anymore!" Craig said angrily.

West was much more interested in the case after his first meeting with Craig. He hadn't heard about the death of Craig's mother and the death of her husband, which made the case more intriguing. West wondered why he hadn't heard of it. Perhaps he really wasn't doing his job, West thought. At that moment, he decided to look more deeply into Craig Sanderson's life.

Mr. West took his position in front of the jury. "Ladies and gentlemen of the jury," he began. "The prosecution has attempted to make my client out to be a beast. However, my client did not commit, nor have anything to do with, the rape and murder of Melanie Stole Gardner. The prosecution claims the evidence points at the defendant, but where is the motive? No one has suggested a reason why the defendant would want this woman dead. The worst thing you as a jury could do would be to put an innocent man in prison or put him to death. And that is what you would be doing if you find the defendant guilty. Melanie and Craig were friends; they had been for a long time. The last thing Melanie would want would be for you to sentence her friend to a horrible, unjust fate."

"If you don't find him guilty, I'll kill that bastard myself!" screamed a woman through hateful tears. Jack recognized her as Melanie's mother. The whole court was shocked.

"Bailiff, remove her!" ordered the judge. The bailiff, a muscular, tall, black man, escorted the grieving woman out of the courtroom. She resisted at first and again screamed at Craig, although it was difficult to understand what she was saying. The court adjourned for the day.

Joseph West went back to his home that night and thought over all of the information he had learned so far about his client. He may not have completely believed Craig yet, but he certainly wasn't positive of his guilt. He did a background check on Craig's life and family the night after he had met Craig in prison, the night he had learned about the horrific death of Craig's mother.

What West had learned through his research of the case was that Craig's mother was stabbed in the heart, just like Melanie Gardner. The wounds presented in the autopsy report looked exactly the same for both Craig's mother and Melanie and were both very distinct wounds. This could mean only one thing: the knife that was used in each murder was unique and was either the same knife used or at least a virtually identical one. There had to be a connection, and Craig was the only connection that seemed to fit. West didn't know how he would get the jury to see otherwise.

With further research into Craig's mother's case, West learned quite a few things. Number one: Mr. and Mrs. Sanderson had been divorced long ago with the cause being infidelity. Mr. Sanderson had demanded the divorce after catching his former wife with another man, the same man she had been with ever since—David Cooper. West didn't bother to look too deeply into David Cooper's life. After all, what possible relevance could he have to the case? No, all that mattered was the reason, the motive.

Number two: Craig's mother and David Cooper had indeed moved into a house in Colorado a year ago like Craig had said. The police report that was filed showed that the murder scene, the bedroom the two shared, was a mess. Furniture had been knocked over, and glasses and dishes shattered on the floor. Craig's mother had bruises, cuts, and strangle marks all over her body. It seemed by the mess and markings that a fight had broken out between the two. The markings showed that David had beaten her, and then apparently had stabbed her in the chest. A knife was still in David's dead hand: however, curiously the knife did not match the stab wound on her chest. The stab wound was very distinct. It must have come from a very unique knife, certainly not the one in David Cooper's hand. David had been found dead, bloody alongside Craig's mother. He had been shot in the head and died almost instantly.

Craig's mother was found with a handgun near her body. Friends of Cooper confirmed that they were aware that David owned a gun and recognized the one near her body as David's. She likely bled to death on the floor, unable to move from her stab wound. She died curled up in a ball in the corner of the room. It was reported as a double homicide in which they took each other's lives; both also had extremely high blood-alcohol content levels.

* * * * * * * * * *

After the first day of the trial, Jack Gardner went back to his large, elegant home in Long Island, New York. His house was three stories tall with a very opulent look to it. The house was white with four large column pillars outside the front door making it vaguely resemble the White House. It was still the kind of house you drove by and thought someone important had to live there. On the inside, it was just as spectacular. A spiral staircase led to the upstairs, which ended with a banister leading over the living room, which framed a hallway to the many different rooms and sections of the house.

He sat down on his large, comfortable leather couch and took off his glasses, placing them on the glass table in front of him. He touched both sides of the glass table four times before leaning back into his couch and relaxing. He looked around his house at all his possessions he had earned: his luxurious house, his big-screen television, everything he had. Indeed, he had earned them with all of his hard work in school. Yes, he deserved everything he had, but somehow all of his possessions seemed empty without his Melanie to enjoy them with. It was as though everything in his life was better with her in it, and now without her, everything seemed less fulfilling.

"Hi, Jack. How was the trial today?" came a soft voice that had just entered the room he was occupying.

"Oh. Hey, Brianne. It was fine, nothing exciting." Brianne was a girl Jack had recently started seeing since Melanie had been murdered.

Although Jack was amused by Brianne, he loved Melanie, and she had and always would be his one and only. Brianne was merely a substitute.

She was a very attractive girl. It was a wonder to Jack that she wasn't a model; she was absolutely gorgeous. She was about five feet, five inches tall with brown hair and the deepest brown eyes he ever saw. They alone would have made Jack fall in love with her if he hadn't been enslaved to Melanie's love. Brianne had a perfect nose and lips, with the most stunning smile Jack had ever seen. Her skin was tan and seemed to glow in absolute perfection. However, Jack didn't care about any of this. He was reminded of this every time he looked at his wedding ring. The similar ring he had given Melanie, which had been found at the crime scene, right next to Melanie's body on the night of the murder. The police had no idea why or how the ring had come off. Craig clearly must have taken it off; perhaps he was jealous.

Jack was at the crime scene; however, he had not been in the room to witness what had happened to the ring. He had been in the next room, helpless, nearly bleeding to death. Brianne had no idea about the real nature of the trial. Jack had told her he was attending it because he had witnessed a robbery, and Brianne believed him. Why wouldn't she? She had no reason not to. Luckily for Jack, Brianne did not like going to the courthouse since serving several days as a juror for a drunk-driving case. Jack didn't tell her the truth because he didn't want to worry her with what had happened to Melanie. Perhaps it would make him less appealing, and Jack liked having her around. It made him feel less alone.

"Are you tired?" Brianne asked.

"Not too tired."

"Meet me in the bedroom in ten minutes?"

"Count on it."

Jack drank down a couple of glasses of whiskey before entering the bedroom and closing the doors behind him, even though no one else was in the large home.

Chapter 2

Strangers Become Lovers

College for Craig and Jack was fairly typical. Their days and nights revolved around studying, partying, and sleeping—a continuous cycle.

"You ready for this party, man?" Craig said with a big grin as they sat in their small, two-bedroom house, anticipating a big Saturday night.

"You know it," replied Jack. "I'm looking to get a girl tonight."

"Ha ha. Don't get your hopes up, Jack. You haven't really been pulling them down lately."

"Yeah, well, I'm in a slump. Not everyone can always be as good with the ladies as you."

"Lord knows that's true," Craig said, and they both laughed together. "Do I feel another bet coming on?"

"I thought you would never ask."

"All right, so what's it going to be this time?"

"I'll pick the girl, we both get our fair share of time to talk to her, and whoever gets furthest with her by the end of the night wins," Jack suggested.

"You always get to pick the girl. It's my turn this time."

"All right, fine."

"I know this one girl who will be there, I'm pretty sure we can both get as far as we want if you know what I mean." Craig said.

"Great, you're trying to hook me up with a prostitute?" Jack laughed.

"Not a prostitute," Craig replied, "just a girl who likes to have a good time."

"What's her name?"

"Melanie Stole. She's in one of my classes."

"Okay, fine," Jack said. You get to talk to her for a while, and then you have to agree to introduce me, and we'll see who comes out on top at the end of the night."

"Or bottom," Craig said with a smile.

They walked down the street a couple of blocks to the house hosting the party. Most of the houses around campus were occupied by kids who went to the school, so parties were a frequent occasion. Craig and Jack walked up to the house that was flooded with people coming and going. Many kids were on the front yard drinking beer and smoking cigarettes and marijuana. The two friends walked up the front steps to the front door that was already open. They could hear music blasting from within the house, raising Craig's and Jack's adrenalin levels. The house wasn't particularly spacious, making the place appear to be even more crowded. They had a hard time walking through the house, as there was hardly enough room to move throughout the crowd. Everyone was taking shots left and right and talking in drunken tongues. "Hey, Jack!" someone called, clearly drunk.

"Hey, um ... What's up?" Jack knew the kid was in one of his classes, but he could not remember his name.

"The keg's in the back, man!" the drunken idiot shouted.

"All right, thanks. I'll talk to you later."

Craig and Jack both walked outside to the backyard and stood in the back of the line of people waiting to get to the keg. When they reached the front of the line they both filled their plastic cups with beer. Craig finished drinking it no more than ten seconds after it was filled. He refilled the cup.

"You'd better slow down, Craig. I'm not taking care of your ass again if you black out, drunk," Jack said.

"Relax! I know my limit," Craig said excitedly.

Craig continued to throw down beer after beer throughout the night while Jack refrained from drinking, as he knew Craig would be in need of his help later on in the night. A couple of hours went by before Jack received any excitement.

"Oh no! I'm sorry!" came a soft voice from behind Jack. Jack turned around and saw that a blonde girl had bumped into him and spilled her beer all over him. Jack would have been mad if it had been someone else who had spilled on him, but it was very difficult for Jack to have any feelings of anger when it came to a female.

"Oh, don't worry about it," replied Jack in as nice and friendly of a voice as he could.

"No, I feel terrible," said the girl.

"Really, it's okay," Jack assured her.

"Melanie!" Craig said as he stumbled over toward her and Jack.

"Whoa! Take it easy, Craig," Melanie replied. "Had a little too much to drink, have you?"

"No, not at all. I'm perfectly sober!" But his behavior suggested otherwise.

"He's been drinking nonstop for a couple hours now," Jack said.

"Oh, wow. Well, I hope he's all right." Melanie sounded worried.

"Yeah, he'll be fine."

"I'm going to go get some more beer!" Craig yelled and ran off after the keg.

"Don't you think you should stop him?" Melanie asked.

"No, trust me, it will be no use. He won't listen to anyone once he starts drinking, and he'll be just fine."

"So what's your name?" Melanie asked.

"Jack Gardner, and yours?"

"I'm Melanie Stole."

"Well, it's nice to meet you, Melanie Stole."

"Likewise."

"Hey, um I have to go to my house really quick to pick up my car for something. Would you like to go with me?" Jack asked.

"Sure, I suppose. If we're going to pick up your car then how are we getting to your house?"

"My house is only a couple of blocks away, so it won't be a long walk."

"If your house is so close then what do you need your car for?" Melanie asked.

"You'll see."

"Well, all right then," said Melanie. "Let's go."

Jack and Melanie walked along the street that was deserted since it was nearing midnight. It was a cloudy night. Although the stars weren't shining brightly, and there was no moon in the sky, it was still a very peaceful setting. The branches of the many trees on the side of the road swayed in the light but cool breeze. Jack looked at Melanie, and he had to admit that Craig was right. She seemed like the kind of girl that Jack could easily score with if he wanted. She was wearing a short jean skirt and a tight tank top.

Jack had always been able to talk to women and had always been pretty good at it. He had charmed many girls into relationships in the past, even though none of them had exactly worked out.

"So how long have you known Craig?" Melanie asked.

"Well, me and him go back a while. Our parents were really close when we were young, so we sort of grew up together," Jack replied.

"Oh, so you're good friends?"

"Yeah, we are now. We weren't really friends at all back then, though. Our parents tried hard to make us friends, but we never clicked. We pretty much hated each other actually."

"So how did you become friends and both end up staying in New York then?"

"Well, Craig's parents went through a divorce when we were ten, and he stayed with his mom here in New York. The fact that we ended up at the same college was just a coincidence. I didn't even know he was going to Hofstra until I ran into him sophomore year."

"Oh, really?"

"Yeah, it's really quite amazing that Craig even got into college with everything he had to go through."

"What do you mean by that?" Melanie asked curiously as they continued to walk closer to Jack and Craig's house.

"Well, to be honest, his mom is a complete alcoholic. All throughout his teenage years he had to watch his mother drown herself in liquor while getting beat by her boyfriend to make it worse."

"Oh my God!" Melanie said with a gasp. "I thought your parents were friends with his."

"Yeah, well the alcoholism didn't start until around the time of Craig's parents' divorce. Once the divorce happened, our parents stopped talking completely. Craig used to tell me that he would sleep in his backyard rather than take the abuse he got from them. They didn't notice he was gone anyways. Amazingly, he was able to get through high school and into college, even with all that bullshit going on."

"That's terrible, what he had to go through." She sighed.

"Yeah, but it made the kid tougher than bricks. Look, don't tell anyone anything about Craig. I'm the only one who really knows his history, and he's very personal. He hasn't really trusted anyone in this world except me lately. I can't even believe I told you."

"It's okay, Jack, you can trust me."

Jack didn't know what it was. He definitely wasn't accustomed to trusting females anymore, but he felt he could trust Melanie with anything, despite the fact he had met her less than an hour earlier. It was just something in her eyes, a certain innocence. They almost began to tear as Jack told the story about Craig's life. You could see the water building up, making her green eyes look even brighter than usual.

Before Jack knew it, they were back at his house. "Hold on, let me just go get the car real quick." Jack ran inside the small two-bedroom house, and moments later the garage door opened. Jack backed out the small two-door coupe, telling Melanie to get in. The drive back was much faster than the walk to the house, and they were back in no time.

"Why did we need the car again?" Melanie asked.

"You'll see very soon," he replied. Jack parked the car across the street from where the party was, and they both walked over to the house. No people were outside in the front yard anymore, and it appeared that the majority of the people had gone home.

"It looks like the party is pretty much over," Melanie said as they entered the house. However, as they entered the kitchen it was apparent that there were still the extreme drinkers doing what they did best. All of them were still throwing down shots of liquor and drinking beer, despite the fact that it was almost one o'clock in the morning.

"Hey, Jack! Where have you been?" It was the drunken idiot from earlier in the night. "Want a shot?"

"Yeah, just save it for me. I'll come get it in a little while," Jack replied. "Do you know where Craig is?"

"Oh, yeah, he's just taking a nap!" the idiot stammered, clearly talking much louder than necessary due to the alcohol.

"Taking a nap, where?"

"Oh, um ... over in the bathroom."

"Great," Jack said while walking over to the bathroom.

Jack opened the door and saw his best friend lying face down on the bathroom floor with all of his clothes off except for his underwear. Craig seemed to be completely motionless. His legs were spread a part while his arms were around the base of the toilet, almost as though he was hugging it. His face was burrowed into the base of the toilet, and Jack immediately rolled him over.

"Craig. Craig, are you all right?" Jack said trying to wake him up while slightly slapping him on the cheek. Craig's head rolled around as if there was no life in him. Jack tilted Craig's head and noticed that Craig's eyes were nearly shut and had rolled back into his head. "Why the hell are his clothes off?" Jack asked.

"He was running around taking them off," one of the partiers said.

"Yeah, it was pretty hot in here," one of the guys said while they all chuckled.

Jack tried to lift Craig up, which was very difficult as Craig's head snapped back and hung down as if it was the weight of a bowling ball. Jack carried him, still unclothed, out of the bathroom and out of the house even though it was a great struggle. Craig had thrown up all over himself and had even been lying in a mess of his own vomit on the bathroom floor. Most likely he was rolling around in it before he passed out. He continued to spit up and drool as Jack carried him. Jack laid him in the back seat of the car and then bent over, resting his hands on his knees, trying to catch his breath. Craig was much larger than Jack, and it was quite impressive that Jack carried him all of that way under the circumstances.

"Is he going to be all right?" Melanie asked.

"Yeah, he should be fine. Now you see why we needed the car though."

"You knew this was going to happen?" Melanie asked.

"Yeah, well it's not the first time. He often drinks too much, and I could just tell it was going to be one of those nights. I didn't expect it to be this bad though."

"Oh my," said Melanie.

Both of them got in the car, and within moments they were back at Jack and Craig's house. Melanie and Jack got out of the car, and Jack attempted to lift Craig out of the car. This was a much more difficult task than putting him in the car, especially since it was only a two-door car. "Do you want me to help you?" Melanie asked.

"No, I'll just wake him up," Jack responded. "Hey, Craig. Come on, Craig, wake up." Jack shook Craig a little to see if he would wake but it was without success. Melanie shot Jack a look as to say, "Are you sure you don't need my help?"

"All right," Jack said with a smile. "I suppose I do need your help."

"No problem. What would you like me to do?"

"Just help me pull him out by his arms if you can." Jack grabbed a hold of Craig's right arm and Melanie took the left. They began to pull him out by the arms when the force of the pull awakened Craig as his head bounced off the interior panel of the car door.

"Where am I?" Craig muttered.

"You're back at home," Jack answered. "Looks like you had a bit too much to drink."

"I didn't even drink tonight," Craig said with a smile even though his eyes were still closed. It was quite apparent that he was still out of it.

"Come on, Craig, let's get you in the house," Jack said.

Craig stumbled out from the back of the car, practically crawling out on his hands and knees. Jack lifted Craig to his feet.

"Hey, Melanie!" Craig yelled.

"Hi there," she responded. However, Craig did not hear her. His eyes rolled back into his head, and Jack caught him before he hit the ground.

"Great," Jack muttered. "I'll just carry him into the house. Can you go open the door for me?" Jack gave Melanie the keys, and she walked over to open the front door. As soon as she walked up the steps to the front door and was under the overhang that stretched out over the porch, it started pouring rain. "You've got to be kidding!" Jack said.

Melanie opened the door and watched as Jack attempted to lift his large, helpless friend. Jack lifted Craig up after much difficulty and began walking toward the door as fast as he could. He had gone no more than five steps before he slipped on the now wet, slick walkway that led up to his house. He fell onto his back, and Craig landed directly on top of him, still not moving. Melanie began to laugh. She wasn't trying to be rude, but the site of the whole thing was quite comical.

"That's not funny!" Jack said to Melanie even though she could not even see him. He was completely covered by the much bigger Craig, making Melanie laugh even harder. Jack and Craig continued to get rained on while Jack rolled Craig off himself. He rose to his feet and attempted to pick up Craig for the second time.

"Need a little help?" Melanie asked, still smiling except now she was out in the open and getting poured on just like Jack and Craig.

"What are you doing?" Jack exclaimed. "Quick, get back under the overhang! You're going to catch a cold!"

"Whoa, relax, Jack. I love the rain," Melanie said cheerfully, tilting her head back, embracing the water hitting her face.

"You're insane," Jack said. "Quick grab his legs, I'll lift him by his arms."

The two of them lifted Craig, which was extremely difficult for Melanie. She could not lift his legs very high off the ground, and it took them quite some time before they were able to get Craig safely in the house.

The three of them were now completely soaked from the rain and freezing cold. Jack and Melanie were exhausted and took a seat at the kitchen table after dragging Craig onto the living room floor.

"Are we home yet?" Craig muttered just after Jack and Melanie had sat down. It seemed as though all of that rain had woken him up.

"Now you wake up!" Jack shouted while panting.

Craig stumbled up to his feet, having a lot of trouble with his balance.

"I think I'm going to go to bed now," Craig said as he walked into his room and shut the door after him. He immediately collapsed on his bed, shoes on and all, and slept peacefully through the rest of the night, not moving an inch.

"Interesting night, huh?" Jack said.

"Yeah, you're telling me," Melanie replied. Her response was followed by a small period of awkward silence in which both looked around not knowing what to say.

"Do you need a ride home?" Jack asked.

"Are you trying to get rid of me?" Melanie asked playfully.

"No, but it's getting late, and I don't want to keep you here if you need to be heading home."

"I'm in no hurry."

"All right, well at least let me get you some warm clothes."

He went into his bedroom and came out moments later with black sweatpants and a gray sweatshirt. Melanie thanked Jack for the clothes and went into the bathroom to change. By the time she had come back from the bathroom, Jack had a lovely fire going. Jack's clothes were a bit large on Melanie, as would be expected, but she still looked quite attractive in them. Melanie came and sat next to Jack who was sitting on the carpeted floor near the fire. The room looked extremely peaceful with the lights off and the blazing fire sending a light glow throughout the room.

"So, do you and Craig know each other well?" Jack asked.

"Oh, not really," Melanie replied. "He's in one of my classes and we talk a bit, but that's about it."

"Yeah, he told me he's been trying to get with you for a while."

"Yeah, I know," Melanie said with a laugh. "He is quite a character and very attractive I might add, but he's not exactly my type."

"What is your type then?"

"I don't know how to describe it," said Melanie. "It's just a feeling I get when I know."

Jack and Melanie talked for a few more hours, throwing more logs on the fire when needed. It seemed as the night went on Jack and Melanie became much more comfortable with each other and opened up to one another quite a bit. Jack couldn't explain why, but Melanie made him feel as though she was completing a part of him that had been missing for a long time. The night couldn't have gone more perfectly for Jack as they finished the night with a romantic kiss in front of the fire. The bet that Jack and Craig had made was nowhere near Jack's mind. Never had he thought when he went to that party that night he would spend his night with such an amazing girl.

Eventually the two of them let the fire die down.

"Would you like to stay here for the night?" Jack asked.

"Yeah, that sounds good," Melanie replied.

The two of them spent the remainder of the night innocently sleeping in Jack's bed. Attempting a sexual advance was not even an option to Jack, for when it came to Melanie, he saw much more than sexuality. It was almost as though she was too good to be true, and Jack wanted to treat her respectfully. Jack spent the night with Melanie in his arms with the strangest feeling that he would be with this girl for the rest of his life.

The officer turned the page.

Chapter 3

Guilty Until Proven Innocent

"Will the prosecution please call its first witness?" ordered Judge Black. Cynthia Miller, the woman who had delivered the opening statement, stood up. She was wearing an outfit that was eerily similar to her outfit of the previous day and looked just as professional.

"The prosecution calls Officer Frank Peterson to the stand." An overweight, white male rose from the seats. He was bald except for the hair around the sides of his head and had an extremely wide face with no evidence of a neck. He walked up to the witness stand, and the bailiff presented him with the bible. Officer Peterson raised his right hand and swore that all statements he would make would be the absolute truth.

"Please state your name and age for the jury," said the prosecutor.

"Frank Peterson, age forty-two."

"Could you state your occupation please?"

"I am a precinct chief for the New York City Police Department," said Mr. Peterson.

"And was the defendant working under your unit and supervision during the time of the alleged murder?"

"Yes, Craig was in my unit."

"How would you describe the defendant's personality while under your unit?" continued Ms. Miller.

"Craig always appeared to be diligent, always did as I told him, although he never really seemed to talk to anyone."

"Did the defendant appear to be happy?"

"No, not really. I often asked Craig what was troubling him, and he would always tell me it was personal business."

"Mr. Peterson, did the defendant make you aware that he would be flying across the country on the night of October the twenty-fourth, the night of the murder?"

"No, he didn't inform me of anything actually. As a matter of fact, he was scheduled to work that night."

"So, Mr. Peterson, would you say that the flight was completely unexpected?"

"Yes, I suppose so. I had no idea about it."

"The defendant had purchased a ticket a few days before the night of the flight. Why do you think he would want to keep it a secret from you?"

"Perhaps he didn't want me to know what he was up to," replied the officer.

"Were you aware of the defendant's criminal record prior to employing him?"

"Yes, I was aware."

"Then why did you hire him?"

"I'm not sure," the officer replied. "I just saw something in him and decided to take a chance. I thought he could do troubled kids some good."

"Do you still have that good feeling toward the defendant?"

"No, I can't say that I do."

"No further questions your honor."

Throughout the entire interrogation Jack had not been listening; he had been eyeing Craig like a hawk. The whole time he was remembering the events that led up to Craig becoming a cop. It was years ago, during Craig's and Jack's last year in college.

* * * * * * * * * *

"I just don't know if this whole college thing is working out for me," Craig said while talking on the phone with Jack.

"What do you mean by that?" Jack questioned.

"I don't know. It's just becoming too stressful. I don't think I'm cut out for college. I think I would be better off if I protected my mom, you know?"

"What the hell are you talking about? You've already gone through three and a half years. Why throw it all away in your last semester?" It was a wonderful spring day, Jack noticed while staring out the window. The flowers had all reached their bloom, and the birds were chirping away. It was only spoiled for Jack due to Craig's news. "Do you really think your mom gives a shit? She's not going to change at all."

"I have to try," Craig said somberly. "I can't just sit around at school while she slowly kills herself! I just think it would be better if I stayed home and helped her get her life back together. She can't do this without me."

"I don't give a shit, Craig. No matter what your problems are, it's not worth it to throw it all away."

"Will you just listen to what's going on? I need some advice," Craig pleaded.

"No. I'm not going to listen because no matter what the problem is, it is not worth throwing away your education." Jack hung up the phone.

Less than a week later Craig dropped out of school. He had not earned his diploma, and over the next few years he did very little, very little good at least, while Jack continued on to law school. Jack and Craig no longer lived together after Craig dropped out of college. It wasn't because Jack was angry with him, but instead because Craig didn't want to live with Jack anymore. Craig hadn't told Jack why he had his sudden change of heart. He simply told Jack that he couldn't live with him anymore and that things might be better out on his own.

However, things didn't get better for Craig. He got involved in some petty crime from small-scale robbery to battery. Things did not go well for him as he struggled with finding a place to live. Without a job he was unable to pay the rent, jumping around to different apartments constantly. When it seemed that he had hit rock bottom, he had nowhere to turn. He was out of money and had absolutely nowhere to go; life seemed hopeless. However, just when he had hit bottom, Jack took him back in. He allowed Craig to stay at his place rent-free and even paid for his food and clothes for several months. Jack made Craig get a job and start a new life for himself. Yes, Jack had saved Craig's life despite Craig's attempts to shut him out.

Before long, Craig decided he wanted to be a police officer so that he could help others turn their lives around as well. It wasn't an easy process for Craig to become an officer. With his criminal record, it was nearly impossible for him to even be considered to become a law enforcement officer. But Frank Peterson saw something in him. He pulled a few strings and called in more than a few favors to give Craig Sanderson a chance. It took Craig a long period of training with the police academy and hard work before he earned the right to be a police officer.

But he wasn't on the job more than a month before his life changed forever. Just a month of being on the force and he was now being charged with murder.

* * * * * * * * * *

"Will the defense proceed to cross examination?" said Judge Black.

"Yes, your honor," replied West as he walked over to approach the bench. "Mr. Peterson, how long had the defendant been working in the police force?"

"I believe he had only been there about a month," Peterson replied.

"And you were not aware that the defendant was taking a plane trip?"

"No, Craig had not informed me of his activities."

"I see," said West, pacing back and forth in front of the officer. "Were you aware that Craig's mother was murdered just days before?"

"Yes, I was quite aware. The Denver Police Department had informed me of the incident right after it happened."

"Were you aware of the fact that Craig's mother's funeral was scheduled on October twenty-fifth, the very next day?"

"No, I was not aware of when the actual funeral was scheduled. Craig never told me," replied the officer.

"Let me ask you something, Mr. Peterson," continued West. "You said Craig was always quiet and kept to himself, right?"

"That's correct."

"Would a quiet man, such as Craig, who never even gave a hello, go about telling everyone that his mother was murdered?"

"No, I suppose he wouldn't."

"If your mother was brutally murdered by her husband, would you want to tell anyone?" West asked.

"No, I suppose I wouldn't."

"If your mother was murdered, would you not fly to her funeral?"

"Of course I would!" Officer Peterson snapped back as if he was offended.

"Then isn't it possible that Craig actually *was* simply going to attend his mother's funeral?"

"Yes, I suppose so," Officer Peterson mumbled.

"Nothing further, your honor," West said.

* * * * * * * * * *

At the end of the day, Jack returned to his home and was greeted by Brianne as usual. However, he wasn't in the mood to talk to her. He didn't want any sexual services from her tonight. "I'd rather just be by myself tonight, Brianne. I'm sorry."

"I see," replied Brianne, sounding hurt. "Well, fine then." And she walked in their room and shut the door behind her.

It was still startling to Jack that he had asked Brianne to move in with him since they had only been seeing each other for about a month. Truth be told, Jack had talked her into moving in with him. He was sick of being lonely, and Brianne helped a lot with that. Also, Brianne had not been the most financially set person, so it was not hard for Jack to persuade her to come and live rent-free. In no way was Brianne using Jack. She truly cared about him despite the short amount of time they had been together. Jack cared about Brianne too, but it was hard for him to think of her as his significant other when his heart still burned for Melanie.

That night, Jack decided to sleep in the guest bedroom. Lately he had been having dreams about the past that were haunting him, dreams of times he spent together with Melanie. Each time he would wake up feeling as though she was alive until reality settled in. Tonight was no different. He said his prayers before going to sleep, just as he always did. He repeated the same prayers every night, never changing them; always praying for his family and friends' safety and everything else he truly cared about. He fell asleep on the guestroom bed and slipped deep into his dreams. He dreamed back to his college days, when he and Craig had been best friends. Back to the night when he first met Melanie Stole, the same night she spent the night in his bed, wrapped tightly in his arms.

Chapter 4

A Family Meeting

With a population of over eight million, New York City was the most populated city in the United States, and one of the highest populated cities in the entire world. Throughout its 321 square miles, New York City was home to large amounts of both domestic and international finance. Immigrants flocked to the Big Apple, helping to provide the great diversity found in the city. Walking to work every morning through the busy streets of New York, one would expect to see familiar faces. However, with the mass amounts of tourists and inhabitants, one was likely to never see the same stranger twice. With all the large city lights and attractions, the dangerous and chaotic urban streets, one would be surprised to learn that New York City had the lowest crime rate among the top twenty-five most populated American cities. However, everywhere one went there was bound to be heinous acts of violence, the kind of degrading activity that only came around every once in a while, although one prayed it never would.

Hofstra University was located in New York, in Hempstead, Long Island. It was a private school of about thirteen thousand students, known primarily for academics in liberal arts, business, and law fields. Jack Gardner was enrolled and studying under the university's undergraduate program for its law school. It had been a very difficult decision for Jack when he considered which college to attend. He knew for sure he wanted to stay in New York to be close to his family, but he didn't know which to choose. He had always been a rather indecisive person. He was accepted into other fine schools, such as New York University and Syracuse University, but ended up at Hofstra the following fall.

His decision to attend Hofstra University was not based on merits or academic reputation, however. His eventual choice was based off school mascots, as crazy as that sounded. Pride was perhaps the most important virtue to Jack Gardner. He swore to himself that through all of his relationships, whether it was with a woman or his friends, he would always keep his pride and not let anyone take advantage of him. When he found out that Hofstra's complete name was Hofstra University Pride, he made his decision. He felt that it was a sign, and whether it was or wasn't, he ended up making a decision that would change his life forever.

Jack was by no means just a standard twenty-two -year-old senior. He was exceptional. Although not the valedictorian, he was without question in the top of his class when it came to merits. His grades were superb and a high-paying job was never out of mind. He was planning on pursuing a career with a successful law firm and was more than likely a shoe- in for the job. Jack did what he needed to do in order to ensure a successful life for himself, along with his girlfriend, and hopefully his eventual wife, Melanie. Jack's best friend was nothing like him. Craig struggled to maintain a decent enough GPA to not get kicked out of school. It's not that he didn't care; he just wasn't the student type like Jack.

Melanie Stole was in the same class as Jack and Craig. Craig had pursued her shortly before Jack and Melanie had met. Craig was not seriously into her or anything. It was merely a physical attraction, and he was not upset when she ended up wanting a relationship with Jack. She wasn't the prettiest girl in the school, but she still had a certain physical attractiveness about her. She was about five feet, five inches tall with golden blonde hair, green eyes, and full lips. She had a nice set of teeth from the braces she had worn in her earlier years and a cute smile to go with them. Her body was physically the most attractive asset of hers. She had voluptuous curves in the right places, while still being slender. However, her reputation was one that was difficult for some to look past. Some mistakes, as she called them, in her freshman year at college gave her a reputation as a rather promiscuous woman. The men at Hofstra often could not look past this. They didn't want a relationship with her; they simply looked for the fastest way to get her undressed. Despite her reputation, one that Melanie claimed was mostly undeserved, Jack attempted to look past what people said about her. Eventually, they were able to put it behind them both, and Jack gave her the chance she wanted—a chance to be in a meaningful relationship for the first time.

Jack and Melanie had been seeing each other for two years by now, and they were as close as a couple could get. They truly had become best friends, even though they fought all the time. Jack would say that he and Craig were best friends, except they had become more of brothers than anything else. In a way, Jack's entire family had taken Craig in as their own, Jack's mother in particular. She almost considered Craig her fourth son.

Jack's brother Mark was two years older than Jack. Mark had always secretly been someone that Jack greatly looked up to. It wasn't that Jack would have been slow to admit to it, but perhaps they didn't have a close enough relationship to where his admiration could be shown. Growing up as young children, the two looked much alike and were even occasionally asked if they were twins by strangers. Somewhere over the years, they gradually began to look less like one another. However, while they might not have looked similar enough to be twins, there was no doubt they were related. Mark Gardner was two inches shorter than Jack. His hair was about the same length as Jack's, although it was a lighter shade of brown. Mark had hazel eyes and was slightly lighter skinned than his younger brother. As smart as Jack was in school, he did not measure up to his older brother. Mark knew pretty much everything about everything, or at least it seemed that way to Jack. On top of being wise, both in and out of the classroom or workplace or wherever else it mattered, Mark was an athletic man like the rest of the Gardner family.

Jack never felt like his older brother liked him very much, at least not like a friend. Sure, he had done everything a good brother should do: told him to stay away from alcohol until he was in college (although Mark was known to drink plenty himself), talked to him about sex and made sure he was being safe, and everything else an older brother did to watch out for his dumber, younger brother. But Jack didn't feel like Mark wanted him as a friend. Jack knew his brother would be there for him, to have his back in a time of need, and he hoped his brother knew that he would do the same for him, probably even a lot more. Jack figured Mark had no knowledge of Jack's view of their relationship; he figured no one realized it besides himself. For some reason, most likely the fact that the two had shared their whole childhood together, Jack felt that he could not be happy if his brother Mark was in any type of pain whatsoever. Perhaps this had something to do with Jack's childhood recollections of Mark sticking up for him when neighborhood kids would pick on him because he was smaller. Nevertheless, Jack desperately wanted Mark to know how much he cared about him, even though he knew he would never be able to tell him.

They had a brother named Chris who was nearly six years younger than Jack. Naturally, having the gap in age made it difficult for Chris and Jack to form a special brotherly bond like Jack felt for Mark. It took Jack until he was nineteen years old before any type of bond was formed. Jack remembered coming home from his first year at Hofstra University for summer vacation. It seemed as though his little brother had completely grown up in only the one year that Jack had been gone. Chris was no longer the small little child that Jack used to be so much bigger than. The thirteen-year-old kid at the time was nearly the same height as Jack and seemed as though he had grown three years older in only one year.

That summer Chris evolved from the younger brother to another one of Jack's friends. The two basically shared a room at the Gardner household because the family computer was located in Jack's bedroom. Chris would talk to his friends over the Internet much of the day to keep in close contact over summer vacation, while Jack used his laptop to do the same. Being together so often forced them to talk and hang out more as friends than they ever had before; the age gap had been closed. However, Jack couldn't say that it was just a friendship. With Chris growing up so fast, Jack, for the first time, felt what it was like to be an older brother. He felt the responsibility of watching out for his younger brother and protecting him. Three years later, the sixteen-year-old Chris was six feet, two inches tall. He had dirty blonde hair, not resembling his two brothers in any way. His eyes were a very distinct blue, completely different from his brothers' darker colors. He looked much like his father, who was also six feet, two inches tall, with brownish-blonde hair and hints of red.

Jack's father, the strong head of the household, had built a more than comfortable life for his family. If Jack could choose one person to aspire to, one person he wished he could amount to in his life, he would pick his father, Mr. Gardner. In fact, he wished he could amount to half of what his dad had become. He was a very successful CPA and had even risen up to be a partner in the biggest accounting firm in Long Island (a firm that Mark now worked for). He made much more than a healthy income but wasn't considered rich. His large paycheck, however, was not what Jack particularly admired and respected so much, but rather the way that he made his paycheck.

Mr. Gardner woke up every morning before the sun to drive thirty minutes to his office to work all day until the sun had gone down, dealing with the stresses of business and clients, and then drive thirty minutes back home. This clearly seemed to be enough to gain one's respect, but Mr. Gardner wasn't finished yet. He always found more work to do, even with the minimal amount of time he had at home. Whether it was doing yard work, fixing a sink, or whatever else, Jack's father did it all. He had financially presented his children with opportunities that were greater than what he had as a child. This included opportunities for his sons to go to expensive, private colleges, paving the way for them to obtain successful, well-paying jobs.

On top of this, he had still somehow found the time to coach all three sons in three different sports (basketball, baseball, and soccer), for much of their ten-year elementary and middle school careers. Altogether, this would mean that each son played on about thirty different sports teams. That totaled ninety different sports teams that the Gardner boys had played on. And Mr. Gardner coached half of these, making it forty-five teams that he dedicated his time and effort into, doing the best possible job that he could do. His teams always did well too. He was quite athletic and knowledgeable about the sports that he coached, teaching his sons everything he knew about the games, particularly basketball, the sport of choice among all the boys. They had all played basketball throughout high school and all had their fair share of success.

Although Mr. Gardner was now forty-nine, he was still in great shape. He weighed nearly 190 pounds, as he was tall and also broad, but wasn't overweight in any way. He found joy in working out and keeping a good figure, mainly by visiting the gym frequently and also biking. He had picked up biking about three years ago and started doing it more and more competitively until he was very good at it. Riding up mountains and biking over forty miles was no problem for him. He was a very strong and proud man. Jack always found that it was hard to crack jokes at him because sometimes his pride would take it as an insult. Being as strong as he was, Jack had never in his life seen his father cry, and he thought surely he never would. He was indeed the strong head of the household, but where would the Gardner family be without Jack's mother, Mrs. Gardner?

She was nothing like her husband. Instead, she was almost a mirror image of her son, Jack. She shared his slightly darker skin color than the rest of the family and had many similarities in facial features. She was short, about five feet, two inches in height and weighed only 110 pounds, which was where Jack and Mark got their lack of great height. She had brownish-blonde hair, which had been dyed from its original darker state of brown, much similar to Jack's. Perhaps the only characteristic she shared with Mr. Gardner was her athleticism.

Growing up as a child, she had always been a bit of a tomboy. Instead of playing with dolls with the girls, she spent her childhood days roughing it up with the boys in whatever sport they were playing. She could hold her own too, oftentimes being better than a lot of the boys. Even though she was extremely small, she was tough, and at forty-nine she was very much involved with athletics and exercising. She ran in the park daily, had played softball for years but recently gave it a rest, and played tennis with Jack whenever they found some spare time. She dressed nicely but kept it simple. She did not wear any jewelry, at least Jack had never seen her wear any, except perhaps for rare special occasions. Her clothes were mainly sporty: shorts and T-shirts, jeans, and sweaters. She rarely wore skirts or dresses, again unless it was for a special occasion. As sporty as she was, she was just as attractive. She was more in shape for her age than any woman Jack had recalled seeing and she was also one of the most attractive—certainly prettier than all of his friends' mothers, not to mention she had been the homecoming queen in her high school days.

In terms of personality, Mrs. Gardner was much different from her husband also. She didn't have quite the same determination for the workplace. Instead, her joy came from relaxing and truly enjoying life in the outdoors. She was not in the workforce, but she definitely had a job. She worked hard to keep an efficient house running, not an easy task when you had three sons. She was perhaps the nicest and most caring woman in the world, especially when it came to her boys. She had a nice sense of humor and usually didn't take things too seriously. Only those closest to her knew of her great fear of losing her loved ones. Besides this fear, her laid-back personality made the right balance to Mr. Gardner's personality and Jack had to admit he was always extremely privileged to have been blessed with parents like Mr. and Mrs. Gardner.

Jack, Craig, and Melanie, in their senior year at Hofstra, were now out for winter break. The next month or so Jack Gardner planned on staying with his family in New York City until the spring semester began. Craig Sanderson planned on spending some time with the Gardner family, and would also be visiting his mom who was now living with her boyfriend, David Cooper. He dreaded this as this man had driven his already off-the-wall mother into severe alcoholism and occasional drug use. Craig knew Cooper didn't treat his mother right and that she could perhaps get her life, a life that was once sober and healthy, back together again if her boyfriend was out of her life. Regardless, he never acted on his anger toward David Cooper. He figured his mother was a grown woman; she wouldn't have listened to him anyway. Since Craig and Jack both had places to go, they decided to leave the house they shared together in Long Island near campus. Melanie Stole and her family were originally from Tucson, Arizona, but Melanie had moved into a house of her own in Long Island after receiving a partial academic scholarship to Hofstra. Since Melanie had no family in New York, she planned on staying in her house in Long Island. After all, it wasn't a very long drive to New York City to see her boyfriend, Jack. However, Jack decided not to invite Melanie over to the Gardner house.

Jack always got the impression that his mother would never think any girl was good enough for him. It seemed that every time he liked a girl, Mrs. Gardner was quick to judge her with a negative opinion. Perhaps she just didn't want to lose her son to another woman.

"It's about time we got out for break. School was starting to drive me insane," Craig said as they drove to the Gardner house after packing up and leaving school for the holidays. Jack was traveling a bit faster than the posted legal limit in his black Toyota, quite anxious to see his family. It was a nice two–door car with a leather interior and wood trim around the dashboard. Although it was a Toyota, it was still a sporty model. The car was nothing extraordinary, but Jack felt lucky to have it. In the passenger seat was his best friend, Craig, who was leaning against the car door with his arm out the window.

"I know," Jack replied. "We ought to enjoy it though. Just wait, before we know it we'll have to be out in that place they call the *real world*."

"Yeah, well right now I feel like I'd rather be there than in school. We'll see if I can even survive another semester."

"Shut up, Craig! Don't talk like that!" Jack snapped. "You're finishing school and you're getting your diploma." Craig remained quiet. He didn't feel like listening to another lecture from his friend.

After only a short while, the two of them had arrived at the Gardner household in New York City. The house was a spacious one considering its location was in such a large city. The Gardners owned about an acre of land in a New York suburb, most of which was a gradual dirt down slope in the backyard. The house was single story but was deceptively much larger than it looked from the outside. It was a peach-like color but had a darker color bordering the large windows through which one could view the family room, kitchen, and living room from the front walkway.

The front yard started with a vertical, rectangular strip of grass on the left side of the house that was about ten by thirty feet. In front of this lawn was a brick mailbox that Mr. Gardner had built with his own two hands ten years earlier. To the right of this, in front of the three-car garage, was an inclined cement driveway leading to the garage. Still farther on the right of this was a horizontal oval lawn of grass that was surrounded by bushes and plants that Mrs. Gardner maintained very nicely. In front of the lawn and the variety of plants was a fake water well that Mr. Gardner had also built himself. The house was in a court that was made up of only three houses, all of them widely spread out with the Gardner house in the middle.

Jack pulled up along the street curb and parked his car as Mark Gardner's car was already parked in the driveway—a spot Jack had always parked in while living in the house. The two of them walked up the driveway and to the right along a path that led up to the front door. It felt good for Jack to be home. For the next month, he wouldn't have to worry about the pressures of school or upcoming graduate school. No, he wouldn't have to worry about anything. He could just relax and spend time with those he loved most: his family, his best friend, and his girlfriend.

"Jack! It's great to see you!" Mrs. Gardner exclaimed, giving her son a big hug. She was literally beaming from ear to ear. Not seeing Jack was one of the hardest things she had to deal with. He remembered during his freshman year she called him in tears about how she missed him and that he needed to call her more often. To Jack, not a single thing on this planet broke his heart more than seeing his mom cry, especially if he was the reason she was crying.

"You too Mom, I missed you." Jack reciprocated her hug and gave his mom a quick kiss on the cheek.

"Oh, and Craig, how nice that you came too!" Mrs. Gardner gave him a hug as well, having a little difficulty reaching his tall torso but seeming pleased to see him also.

"You too, Mrs. Gardner," was Craig's reply. "You're looking good aren't you?"

Mrs. Gardner gave him a smile but turned around without giving a reply. Straight ahead through the doorway was a semi-elegant dining room. It had a nice large wooden table with a chandelier hanging directly over the middle. Cabinets on the wall held fine sets of glasses and silverware. The two of them followed her into the hardwood kitchen, which was just to the left of the dining room separated by a wall. Inside the kitchen was a smaller wooden table upon which the Gardners normally dined; the large dining room table was used only for special occasions or when there were more people. The kitchen table overlooked the front yard through a large window and just to the side was a white pantry that held much of the Gardners' food. However, plenty of food was already on the kitchen counter.

The counter was filled with plates of chicken, mashed potatoes, and salad. Mr. Gardner was on the opposite side of the kitchen with his back turned to the new arrivals. He was washing his hands over the sink, clearly cleaning up from the meal he had helped to cook.

"Hey, there, Jack," he said after turning around upon their entrance. "You're just in time for dinner."

"Perfect timing," Jack replied, glad that he didn't have to help cook it but could still enjoy the meal.

"Hey, Craig, how's it going?"

"Good, sir, how are you?" Craig's father had always taught Craig to be overly polite, even when it came to people he was familiar with. He even referred to his own father only by "sir."

"I'm doing pretty well," Mr. Gardner responded.

Craig and Jack walked through the kitchen to the family room where Jack's brother, Mark, and his wife, Dianne, were sitting on a sofa. No walls separated the kitchen from the family room, only the transition from the hardwood kitchen floor to the blue-carpeted family room floor. There were two dark blue sofas and a lighter blue, cushioned, reclining chair, the latter being everyone's favorite seat. Mark and Dianne were on one sofa, so Craig and Jack took a seat on the other unoccupied sofa. On the opposite side of the room, as far away from the kitchen as possible, a fireplace was trimmed in silver metal; the Gardners never used it though. It was built into a big brick chimney that went all the way to the ceiling. Above the fireplace was a mantel holding up many of the Gardners' pictures and above that was a silver, circular clock. To the left of the chimney was a big-screen, silver television that matched nicely with the fireplace.

The brothers acknowledged each other but did not say hi. Ever since Mark and Dianne had gotten married two years earlier, Jack found that the two of them talked progressively less and less. They had a six-month-old baby boy, which Jack hadn't noticed resting in Dianne's arms, sucking on a bottle of milk.

After Mrs. Gardner had finished setting the dining room table (the kitchen table was too small for seven people), she called everyone to come and have a seat. After yelling a couple of times at Chris to join them, he finally made his debut, coming out of his room where he was watching television. It seemed to Jack that he had grown even more than he remembered. It was weird for Jack to see his six-years-younger brother taller than himself.

"So how did this last semester go, boys?" Mrs. Gardner asked.

"Glad it's over, but I know I did well," Jack replied while taking a big bite from his chicken leg.

Craig waited until he was finished chewing. "Just thank God I survived. I never know if I'll make it through each semester." Mrs. Gardner laughed, unaware that Craig was perfectly serious. "Mrs. and Mr. Gardner, I know this is rude, but do you think I could stay here these first couple nights?"

Jack looked surprised as Craig had not even mentioned this idea to him.

"Well, sure, Craig, you're always welcome to stay with us, you know that. But don't you want to see your mother?" Mrs. Gardner asked.

"It's hard to call the mother I have now the mother I used to have, but yeah, I want to see her. I just don't want to while you-know-who is there. He's supposedly leaving to go to Colorado to look for houses for a couple days. I'd rather go visit once he's out of the house."

Jack's parents knew exactly what Craig was talking about. Everyone in Craig's life knew about the terrible reputation of her boyfriend, David, and how Craig's mother had picked up drinking upon becoming an item with him.

"All right, well, stay as long as you would like. You can stay in Mark's old room," Mrs. Gardner replied.

"Thank you so much." Craig sounded sincere and he meant it. The table grew awkwardly silent for several moments as no one knew quite what to say. After all, it was a very uncomfortable subject.

"Have you been taking your pills, Jack?" Mrs. Gardner asked.

"Yes, Mom."

"And have they been doing the job?"

"Yes, I haven't had any reoccurrences in a long time, you know that." Jack wanted someone to change the subject as fast as possible. Jack had a rather serious case of obsessive-compulsive disorder, mainly which went on during his teenage years. He didn't feel very comfortable talking about it, but he had been put on medication two years ago and after several sessions of therapy he had gotten over his problem. However, he was unaware that soon it would come back to be worse than ever.

Over the course of dinner, the Gardners discussed school, Mark's and Mr. Gardner's jobs at the office, sports, and anything else they could think of.

After cleaning the dishes and table, the now five of them watched some television. Mark and Dianne had gone back to their apartment, which was less than a half hour away.

That night along with the next went along uneventfully. Craig stayed with the Gardners, sleeping in Mark's old bedroom as Mrs. Gardner had suggested. The day bed in Mark's old room wasn't the most comfortable, but it was plenty good for Craig. Mark's old bedroom was the first stop along a hallway that included Jack's bedroom in the middle and Chris' room at the end. In between Jack's and Chris' rooms was a bathroom on the opposite side of the hall. Before the hallway began there was a half bathroom, which the Gardners referred to as the "guest bathroom." The end of the hallway led into the master bedroom where Mr. and Mrs. Gardner slept. Their bedroom was perhaps three times the size of the boys' bedrooms with a master bathroom in the back section of the room.

After just a couple days of being home, Jack was beginning to miss Melanie. It hadn't been often that they had spent nights apart from each other in a long time. They had recently celebrated their two-year anniversary, two years that had been extremely rocky for their relationship. They had separated several times, said many things they didn't mean (or maybe they did mean some of them), yet they believed they loved each other and always quickly got back together because of it.

The officer turned the page.

Chapter 5

The Facts Are Told

Jack woke up with the sun, rolling over to his left and putting his arms around the empty space on the bed before realizing that he was no longer in his little house back at college and his Melanie was not there with him. His heart suddenly sunk as it always did after dreaming of her. His dreams were so real that the harsh realities of life were easily forgotten and replaced by his dreams, waking up every time to think she was still around.

"I hope you had a good sleep last night." Brianne had entered the guestroom and stood just inside the doorway with her arms folded, still seeming upset that Jack had not slept with her the night before.

"I had a fantastic sleep," Jack said.

"You'd better get a move on. You're going to be late for court."

Jack looked over at the clock and realized he only had an hour before the trial was to begin. He quickly got ready and rushed over to the courthouse, touching each side of the entrance door to the courtroom four times before entering. He made it just in time.

"Will the prosecution call its next witness?" Judge Chadsworth Black ordered.

Ms. Miller rose from the prosecution stand. "The prosecution calls Officer Travis Denton to the stand," she said.

A young man in his early twenties stood up and walked toward the bench. He was wearing what appeared to be a cheap suit and tie but was very handsome nonetheless. He had strong but pleasant features with short brown hair and a winning smile.

"Mr. Denton, do you swear to tell the truth, the whole truth, and nothing but the truth, so help you God?" the bailiff said.

"I do," replied Mr. Denton, taking a seat at the witness stand.

"Can you state your name and occupation for the jury?"

"My name is Travis Denton, and I am an officer of the New York City Police Department."

"And were you on duty the night of October the twenty-fourth?" Ms. Miller asked.

"Yes, I was."

"Were you the officer who appeared at the Melanie Gardner crime scene?"

"Yes, I arrived at the scene of the crime after being called," Denton replied.

"Who called the police reporting the incident?"

"One of the victims of the attack was able to get free long enough to call. Jack Gardner."

"Ladies and gentlemen of the jury, we have a recording of the phone call made by Jack Gardner to the police station that night," said the prosecutor. With the permission of Judge Black, I would like to play the recording for you."

"Proceed," said the Judge.

Cynthia Miller walked over from behind her bench and pulled out a black tape recorder. She pressed the play button on the recorder and the voice of the police dispatch operator began.

"911, what's your emergency?"

"Help … I'm bleeding to death," came Jack's voice in a low, chilling whisper.

"Where is your location?" the operator asked.

"I've been stabbed in the chest!" Jack yelled. "And I think he's still in the house! I think he just raped my wife!" Jack spoke through moaning shrieks of pain. "She may be dead!"

"We have a fix on the source of your call and are on our way," the operator said.

The entire courtroom looked horrified, as you would expect, after hearing Jack's shrieks of immense pain. A cold shiver ran down Jack's spine as he heard the tape being played. This was naturally followed by a feeling of utter repulsion after recalling the events of that night. He touched each side of the pew he was sitting in four times.

"Mr. Denton, what time did you arrive at the scene?" asked Cynthia Miller.

"It must have been about nine thirty at night."

"Could you describe what happened and what you saw at the scene of the crime?"

"I arrived at the house the call came from," Denton began. "I was very cautious, as the suspect was thought to still be in the house. I couldn't be too cautious, though, because someone's life could have been at stake."

Travis Denton busted in the front door of the three-bedroom house, holding his gun up around his shoulder so that the shaft of the gun was pointed at the ceiling. The living room was carpeted in a beige color and the walls were a solid white. A brown loveseat was against the left wall and a matching chair was next to it with a window exposing the backyard on the wall straight ahead of the doorway. A tall gold lamp stood in the far left corner of the room and a small television sat on a stand in the far right corner. Just beyond the right corner was a flight of stairs leading to the second story of the house and just to the right of the stairs was the kitchen. He walked sideways slowly and carefully through the living room and into the kitchen, looking for any sign of movement. The kitchen was rather small and was quite ordinary. A sink with a window over it showed the side lawn and a microwave oven next to it. Across the kitchen was a large white fridge that appeared even larger due to the small size of the kitchen. Also, of course, cabinets encircled the kitchen.

The coast seemed to be clear so far. There were no other rooms downstairs except a door leading to the garage. However, assuming no phone was accessible in the garage, the officer decided to check upstairs. He walked up the stairs and saw three bedroom doorways. Two were on the left and one on the right, without any hallways. Since only one room was on the right, Denton surmised that the bedroom on the right was much larger than the two on the left. It was clearly the master bedroom. Travis Denton pushed open the door to the bedroom, which was only halfway open. When the door opened, Denton saw the most disturbing image he had ever seen and would ever see in his life. The site of it was repulsive enough for anyone to have vomited right where they stood.

Upon entering the room, Travis Denton saw sprawled out on the white king-size bed a naked girl lying on her back with her legs and arms both spread. "Holy shit," Denton gasped. He ran over to the bedside to get a better look at the girl. She wasn't completely naked, but the white dress she had been wearing had been ripped so much that it gave the appearance that she was. The articles of clothing were barely hanging from her motionless body. Melanie Gardner lay in a pool of her own blood covering the entire bed. Blood was all over her chest and stomach and it was almost impossible to see any piece of flesh of her torso. Her eyes were wide open and Denton could see a stab wound right through her heart. Scattered blotches of blood were on her face and her blonde hair was all over the place. Denton felt her wrist for a pulse, but he knew it was useless. "I need some backup quick!" Denton called over his radio.

He heard a noise coming from outside the room. He walked out of the room and heard what sounded to be someone moving very slowly and panting. He walked toward the noise and into one of the smaller bedrooms. There he saw Jack Gardner crawling toward him on his hands and knees. Jack's mouth was open and panting for breath as blood dripped out of it. "Get over here now!" Denton screamed into his radio, insisting on the backup. Jack collapsed right next to the officer's feet and Denton bent over to get a better look at him. It was clear that Jack had been stabbed a few times.

"What have we got here, Denton?" said Officer Frank Peterson, the precinct chief who had just arrived on the scene.

"This man is bleeding to death. We need an ambulance right now," Denton replied.

"What happened from there Mr. Denton?" asked the prosecutor.

"An ambulance was called and came to get Jack. He was put on the stretcher and taken away. Then I answered some questions, and the specialists came in to look for pieces of evidence."

"Your honor, I would like to call specialist Henry Wilson to the stand."

"Would the defense like to cross examine?" Judge Black asked.

Joseph West didn't see any reason for the police officer to be lying about what he saw. He figured he would ask him to take the stand again if he saw the need. "No questions at this time, your honor."

Travis Denton got off the stand and walked back to take his seat. Henry Wilson, an older male in his mid-fifties with a full head of grayish-black hair, walked toward the stand. The bailiff swore him in and Wilson took the stand.

"Could you please state your name and profession for the jury?" Ms. Miller asked.

"Henry Wilson, lieutenant for the FBI."

"Lieutenant Wilson, why would the FBI have been called into this case? Wouldn't this case be investigated by NYPD detectives?"

"Initially the case was NYPD," Wilson began. "However, once Officer Peterson reported to his superiors that the knife wounds found on Melanie Gardner were similar to the wounds he had heard were found on Craig's mother, the FBI was called in."

"Did you investigate the crime scene for evidence and clues?" asked Ms. Miller.

"Yes, me and my crew surveyed the area," Wilson answered.

"What did you find upon your investigation?"

"When we searched the house, we found a couple clues. First, we found a few sets of fingerprints on the walls of the master bedroom. The prints belonged to Jack Gardner and Melanie Gardner as you would expect. However, there was a third set of prints. The prints matched those of the defendant, Craig Sanderson."

"What else did you find?" asked the prosecutor.

"Within a couple of hours we were able to find a large amount of semen on the bed and on the floor, which we naturally expected to be that of Jack Gardner," said Wilson.

"And was it Jack Gardner's?"

"Well, most of it was," said Wilson. "However, Jack Gardner's story was that Craig Sanderson had raped Melanie, so we had to search very carefully. With further searching we were able to find a small amount of semen which definitely matched the DNA of that of the defendant, Craig Sanderson."

"Mr. Wilson, what possible explanation could there be for the defendant's semen to be in the bed of the victim? Is it reasonable to think that it is merely coincidence that the defendant was witnessed committing a rape and that his semen was found in the victim's bed?"

"Objection!" yelled West.

"Sustained," replied the judge, although it didn't really make any difference. When the judge said, "Sustained," the jury was to disregard all information that the attorney had said, but that was an impossibility. The damage had been done. The jury had heard it and could take it into consideration, regardless of the judge's orders, and the prosecutor knew this.

"Did you find any other evidence?" asked Ms. Miller.

"Yes," said Mr. Wilson. "The strangest clue of all was that along the bedside on a small dresser was a wedding ring. Later, Jack Gardner identified it as the ring he had given his wife just weeks before."

"In your opinion, what does this show?"

"Well, it's hard to say really," said Wilson. "I guess you could say it is possible the ring just came off during the struggle of the incident. But the fact that it was placed so nicely on the dresser makes it seem pretty clear that it was taken off and placed there."

"Thank you. No further questions," said Cynthia Miller, taking a seat at her bench and sipping from a glass of water as was her routine.

"Would the defense like to cross-examine this witness?" asked Judge Black.

"Yes, I would like to ask Mr. Wilson a few questions," said Joseph West. He rose from his bench and walked toward Mr. Wilson and the witness stand.

"Mr. Wilson, you said you found handprints of the defendant on the walls of the bedroom," West began.

"That's correct," replied Wilson.

"Well, it is a well-known fact that Craig, Jack, and Melanie were all good friends. Don't you think that these prints could have come anytime over the year that Melanie had been residing there?" asked West.

"Well, yes, except for the fact that these were the only fingerprints present. This made us curious. Upon questioning him, Jack Gardner told us that Melanie had painted the room just eight weeks before the incident, which means that all previous handprints would have been painted over. The only prints that would have been present would have been those who had touched the wall in the last eight weeks. When we questioned the defendant, however, he claimed he had not been to Melanie's house in much over eight weeks."

"How do you know that the room was ever actually painted and Craig's prints were not from over eight weeks ago when he had visited?"

"The prints were much too clear and vivid to have been there from eight weeks ago anyways. Clearly the prints from these three people had been very recent."

"Mr. Wilson, you said that you found semen belonging to the defendant, ultimately suggesting the defendant may have raped Melanie. But, first of all, how do we know Melanie and Craig weren't intimate with each other?"

"That's really not my place to say. I have no idea. I'm just presenting facts."

"Well, here's another fact. Isn't it true that there were no strangle marks on Melanie? Isn't it true that there was no sign whatsoever of a forced entry?"

"That's quite correct. However, that doesn't mean that a rape didn't occur. Her clothes were completely ripped off. We don't suppose the murderer just wanted to look at her body."

"Then how do you explain the lack of any sign of forced entry?"

"Melanie Gardner was already dead when she was raped. The murderer killed her, and then proceeded to take off her clothes and rape her. Thus, no strangle marks or forced entry was necessary."

"How do you know the clothes came off after she was already murdered?

"Take a look at the dress Melanie was wearing. Right where the chest of the dress would be you can clearly see that the knife was stabbed into her heart through the fabric of the dress. There's a slit in the dress at the very same place she was stabbed and the knife fits the cut."

"No further questions your honor," said Joseph West, feeling as though he was getting nowhere in the case.

After court adjourned for the day, Craig Sanderson and Joseph West had a talk about the case. They sat down, Craig still cuffed in chains, inside Craig's jail cell.

"We don't have a chance do we?" asked Craig.

"A couple of things interested me today," West said. "While listening to the recording of the police phone call that Jack made, I realized a few things. First, Jack never stated that his wife had been murdered; he emphasized that she had been raped. He said she may be dead."

"So," said Craig.

"Well, if your wife was murdered wouldn't you mention that first, seeing as it is a little more important? It makes it seem like he cared more about the sexual part," said West.

"He will just say he wasn't in the room when she got murdered," said Craig.

"In the recording, at first, Jack is extra careful to be quiet so that the killer wouldn't hear him making a phone call. But, just a second later he was yelling into the phone with no regard for the killer hearing it. Also, Jack remained talking on the phone for some seconds after. Now the part that doesn't make any sense is why the killer wouldn't have come back into the room and killed Jack. Obviously he must have heard Jack yelling, yet he spared his life."

"Yeah, but the killer might have just left after hearing Jack call the police in fear that the police were on their way. He might have thought he didn't have time to kill Jack."

It was for many of these reasons that Joseph West had grown to seriously and passionately trust Craig Sanderson. He was growing to believe more and more in his innocence despite most of the evidence pointing directly at his client. Perhaps Craig really did kill Melanie Stole Gardner, but not everything was adding up. It was true that West didn't know many of the answers to the situation, but he was going to find out. West was definitely not going to let an innocent man be put to death. He wasn't even completely sure why he had grown to believe Craig's case, but he wasn't going to rest until he found out all of the answers he needed.

* * * * * * * * * *

Now that Travis Denton had given his testimony, he hoped the nightmares would stop. He would help the case in any way that he could, but he was horrified by everything that happened that night. All of his life he had wanted to be a police offer, to help those in serious need. He figured that he would have to fight "bad guys," but never in his life did he anticipate this. He had nightmares every night from the vision of seeing Melanie in the state that she was in; however, rather than cower down and quit, he went the other direction. Denton decided that he would continue to search for clues in the Melanie Gardner case, despite the orders of FBI lieutenant Henry Wilson who told him that it was an open and shut case. Wilson had told Denton that he should let the "big boys" in the FBI take it from there. The problem was, in Denton's opinion, the "big boys" weren't doing all that they could. He remembered the first time he had been questioned by Lieutenant Wilson, the same night of the crime at nearly three in the morning, back at FBI headquarters.

"Let's not kid ourselves," Wilson had said. "There is a direct link between the killing of Mrs. Gardner and the deaths of David Cooper and Craig's mother. Let's be honest. The same person or persons committed both of these murders."

"Yeah, but the killings in Colorado were decided to have been double homicide in which there were no suspects. The two victims killed each other," Denton replied.

"Listen, kid, I've been on the force a long time. Those victims didn't kill one another. The scene was too perfect: a false knife still in David Cooper's hand, the gun still her hand. No, son, real life doesn't work out that way. It only works out that way when someone sets it up. Unfortunately, whoever did it did a good job of it."

"What do you mean?"

"I mean, most everyone in the Denver Police Department knows that the victims didn't kill each other."

"Then why the hell aren't they still looking for clues or something?" Denton began raising his voice. He couldn't believe how cold-hearted the FBI lieutenant was sounding at this point. Didn't he realize that these victims had families? Certainly they couldn't just leave the case to die and let whoever did it get away to possibly kill again.

"Listen, son. You're new on the force right?" said Wilson.

"Yeah, just about a year now. What does that have to do with anything?" Denton responded with pride.

"Maybe you don't know how things work, but let me tell you. The public—all those people who want to know every damn thing about every case, all those people who get so involved in the deaths of people they knew, or even didn't know—they want to hear that the case was solved. They want to believe that the police will always protect them and solve the case so that they can sleep soundly in their little homes. They don't want to believe that killers are out there still lurking about. So, when it came down to it, Denver PD had no suspects, no leads, and had no idea who would have done it. So what else could they do? They told the public how certain they were that the victims took each other's lives and that the case was solved."

"You had no idea at all?"

"Well, at first they questioned Mr. Sanderson. He was the only likely suspect. The two of them had divorced about fifteen years ago."

"For what reason?" Denton asked.

"He caught her getting laid by some rich fellow," Mr. Wilson laughed. "Same one that got killed. But it didn't make any sense. If Mr. Sanderson was so outraged by her affair, why would he wait fifteen years to kill her? It just didn't seem to fit. Plus he was in California at the time, and there were absolutely no clues that led to him. Not to mention, this new murder makes it even more clear that it wasn't him."

"How so?"

"If the same killer was involved in both Colorado and New York, what possible motive could Mr. Sanderson have for murdering this young girl, Melanie Gardner, who lived all the way across the entire United States? There's no plausible explanation for that."

"I suppose you're right," Denton admitted.

"Now what suspects did you and your department come up with?"

"We were able to come up with two main ones so far: Craig Sanderson and," Denton paused for a second. "Jack Gardner."

"Jack Gardner?" The lieutenant seemed surprised. "What suspicions do you have against him?"

"Well, nothing quite feasible yet. But he was the husband of the victim. You know those spousal situations that can arise. You just always have to look into it."

"Jack Gardner didn't kill his wife, son. You don't marry your wife a month before you kill her."

"Maybe a month of marriage was enough to drive him insane," Denton said while laughing out, but Wilson did not reciprocate.

"His marriage drove him crazy enough to kill his wife, and then stab himself several times? I know women can drive you crazy but not that crazy."

"Yeah, I guess you're right," Denton said, surprised of the seriousness in Wilson's voice. Clearly he wasn't interested in anyone else's humor except perhaps his own.

"Listen, not only did he have no apparent motive to kill his wife, but there certainly could be no connection with him and the killings in Colorado. Why would Jack Gardner want to kill his best friend's mother and her husband? It just doesn't add up."

"I suppose you're right," Denton said again.

"The only suspect who makes any sense at this point is Craig Sanderson."

"And what could his motives be?"

"Well," Wilson began. "We may not know his motives yet, but Jack Gardner did witness the acts and was even a victim of the attacks himself. He's the only witness we have and at this point we have to believe him."

Chapter 6

A Close Call for a Sanderson

After three nights of staying at the Gardners' house, Craig decided it was unfortunately time to go visit his mother. It wasn't that he didn't love her, because he did. It was just the fact that he hated seeing her as she was now. She used to be so full of life, so youthful. Now she just sat around the house waiting for her boyfriend to come home from work by drinking her pointless life away. She had quit her job because, well, David was rich enough for her to not have to do any work the rest of her life. She had had a good thing once with Craig's father and Craig couldn't come to grips with why they divorced.

"Thanks for everything, Mrs. Gardner," Craig said while giving her a hug.

"It was great to see you. Give me a call if you need anything." Craig walked out the front door and into the passenger seat of Jack's car. Jack had to drive Craig to his mother's house because Craig didn't have a car of his own. The house that Craig's mother lived in was only fifteen minutes from the Gardners' house. Jack had not yet been there, but when he pulled up to the house he was quite impressed with the house. It was a three-story house made primarily of bricks. A paved walkway led up the middle of a perfectly cut lawn to the front of the house. The house was covered with windows and balconies were across the top story of the house.

"You sure you don't want me to come in with you?" Jack asked.

"Sure, if you want. I could always use more support," Craig said, sounding more thankful than he wanted to lead on.

"All right." Jack and Craig stood outside the house with his school bags in his hand. Craig gave Jack a look and then took a deep breath as he hoped that what he found inside the house would not be as bad as he expected. He rang the doorbell and waited several moments, but there was no reply.

"Maybe she's not here," Jack suggested. He attempted to open the door himself and to his surprise, the large white door opened. He pushed it open and inside he found himself on a marble walkway with white carpet on each side that led up to a marble staircase to the upstairs. Another staircase just to the side led down to the basement. Each level of the house was equally magnificent. Jack knew David was rich, but this was even more than he expected. French-looking paintings hung on the white walls of the house and were framed by sterling silver. The carpet was perfectly clean as though it were maintained daily. In fact, the whole house seemed spotless. Silver chandeliers hung from the enormous ceilings in every room. Clearly Craig knew why his mother stayed with this man. He knew it couldn't have been for love. After all, how could she love someone who neglected her like David Cooper?

When they walked past the stairs they ended up in what appeared to be the living room. They saw a large plasma flat-screen television on the wall surrounded by big black speakers and a complete stereo and DVD system. However, what they saw lying on the sofa was much worse than Craig had anticipated. He saw his mother, or at least something that resembled his mother, sprawled out on the long couch that was shaped like an arch around half the room, making it about the length of two couches although it was only one.

She was lying on her back with her head held back as though she was looking at the ceiling, except her eyes were shut and her mouth was wide open. Both legs were on the couch, but one of her arms was hanging off the couch and on the floor, clearly a more than uncomfortable sleeping arrangement. Her face seemed much more aged than Craig had remembered. She had sharp wrinkles, more than someone her age should have. Her hair was still dark brown, but her skin was much paler than Craig remembered. She had been a very pretty lady once upon a time. She was wearing expensive jewelry, something Craig was not used to seeing on his mother. He knew that she was always into that kind of stuff, but they never had that kind of money growing up. Diamond necklaces and earrings shone from her lifeless face, and her fingers sparkled from her rings in the light. The jewelry seemed far too extravagant for the clothes she was wearing, jeans and a T-shirt.

Craig ran toward his mother to check her pulse. Next to her body, on the floor, was an empty bottle of Jack Daniels whiskey and some scattered pills that Craig recognized.

"Wake up, Mom!" Craig screamed, kneeling beside her and shaking her in an attempt to wake her. She had a pulse, but her eyes weren't opening and her body remained motionless. "God damn it, Mom!" Craig jumped up and grabbed the phone that was sitting on a dresser at the end of the sofa. He dialed 911 and demanded an ambulance be sent immediately.

Craig picked his mom up over his shoulder without difficulty; she weighed significantly less than Craig had remembered. He brought her outside, still over his shoulder, so that he didn't waste any time when the ambulance arrived. Before long he heard the sirens and saw the paramedics racing out of the back of the van with a stretcher.

"Quick, put her on," one of them ordered Craig.

Craig did as he was told and before he knew it they had her lifted into the back of the ambulance and had told both he and Jack to hop in. They shut the doors behind them and sped off for the hospital before either Craig or Jack had a chance to take a seat.

"What happened?" the paramedic asked. He was fairly short, well below six feet, and looked as though he was the oldest one on the unit. He had a gray mustache and matching gray hair that was combed over from one side to the other.

"I'm not sure exactly. I came home and found her like this. An open empty bottle of whiskey was next to her and pills were spilled on the ground."

"What kind of pills?"

"Antidepressants."

"Looks like she overdosed," the paramedic said to his partners. They began sticking tubes down her throat, which was almost impossible for Craig to watch. What had his once fun-loving mother come to?

Once they reached the hospital, they pulled her out quickly and wheeled the stretcher out of the van. They ran into the hospital in a hurry, straight to the emergency room.

"Wait here in the waiting room," the older paramedic told Craig.

"No, I need to see if she's all right!" Craig attempted to move past the smaller paramedic. However, even with his size and age, he was still able to restrain Craig.

"Those guys know what they're doing. She's going to be fine."

Craig took a step back and tried to take a deep breath. He didn't know how the paramedic could be so calm about this. He had probably seen much worse in all his years.

"What relation is she to you?" the paramedic asked gently.

"She was my mother."

"Was? Don't worry, son, we'll save her. She's going to be fine."

"Oh, yeah. I mean she *is* my mother."

"Just sit tight, okay? Go read a magazine, go to the bathroom, and splash some water in your face, or whatever you need to do." Craig could tell this man was used to dealing with unruly people. "The nurses will come and tell you when you can see her as soon as possible."

"Thanks." Craig and Jack walked over to the waiting room, which contained a mixture of occupied and empty seats.

Jack looked at the faces of the others and wondered how many lives might be affected if one of those people lost their loved one today. How many of them would not go back home with the patient they had come with? Hell, perhaps Craig should be wondering the same. Who knew if Craig's mother would make it out alive? Who knew if she even wanted to? Clearly she had taken several more antidepressants than prescribed.

Craig knew she had been taking them. She told him that it wasn't for anything serious and that they just helped her to feel better. Jack looked over at Craig who had not spoken a word to him since they reached the hospital. As Craig sat there, not speaking, simply biting his fingernails, Jack wondered what he was thinking. What is someone to think when his mother was in such condition?

After about an hour, a nurse came out to speak with Craig. "Excuse me, Mr. Sanderson?" an overweight, middle-aged woman with black curly hair said.

"Yes, that's me."

"Dr. Ferris would like to speak with you. Come with me." The nurse led him into an office where a thin man with glasses was waiting for him. He had light brown hair and was smiling before Craig even entered the room. Jack was told to stay in the waiting room along with all the other non- relative visitors.

"Hey, Craig, how are you doing?" Dr. Ferris asked.

How the hell do you think I'm doing? Craig thought. *I'm in a damn hospital.* Craig held his breath at first though as he didn't want to upset the doctor who was trying to save his mom's life. He just couldn't see what there could be to smile about. Craig almost took it as an insult. "I'm fine," he finally replied.

"Well, I'm not going to lie to you," the doctor said quickly changing his tone from friendly to serious. "It was a close call, but she has regained consciousness." Craig's heart almost dropped straight out of his chest and onto the floor. "She's not yet in stable condition, but we think she will be fine."

"Can I see her now?"

"Yes, follow me."

Craig followed the doctor down the hospital hall past several other patients' rooms and couldn't help but look into the rooms and wonder how many of them would be all right and how many of their lives were already gone regardless of what the doctors did. Walking down the hallway was a cold feeling, almost like he was walking through a graveyard. It was like he knew so many terrible things could be happening in the building and there was nothing he could do about it. He remembered how Jack always expressed his uneasiness toward hospitals. Jack was the type of person who, if he saw a stranger suffering, as so many are in hospitals, his heart would go out to that person as if he or she were a member of his own family, and Jack's whole day would be ruined worrying about every single patient and family member in the place. Craig wouldn't consider himself to be that sympathetic toward others he didn't know, but he felt uneasy being there nonetheless.

It was an awkward feeling for Craig to know that twenty-two years ago his mom had been in the hospital giving him life, and now twenty-two years later he was in the hospital trying to give her life back to her.; guess they were even.

The doctor led Craig into a completely white room with nothing on the walls except a framed award of some kind. Craig didn't pay attention to it. Naturally, his focus was centered on the figure lying helplessly in the hospital bed ahead of him. Tubes were hooked up from a machine to her body and her eyes were barely open, almost in a squint, except that they were looking up toward the ceiling. She didn't look at Craig while he was standing in the doorway. She was too embarrassed for Craig to see her in such a condition. If it were Jack standing in that doorway and Mrs. Gardner were lying on the bed, he would have run over and wrapped his arms around her. He would have cried and thanked God that she was still alive. Not Craig, however. He was too disappointed in his mother at this point, almost ashamed of her.

After seeing that his mother was alive and would be all right, he no longer wanted to talk to her. He walked back to the waiting room and thought about the awful situation in front of him.

He waited there for seven hours until she was released from the hospital and allowed to go back home. Not a word was spoken on the drive home. Craig sat in the passenger seat and stared out of his window. Craig's mother sat behind the driver's seat and stared out of her window in the same fashion. They continued to do so until Jack had reached her house. Craig's mother walked toward the front door without saying a word to Jack. Craig stayed behind, outside the car, leaning over the driver's side window to talk to Jack. "Thanks a lot. I don't know what got into her."

"Listen, Craig, if you need anything, be sure to call me. I don't care what hour."

"Thanks. We'll be fine, though." Craig walked back into the house and Jack drove back to Long Island to Melanie's house, where he had anticipated he would be spending the majority of his evening before his night changed for the worse.

Craig shut the front door, which his mother had left open. It was now one o'clock in the morning, and both he and his mother were tired. Craig decided he would wait until morning to scold his mother. She had already lain down on the couch with her eyes shut, but Craig knew she couldn't be asleep yet. Regardless, he picked her up and carried her upstairs to her bedroom. After he had tucked her in, Craig went back down the stairs and lay down on the couch where the night had first begun until he fell asleep.

* * * * * * * * * *

Jack got back to Melanie's house about an hour later. The true tragedy of the situation had not fully reached Jack until he was away from it. *Poor Craig*, he thought. He wondered what he would do if it were his mother and thought about how lucky he was to have a mother like Mrs. Gardner.

"It's horrible," Melanie said after sitting down on her living room couch next to Jack. She had gotten a cold beer from the refrigerator for the both of them, which was greatly needed. After she sat down, Jack could see that a stream of water had leaked from Melanie's eyes.

"Don't cry, Mel," Jack said sympathetically as he put his arms around her to give her some comfort.

"I can't help it," Melanie blurted through her tears. Jack was used to seeing her cry. She had cried through several movies they had watched where she shed tears simply because Bambi's mother or Mufasa, the lion king, died. Also, he had seen her cry all the times her and Jack had broken up, when she bawled her eyes out even though she knew that most likely they would be back together within twenty-four hours. "I just wish there was something I could do to help."

"There's nothing we can do about his mother. She won't change. We just have to make sure he knows that we're here for him."

"How exactly did she get like this?"

"I'm not sure. I think it's something that had progressively gotten worse over the last ten years or so," Jack replied. "Once Craig's parents got divorced and she started seeing that asshole, David Cooper, her whole life turned around for the worse. I remember when I used to see her everyday when I was ten; boy, has she changed. She used to be very pretty. She had always been slender, but it used to be in a good way. Now she's so skinny, it's almost sick. She used to be so friendly to me. She used to take me to the park, play with me all the time, you know? Tonight, when I picked her up, she didn't say a single word to me or even give me a glance."

"Why did they get a divorce?"

"I'm not really sure. Craig has asked his parents several times, but they never told him an honest answer. But anyway, this rich bastard is bad news. When Craig was a teenager, David used to beat him frequently and his mother could do little to stop it. When she tried to stop it, David just beat him worse and beat her after him. She figured the best thing to do would just be to not provoke him and not stand up for her son. Because of this, Craig ran away from home several times. He told me he started hanging out with some low-lives and things got bad for him. Craig told me about one time when David forced Craig to help him fix a flat tire. Apparently Craig made a mistake and David picked up a crowbar and hit him right over the head and Craig ended up with a large gash in his head. After that, Craig told me he ran away and didn't come back for a month; never told me where he went during that month, though. He was only seventeen. It's just a shame what the kid had to go through, just because his mom decided to date an abusive drunk."

"Why does she stay with him, then?" Melanie questioned.

"I just told you. He's rich."

"Oh, shut up, Jack," Melanie said, sounding annoyed. "You don't know what you're talking about."

"Yeah, well I know more than you think. Anyway, I really need to be going." Jack finished his beer and walked toward the door.

"I'm going to give Craig a call tomorrow and make sure he's doing all right," Melanie said.

"Good idea." Jack gave her a kiss goodbye and got into his car, wishing he didn't have to make the drive back to New York City at three in the morning. He had to, however, because he knew his mother would be wide-awake on the Gardners' living room couch worrying and wondering if he was all right until the moment he walked through the door. The fact that he was twenty-two-years-old was irrelevant to her. She would worry about him until the day she died; just as Jack's grandparents continued to worry about her.

* * * * * * * * * *

Craig awakened before the sun the following morning. Naturally, he wasn't able to get much sleep after the traumatic events that took place last night. He walked up the stairs to his mother's room and slowly opened the door. *Good, she's still breathing,* he thought. Craig gave out a sigh of relief. He wasn't hungry in the least, so he sat on the couch with the television off for two hours before he heard his mother walking down the stairs. She was still wearing the same clothes that she was wearing the previous night, as was Craig. She didn't say a word to Craig, just sat down on the kitchen table and out of Craig's sight. Craig followed her into the kitchen. "Mom, we're going to have to talk about this sometime."

"Talk about what?" she asked, as if she were totally oblivious to what had happened the night before.

"Don't play stupid, Mom."

Craig remembered his father used to say that to him. It was ironic now that Craig was saying it to his mother, a woman forty-six years of age, in a scolding way, as if she were a young child. Yet, as a young child would do, or even a guilty puppy for that matter, she hung her head. If she had a tail, Craig was sure it would be tucked in between her legs. "What happened last night? Didn't you remember I was coming over?"

"No, I guess I forgot. I was lonely. I missed my Davy and the antidepressants just weren't doing their job."

"Your Davy?" Craig said disgustedly. "You missed that jerk enough to almost kill yourself?"

"You try sitting around this damn house all day long every day. It gets lonesome."

"That's no excuse, Mom. You look terrible. You look like you've been getting no sleep." Indeed she did; she had dark bags under her brown eyes. "And," Craig said before pausing, "what the hell is that?" he asked, pointing to her lift bicep. A dark purple bruise covered much of the muscle. He must not have noticed it last night in all the excitement.

"It's nothing."

"Did David do that?" he yelled, getting more and more outraged at the thought of someone hurting his mother.

"It was an accident," she said. "I just got in his way at the wrong time."

"This is bullshit, Mom. You're not putting up with this anymore; you deserve better."

"It's not that simple. I love him."

"Do you really? Because this isn't love. You deserve to be with someone who will treat you right and make you feel good about yourself, not bring you down."

Craig's mother closed her eyes and paused. "You're right, Craig, but it is so hard. I don't want to leave him and I don't think he'll change."

"He won't unless you stand up for yourself. Maybe then he will have to respect you."

"I can't do it on my own," she said as she began to cry.

"You're not doing it alone. I'm staying here with you. I'm not going back to school next semester."

His mother tried to talk him out of it, but it was no use. Craig had already made up his mind. He was dropping out of school, and he was going to help his mom turn her life around. His mother promised her son that she would no longer drink, do drugs of any kind, and would not let her boyfriend push her around anymore. She would start her life anew. Now the only trouble was for Craig to tell Jack, his best friend and someone who had helped him through much of his college experience, about his decision to drop out of school just a semester before graduation.

The officer turned the page.

Chapter 7

Dillon's Beach

The next day Brianne asked Jack if he wanted to take a day off to visit Dillon's Beach. There was no Court session scheduled for this day and Jack thought he could use the serenity of the beach to take his mind off the trial, so he agreed. The constant talk of his former wife was starting to get to him. It was extremely difficult to sit in a courtroom and listen to attorneys and witnesses discuss the details of his wife's murder. Not to mention, sitting in the room with the person responsible for the entire situation and fighting the urge to jump from his seat and beat the shit out of him was the hardest task of all. He hoped this little trip to the beach would be able to calm things down for him a bit.

"Are you ready to go?" Brianne asked. She had come out of the master bedroom holding some blankets, sandwiches in a zip-locked bag, and her bright pink purse. She wore a white tank top, which showed off her breasts slightly, and a rather short jean skirt to match. Her tan legs looked extremely sexy and her toes sparkled with nail polish through her sandals. She was wearing stylish brown sunglasses that matched well with her light brown hair and big brown eyes. Her appearance had a certain sexiness to it, but she still managed to look sweet and innocent.

"Yeah, let me just get changed," Jack replied. He went into the bedroom and changed into more appropriate clothing for the beach environment. He put on a white sleeveless shirt with light colored jean shorts. He took his bathing suit along with him in case the weather was nice enough for a swim.

"All right, I'm ready to go," Jack said, coming out of the bedroom.

The two of them got inside of Jack's expensive, jet-black Mercedes. It was a four-door car with silver lining and chrome wheels. The windows were tinted, making most of the car look dark, the only light coming through the windshield and possibly the sunroof. The inside of the car was just as nice. Black leather covered the seats and the dashboard and doors were beautifully lined by shiny brown wood trim.

Jack drove down the suburban street past all of the other expensive homes. However, all of them failed in comparison to Jack's palace. The drive was not a long one, only about fifteen minutes. Jack's house actually overlooked the Atlantic, but it was on top of a large hill and it took a while to drive down the mountain to the beach. It was a wonder that he did not go there more often to enjoy the beauty of it all. But how could he possibly see beauty in anything at this point in his life?

Jack and Melanie had never gone to the beach despite their five years together. Jack had only recently moved into his palace of a house, about six months ago, and to be honest Melanie had not been at Jack's new house very often when she had been alive. The fact that Melanie and Jack had never been to the beach together was much of the reason Jack agreed to spending this day with Brianne. He figured it would at least be a place where nothing could remind him of her.

Silence filled the majority of the ride. "I think this will be good for you, Jack," said Brianne, breaking the silence.

"And why is that?" Jack said, even though the answer was obvious.

"Well, you've been stuck in that courtroom all the time lately. It would be nice for you to have a relaxing day. Not to mention you've been having those nightmares lately and won't even sleep in bed with me anymore," Brianne said, sounding understanding yet annoyed at the same time. Jack didn't respond, and Brianne didn't seem to mind. Before long they had arrived at the beach.

The weather, which had looked sunny to begin with, did not stay pleasant for long. The moment they hit the sand the clouds overtook the sky, blocking the sun completely and making the beach several shades darker. It was windy but was not terribly cold. Luckily, Jack and Brianne brought a change of clothes in the car just in case. They went back to the car and changed into something a little more suitable for the situation. After getting dressed in sweaters and sweatshirts, they returned to the sand. They walked along the water, which was bluish-gray due to the weather. The beach definitely didn't appear to be anything special on this particular day. However, it wasn't always like that.

Five years ago, when Melanie and Jack first met, she often talked about the greatness of the beach. She talked of a place with powdery white sand, like fresh snow on an early December morning, which was soft under your bare feet. The water was a crystal-clear blue that looked like glass on the surface. There were full green trees just beyond the sand along little mounds and hills covered in green. He was told that when the sky was perfectly blue and cloudless, the sun shined brightly and the slight cool breeze made it the most pleasant place in the world. Several banks were where the water would flow between the green mounds, giving it an island feel. It sounded like heaven. Jack could not see any of this. When he looked at the beach, he couldn't see any of the joy that Melanie had once talked about with such passion. He hated to admit it, but even this place was reminding him of Melanie.

"Come on, Jack, what are you waiting for?" said Brianne. Jack had not realized it, but he had completely stopped walking to look around at the scenery and Brianne was now a ways in front of him.

"Oh, sorry," Jack replied as he walked toward her.

"So, Jack. How is your trial going?" Brianne asked.

"I thought the point of this trip was to forget about the trial," said Jack.

"Yeah, you're right, I'm sorry. I just don't know what else to talk about."

"We can talk about whatever you want."

"All right, let's talk about us then."

Jack seemed taken aback. "What about us?"

"I don't know," Brianne began. "Sometimes I just don't feel like other couples. It's like lately the only time you give me any attention is when you're fucking me!"

"You know I've just been busy lately, Brianne … I love you," Jack lied.

"I know you do," she replied. "I love you too."

It's amazing how some people can convince themselves that they are in love, Jack thought. He had only known her for a few months now; already she was claiming her love for him, and she truly believed that he loved her back. Brianne knew nothing of what true love was. She had never been in love before and had never shared anything to the degree that Jack and Melanie had shared. Jack sometimes thought that the concept of love was impossible and impractical. Hearing people talk about how they were in love often made Jack wonder if there was such a thing as love. If love was as great as it was made out to be, then how could people claim they reached it so easily? All truly great things in life were rare commodities. How could people know if they had reached it? Perhaps they thought they were in love but simply didn't know better because they had not truly been there before?

All of this had changed for Jack after meeting Melanie. He too became one of those hopeless people who believed themselves to be in love without knowing any better that there was no such emotion. After Melanie had passed, Jack regained his senses and returned to his original feelings. If love was true and was the strongest thing in the world, then why couldn't his love protect Melanie?

Jack and Brianne walked hand in hand along the ocean shore as the waves lightly crashed into the large sharp rocks in the distance ahead of them.

"You know, your parents called today," said Brianne.

"What did they want?"

"They're having a family get-together and wanted to know if you could go."

"What did you tell them?"

"Well, I told them you would go of course," said Brianne.

"When is it?"

"Month from now."

"Did they ask you to come too?"

"No," said Brianne.

"Oh, well, don't feel bad. She didn't like any of my exes either."

"Why not?"

"It's kind of a long story. Anyways, what do you want to do now?"

"Let's just walk up to those rocks and try to find somewhere to take a rest," Brianne said. They were now fairly close to the rocks that seemed much more distant just moments before. The large rocks looked ten times bigger once they found themselves next to them. Half of the giant rocks lay in the ocean, while the other half of the rocks remained on the sand. The sand behind the rocks slanted upward toward the rocks like a ramp. Brianne and Jack walked up to the rocks and stood at the edge of them so that they were hanging over the ocean. The ocean was creating a strong but pleasant breeze that was throwing around Brianne's hair in a wild manner. They couldn't have been more than fifteen feet off shore, but the water still appeared to be fairly deep below them.

"Come over here and sit down with me," Brianne insisted. She walked away slightly from the edge and looked for a spot to sit. The rocks were jagged for the most part, but there was enough flat area for them to walk around and to sit comfortably. Jack went over and took his place next to his girlfriend. Although they were no longer at the edge of the rocks, they could still see the waves of the ocean and hear them crashing into the base of the rocks below them.

"So how long are you planning on being off of work?" Brianne asked.

"Just until the case gets over with, I guess," Jack responded. He had not worked since the beginning of the trial.

"How long could a simple case of robbery possibly take?" Brianne questioned. Apparently, she still had no idea of the true nature of the case.

"Well, some new evidence has recently been discovered," Jack said. "Could take another couple months before this whole thing is resolved."

"Oh, I see," Brianne said. She paused for several moments. "Jack," she began. "I know we've only been together for a couple months now, but where is this relationship going?"

"It's going to go wherever you want it to go, all right?" said Jack, although he wasn't really paying attention. He certainly didn't want to be bothered by Brianne's longing to find her true love. It annoyed him that she just couldn't be happy, that she always wanted something more. *Didn't she know that nothing good could come from a couple growing closer together?* Jack thought.

He stared off into the distance, the cool breeze chilling the bones in his body more as he thought about his deceased wife. He noticed a seagull flying around overhead, high above the ocean's surface. It was floating around, wings spread wide, letting the wind throw the bird around as it pleased. Jack wondered what it would be like to be that bird, without a care in the world. It didn't have to deal with emotional attachments and the deaths of loved ones in the same way that humans did. He didn't want to think about it anymore. The point of the day was to keep his mind off Melanie and he had to try his hardest to accomplish that goal. The more he thought about it, the lonelier he felt, and so he moved closer to Brianne.

He scooted a little closer to her and wrapped his arms around her. She responded with a sweet smile. She truly adored him and wanted them to be genuinely happy together. She rested her head against his shoulder, much like a loving couple would. Her long brown hair flew wildly in the wind, tickling Jack's face. She tilted her head up waiting for an arrival of affection. Jack granted her the kiss she was waiting for. At nearly the same time the clouds finally gave way and let the water go as the sky began pouring rain.

"Come with me, Jack," Brianne said as she quickly rose to her feet and pulled Jack by the hand. Jack followed as they climbed down the rocks to a little cave that was created by the surrounding large rocks. The sand underneath their feet was now growing damp as the rain continued to poor down. The giant rocks on one side were slanted all the way down to the sand so that at the ground level there was some dry area if they pressed up all the way against the rocks. The slant served as an overhang of perhaps four feet high.

Brianne and Jack, now soaking wet, lay together in the dry sand and laughed with one another about the current situation. Playful laughter turned into passionate embraces as the two began intimately kissing and Jack rolled over on top of Brianne. He kissed her as though he loved her, while the ocean waves crashed into the rocks outside of their cave. Due to crevices in the rocks, small streams of water leaked into the cave. Jack continued to kiss Brianne while simultaneously unbuttoning her pants, a dual talent that Jack had perfected. After a little struggle to get the tight wet jeans off, Brianne began to take his off as well. They made love in the snowy sand with the water pouring down just inches away from them. It was extremely passionate and romantic until Jack stopped himself in the middle.

"I'm sorry, Brianne," Jack said as he stood up and put his pants back on in the rain. "We really should get going home." Jack began climbing out of the cave and back up to the top of the rocks.

"Jack! What the hell is wrong with you?" Brianne cried while struggling to get her pants on.

"I'm sorry, Brianne. I just really think we should get home. We can continue this another time."

Brianne didn't say another word as they walked back to the car and drove back to their house. She couldn't help the feeling that she wasn't good enough for Jack, which wasn't the case at all. In all actuality, Jack was beginning to feel closer to her than he anticipated, and the thought of falling for another the way he had for Melanie was not something he was prepared to do.

COLLEGE DAYS ...

Chapter 8

An Unfaithful Woman

Craig set the receiver down after the phone line had gone dead on the other end. An outraged Jack did not see eye to eye with Craig on his decision to drop out of school to help his mom. Craig rarely saw Jack get that upset with him, to the point where raising his voice was necessary, but this time Jack was livid. Craig could see where Jack was coming from. He had made it so far through college, through three and a half years of tough work to get where he was, and Jack had helped him much of the way. Then again, Jack couldn't understand given his mother; his entire family. Unlike Craig, Jack was dealt a good hand. He didn't come home to see his mother beaten or passed-out drunk. He didn't come home from college to find his mom knocked out from antidepressants. Perhaps if he had witnessed just one of those events, then Jack would understand.

Craig became more frustrated and even upset with Jack as he thought about the memories more. *Why does all of this happen to me? Why doesn't anything go wrong in his perfect world? It just isn't fair.* Just as Craig's anger was at its highest, it was interrupted by the ring of the phone. He answered it.

"Hey, Craig, it's Melanie." Craig almost forgot to mention Jack's *perfect* girlfriend, Melanie. Why didn't he have one of his own?

"Hey, Melanie, what's going on?"

"I've been worried about you. Jack told me what happened with your mother. I'm so sorry. How are you doing?" Melanie was as sympathetic as ever.

"Awful, I just had a fight with Jack. Have you talked to him lately?"

"A couple hours ago. Why, what happened?"

"Are you with him now?"

"No."

"Can I come over? I really need someone to talk to about this."

"Yeah, sure, Craig."

"All right. I'm going to take the bus. I'll be there in about an hour."

* * * * * * * * * *

Jack hung up the phone with Craig. He couldn't believe what Craig was telling him. What was he thinking? Did he want to ruin his life just months before graduation? Jack couldn't understand it. "After everything I've done for him, how selfish could he be?" He knew it wasn't his decision to tell Craig what to do, but if he didn't, who else would? Jack decided to seek advice elsewhere. "Mom, can I talk to you for a second?"

His mother was lying on a towel, wearing gym shorts and a tank top, on the backyard deck absorbing the sun. Upon Jack's question she jumped up in alert.

"Oh, no! Is everything all right? Is Melanie pregnant?" she asked overly-alarmed.

"No, Mom." Jack gave a smile and shook his head.

"Well, that's a relief. What is it then?"

"Craig's mom was sent to the hospital the other night: drug overdose."

"Oh no, poor Craig."

"Yeah, but that's not exactly what I wanted to talk about."

"Then what is it?"

Jack paused. "It's about Craig. He has this crazy idea to drop out of school."

"What?"

"He thinks he can help his mom change her life around if he stays at home."

"Oh, I see," Mrs. Gardner said. "Well, as noble as that is, Craig has no idea what he's getting into. I've known Craig's mom for a long time, as you know, but even before you were born we were friends. She isn't going to change. She's like this because she wants to be like this. Jack, what I'm about to tell you can never leave this house. I would prefer if you didn't tell anyone in the family either because they have no reason to know."

"All right," Jack said, unsure of where she was going with this.

"I know why Mr. and Mrs. Sanderson separated."

"You do? Why?"

"It's okay, Jack. I know you saw the whole thing happen and I am so sorry. What a terrible thing for a young child to witness."

"I don't know what you're talking about," Jack began to say before being interrupted.

"You don't have to pretend that you don't know anymore. I know you've been pretending to protect Craig from knowing what Mrs. Sanderson did. I should have talked to you earlier, but I thought that maybe you would have forgotten all about it. After all, you were so young when it happened."

"How do you know I didn't forget about it?" Jack asked.

"I see the way you've always looked at her Jack. It's almost as though you despise her."

Jack did not look up at his mother, but spoke softly. "You weren't there, Mom. You didn't see the look in his eyes, the pain, the feeling of betrayal."

"Yes, I know Jack. But I knew much more about the situation than you might think."

"What do you mean?"

"I mean the time that you and Mr. Sanderson walked in on her was not the first."

"There were others? And you knew about them?"

"Yes, Jack, there were several others."

"Why didn't you stop her?" Jack said rather angrily.

"I tried. I told her how lucky she was to have Mr. Sanderson and I told her that she was going to ruin her family. But she didn't stop for the same reason that she will not change now. She pushes those who truly love her, or loved her, away. She thrives off the attention she might get when people feel sorry for her."

"That still doesn't explain why she had the affair though."

"Oh, Jack," she said sweetly. "People have affairs for all different reasons. Personally, I think she was attracted to the youthfulness and riches of that David Cooper. After all, Craig was an unexpected, and in some ways unpleasant, surprise for the Sandersons."

"They didn't want to have a kid?"

"Well, they hadn't planned on it. When Mrs. Sanderson first found out she was pregnant, she didn't tell Mr. Sanderson. She came to me, scared as hell, and told me she didn't know what to do. Her plan was to get an abortion and never tell Mr. Sanderson about it. She said she wasn't ready for all that kid stuff. It took me a whole month to convince her to talk to

Mr. Sanderson and keep the child. Turns out Mr. Sanderson wasn't nearly as scared as Mrs. Sanderson. He wanted to keep the child and thus Craig was born. I think soon after the child came is when she met this David Cooper. Ten years of lies and deception caught up with her, but to tell you the truth, I don't think she minded."

* * * * * * * * * *

Melanie was still sitting in her black sweats and gray sweatshirt when the doorbell rang. Her hair was pulled up into a bun and she had no make-up on her face. She didn't feel the need to get all dolled up. Why would she?

"Hi, Craig," she said, greeting him with a hug. "Come sit down." Craig followed her to the living room couch where they both took a seat. "I can't believe what happened with your mom. I'm so sorry."

"Yeah, it's all right. I don't really want to talk about my mom right now though."

"Then what do you want to talk about?" Melanie said surprised.

"I don't know if you've heard, but I've decided to drop out of school."

"What?" Melanie blurted. Apparently Jack had not told her. "Why would you do that?"

"I feel like this is the only chance I have to change my mom's life around. Maybe if I'm there, then David won't be able to walk all over her and depress her so much. Anyway, Jack thinks I'm making a huge mistake. I wanted to see what you thought about it."

Melanie paused for a long while. "Wow," she said. "I think it's great what you're doing for your mom. Obviously dropping out of school is a huge decision, but when it comes down to it, I think it has to be your decision. You have to do what *you* think is best for you and your family, not what me or Jack think."

"Well, I think my mom's life outweighs a college degree any day," Craig responded.

"Well, there you go then," Melanie said.

Craig smiled. It felt good to finally have someone on his side. He respected Jack's opinion, but this was something that he had to do for himself. Melanie and Craig talked for another hour or so. They talked about many things, most having nothing to do with his mom or school. Talking with Melanie made him feel a lot better, as though he knew for sure he was making the right decision. He almost forgot all about it on the bus ride back to New York City until he arrived at David Cooper's house.

Reality struck Craig when he saw David's red Porsche sitting in the driveway. *Great, this will be interesting,* Craig thought. He always hated seeing David, even if he was in a rare, nice mood. Craig figured it would be an uncomfortable meeting, especially since they hadn't seen each other in quite some time.

The officer turned the page.

Chapter 9

A Mental Disease

The alarm on Jack's clock sounded as he arose to yet another day. He had to wake up earlier than usual as he had scheduled an appointment with his psychologist. Jack Gardner had been seeing a psychologist for several years now. He started attending one during his junior year in high school due to a minor onset of obsessive-compulsive disorder, among other issues. After the death of his wife, Melanie, he knew that he and his psychologist would have many more issues to tackle.

Jack's psychologist, Charles Slovano, was a tall, thin man, about six feet, five in height. He had a full head of thick brown hair, which was matched by a beard and mustache. His glasses, which were held up by the tip of his pointed nose, always seemed to be angled lower than his eyes actually were, as if he was attempting to look scholarly. He did not need to pretend, however, as he had proven himself wise throughout the years.

Jack turned off the alarm and sat up on the side of his bed so that his feet were on the floor. He wasn't wearing any clothes as the night before had been a bit of a wild one. He turned around to see his girlfriend, Brianne, still sound asleep wrapped up in the big white bed sheets. He leaned over and gave her a kiss on the forehead before getting completely out of bed and putting his clothes on. He was careful not to wake her when he left the room as he had not mentioned his psychologist to her yet. He gathered up his keys and wallet and entered his Mercedes. The drive took a little while as he had to drive from his home in Long Island into New York City for his appointment. It was a beautiful spring day, the type of day where one pictured birds chirping and flowers blossoming. He converted the removable top of his expensive car so that he could enjoy the cool breeze against his face.

When Jack arrived in New York City at Slovano Psychological Care, he parked his car and made extra care to lock his doors. His set of keys had a remote control button to lock and unlock the doors. He clicked the lock button four times and then pulled on the handle four times to make sure it was locked. He walked up the steps to the small building and opened the glass doors. He walked up to the secretary who was waiting behind a glass window.

"Hi, I have an appointment to see Dr. Slovano at nine o'clock," Jack told her.

"Hi, Jack. Go ahead and have a seat in the waiting room and he will be seeing you shortly."

Jack walked back and took a seat on a black cushioned chair and waited patiently for the doctor to return. He looked around at the covers of all the magazines sitting on the table for the customers to read but didn't bother to pick any of them up. He noticed the texture of the white painting on the wall. It was textured so that the paint was bumpy, reminding Jack of the walls he had in his bedroom as a young child. He recalled finding random images in the textures, such as animals, people, and anything else. He always had a creative mind.

"Hello, Jack," said Dr. Slovano. "Are you ready?"

"Yeah, Charles, let's do it." Jack touched both of the arms of the chair four times before rising and following Dr. Slovano into his office. Over the years, Jack had learned that people with OCD often find themselves counting things and performing strange rituals which do not make sense to other people. OCD was different for all people who suffered from it. For Jack, he had several rituals that he did routinely without even thinking. It was a very complicated situation, of which often only the person suffering can understand why he did the things he did.

In Jack's case, it all started with numbers when he was about twelve years old. For whatever reason, certain numbers appealed to him, and others did not. The numbers two, four, five, eight, nine, and zero were considered "good" numbers. The numbers: one, three, six, and seven were considered "bad" numbers. When it came to multiple-digit numbers, the last digit was the only number that mattered. The routine that Jack got into was to only do things in repetitions of "good" numbers. He would press the lock button on his keys four times and jiggle the handle on the door four times to make sure it was locked. The four clicks of the button plus the four jiggles of the handle added up to eight, plus the two different objects he used (the button and the door handle) added up to ten. Since zero was a "good" number, this was acceptable. However, if he pressed the key button two times, and jiggled the handle two times, it would all add up to six (two clicks of the button, plus two jiggles of the handle, plus two objects), a "bad" number. This made life rather confusing for Jack, which was why he tended to do things in two sets of activities, in a repetition of four times each. By this point of the explanation most people were either confused as hell or gave up trying to understand. However, Jack rarely talked to anyone about his condition, making him somewhat of a mystery to those around him.

What was even more difficult to understand was why Jack felt he had to do these things. For some reason he felt if he didn't do certain things, if he did something in a "bad" number of repetitions, then maybe something bad would happen to his family. It was as though he was not creating the most perfect situation for himself and so he wanted to make it as perfect as possible. His counting of numbers extended to everything. If he accidentally hit ninety miles per hour on the freeway he would make sure he hit ninety another time so that it was in a repetition of two (ninety plus ninety is 180, plus the two times that he did it added up to 182, a "good number). He made sure while lifting weights to never finish his number of repetitions on a "bad" number, and anything else one could think of. OCD was known to be hereditary as Jack's mother was also a very superstitious person. From Jack's many visits to Dr. Slovano over the years, he was able to control his obsessive-compulsive disorder, but episodes had been coming back to him since the death of his wife. They often came back stronger when he was stressed or worried about something.

Jack soon found himself back inside Dr. Slovano's office. Inside the office was a large leather couch for the patient to lay his troubled spirit upon, and next to it was a large leather chair for the psychologist to sit on. It was exactly the type of psychologist's office Jack had seen in the movies. Files on shelves were hanging on the walls and papers were scattered on desks. Over the years Jack had become extremely comfortable with Dr. Slovano and felt he could pretty much tell him anything. This was the first visit since the death of Jack's wife.

"It's been a while, Jack," said Dr. Slovano. Even if he didn't use big words, the tone of his voice always sounded to be in a dignified manner, just as Jack had remembered.

"Yeah, it has Charles. How have you been?"

"All is well with me. I'm so sorry about your loss," said Dr. Slovano.

"Yeah, me too," said Jack.

"So what should we talk about today?"

"It's been coming back, Charles, my OCD. The pills just aren't doing it anymore."

"And how long have your superstitions, as we'll call them, been coming back?"

"It's been months and months."

"Months?" Dr. Slovano said shocked. "Why didn't you come in for treatment?"

"I've been busy. I guess I just thought there wasn't any cure at this point."

"So then why are you here now?"

"It's been getting outrageous. I have to do something about it immediately. I need you to do something."

"Well, you know there's no magical cure for these kinds of things, Jack. I can talk to you about what you've been experiencing and perhaps try to make you more at ease. Now, as you've told me before, you feel like if you don't follow these superstitions, then something terrible will happen in your life. Is that correct?"

"It's not that something terrible *will* happen, it's that something terrible *could* happen," Jack corrected him.

"So you're telling me that nothing terrible can happen as long as you follow these rituals?"

"The odds are much less likely that something bad will occur, yes. I can't explain to you why this is, it's just the way my mind works," Jack explained.

"I know I've never asked you this Jack, and of course it's none of my business if you chose not to tell me, but do you happen to be a religious person?"

"Yes, in some ways. Why do you ask?" Jack was not sure where Slovano was going with this.

"It's just, often times, obsessive-compulsive disorder can be linked to different religious aspects in my opinion."

"I'm not following."

"Well, religions in a way, while devout members will deny it, are often superstitious. Many people that claim to be deeply involved in religion are actually only that way because they are scared what this almighty God will do to them if they are not devout."

"So you're saying I have OCD because I'm religious?"

"Ha ha, not at all," Charles said with a laugh. "I'm simply saying many of the same patterns exist between the two. Take Christianity for instance. Do you happen to be Christian?"

"Yes."

"All right, well, many Christians, while hating to admit it, are worshiping out of fear. They are scared that if they don't worship in the way that their God wants then they are condemned to eternal damnation. Do you pray a lot?"

"Oh, all the time," Jack replied.

"Many Christians pray for the same reasons that you perform your OCD superstitions."

"And why is that?"

"Because, *why not?* What do you have to lose from praying? If there is a God and you pray, you are doing your God's will, and should be saved in the afterlife. However, even if there isn't a God, what can you lose from praying?"

"Nothing."

"Precisely," Dr. Slovano replied. "You can lose nothing in the same way that you performing your superstitions has nothing for you to lose. Even if they don't better your life in any way, they certainly shouldn't worsen it."

After the doctor finished, silence followed for a couple minutes as Dr. Slovano allowed time for Jack to process his thoughts.

"How does this help me get over my problem?" Jack asked.

"Well, it doesn't unless you search for the true meaning of it all, which is, where did your OCD stem from? Just as religion can often be based off fear, I believe your condition is likewise based solely off fear. I suggest you find out where your fear is stemming from immediately, and what precisely it is that you are afraid of. However, I give you another month to come up with that answer Jack because we are out of time in this session."

"Thanks a lot, Charles. You've certainly given me a lot to think about."

"Until next time Jack."

COLLEGE DAYS ...

Chapter 10

Spousal Abuse

Craig walked up to the front door and took a deep breath, preparing himself for the unpleasant events that were soon to follow. When he opened the door and walked in he could not see anyone, but sure enough he heard David's deep and threatening voice screaming in an outrageous rage. He walked along the marble walkway past the stairs and into the carpeted kitchen.

"You do whatever the hell I tell you to do, got it?" David said. He was standing over the top of Craig's mother with his fists clenched and breathing heavily. She lay under him trembling, holding her hands above her face as if to shield herself from what David was doing to her.

"I'm sorry, David. I know I was supposed to take your suit to the dry cleaners, but I forgot. It won't happen again, I promise."

"Does it look like I give a shit?" David yelled and gave her a backhand across the face just as Craig entered the room. Craig stopped for a moment, stunned by what he saw. He looked at his mother and noticed that her left eye was puffy and her nose was bleeding. Clearly this had been going on for some time before he witnessed David's backhand blow. David stopped upon Craig's entrance into the room. He faced Craig and rolled up the sleeves to his long sleeve buttoned-up shirt, as to say that Craig was next if he didn't leave the room. However, Craig was no longer the teenage boy that David used to beat up. He was a man, just like David.

Without hesitation, Craig ran at the man that he despised so much. In one swoop he lifted David off his feet and slammed him aggressively on the floor. Craig crawled on top of him and began driving fists into David's face as if he were possessed. "Don't- you- ever- touch- my- mother- again!" Craig yelled while he continued to connect into David's jaw, eyes, mouth, and chin. However, it soon was no use in saying anything because David had become unconscious, flat on his back. Regardless, Craig continued his relentless pursuit as if he was going to kill him and, truth be told, he very well might have if it were not for his mother.

"Craig, no!" she screamed, getting onto her feet.

Craig continued to swing as his mother came up from behind him and attempted to pull him off. When Craig resisted, she took her long fingernails and clawed Craig in the cheek so that he was bleeding. She began slapping at him, throwing her arms around frantically until Craig got off her boyfriend.

Craig's mother was now profusely crying. "What the hell are you doing?" she cried hysterically through her tears.

"What are you talking about, Mom? I'm here to protect you."

"I don't need your damn protection! Get the hell out of my house!"

Craig looked his mother deep in her crying eyes. Everything she had told him about changing her life around was a lie. She would remain wasting her life, being nothing more than a doormat for someone else to step all over until the day that she died. As Craig looked into her eyes, thinking about all the memories they shared together, he wondered how many more opportunities he would ever have to look into those eyes.

As he left the house, slamming the door behind him, he thought, *What now? That son of a bitch David would surely not help pay his college tuition now. Where would he go? What now?*

* * * * * * * * * *

"I'm so sorry, Jack. I had to tell him what I thought was right," Melanie said, although she didn't sound at all apologetic. A planned pleasant evening in at Melanie's house, including dinner and possibly renting a movie, had gone bad when Melanie mentioned she advised Craig to drop out of college for his mother.

"How could ending his education be the right thing to do?" Jack said, standing up from the living room couch that the two were sitting on.

"Think about if it were your mother. Wouldn't you want to help her?"

"You don't understand. She's a damn drunk; she has been for fifteen years. A no-good, lying, cheating drunk! No matter what Craig tries to do to help her, she won't change. And if Craig continues to worry about her, then he's going to end up just like her one day!"

"Stop yelling at me, Jack! Maybe you don't always know what's best for him. You're not his damn father!"

Jack grabbed the phone, which was attached by a cord to the wall. He ripped the cord completely out of the wall and threw the phone against the wall, just to the left of where Melanie was sitting. The force of the phone hitting the wall had actually broken the receiver and also chipped some of the white paint off the wall.

"You're so stupid. I don't even know why the hell I was with you!"

"Oh, so now we're broken up?" Melanie cried.

However, it was too late. Jack had stormed out of the house, slamming the door behind him and getting into his car. He drove back to his and Craig's house in Long Island, hoping Craig would be there so that he could have one more chance to talk Craig out of his idiotic decision.

The officer turned the page.

Chapter 11

The Beginning of the End

Craig rushed out of the house wiping the blood off his face. *I have to find a phone,* he thought. He walked around until he reached the local shopping center. To his luck, a pay phone was outside the main grocery store. *Great, now who to call?* Instinctively he thought of Jack, the one who had always been there to solve his problem had to be the obvious choice, despite the fact that Jack was mad at him. Craig was so furious he needed someone to calm him down, and he needed it now.

He deposited some coins and dialed the number to the house that both he and Jack owned. No one answered. "Maybe he's at Melanie's house," he guessed. He dialed her number and this time there was a response.

"Hello?" came Melanie's irritated voice over the phone.

"Melanie? It's Craig. Is Jack there?"

"No, you just missed the asshole," Melanie said, still heated from her fight with her boyfriend. "He just left."

"Oh, all right. Well, I guess I'll talk to you later then." Craig was about to hang up the receiver when Melanie responded.

"Is there anything I can help you with?"

"Well, I was looking for a ride, possibly even a place to hang out for a while."

"Is there anything wrong?"

"It's my mom," Craig said angrily, as if Melanie was the person he was upset with. "She's been beaten again. This time I'm never going back. I need a place to stay until I figure this out."

"Oh my God! Where are you?"

"The shopping center."

"The one on Tracy Boulevard?" she asked. " I'll be right there."

Craig took a seat on the curb outside the grocery store and thought in dismay about what had just happened at his mother's house. His own mother, turning his back on him? He would have never guessed in a million years.

"Excuse me, sir." A grocery store clerk had come outside to speak with Craig. He was a mature man, perhaps in his upper thirties, with blond hair that was combed back nicely. "I'm sorry, but I'm going to have to ask you to move along. We don't allow people to sit in front of the store."

"Son of a bitch," Craig muttered under his breath but got up and moved nonetheless. He walked down the shopping center a little farther but did not sit down this time. "The nerve of that guy to kick me away from the store as if I was a homeless beggar. I guess that's what I'm becoming though. With no way to pay for college, I'll have to drop out of school anyway. I can't afford another semester on my own. Not to mention I'm not sure if I'll have enough money to even pay the rent."

Sometime, whether it was soon due to a lack of rent money or later due to a lack of a degree, he was sure he would become one of those homeless beggars. However, he would rather beg all of his life, or even die for that matter, before he would suck up to David and beg him to pay for tuition once again.

Melanie swooped into the parking lot in her small, white two-door Honda Accord. Craig opened the passenger door and hopped in right as Melanie took off. She drove as if Craig had just robbed a bank and she was driving the get-away car.

"Tell me what happened," Melanie demanded immediately.

"That son of a bitch David is what happened."

"What did he do to your mom?"

"All I saw was a slap in the face," Craig said. "But there was more."

"Well, this isn't the first time is it?"

"I'm pretty sure it isn't. But this is the first time I saw it in person."

Before long they had reached Melanie's house, the same house that just minutes before Jack had stormed out of. Melanie unlocked the door and walked into the kitchen with Craig following close behind. "I need a drink," she said. "How about you?"

"Thanks, but I don't drink anymore. Don't really want that stuff around me. I've seen how it ruined my mom's life."

"You don't mind if I drink do you?"

"Go right ahead," he said approvingly.

Melanie pulled a beer from the refrigerator before going into the living room and taking a seat on the sofa. Craig followed.

"So you left right after you saw him hit her?"

"Not exactly," Craig began, but he was interrupted by a telephone ring. "Is that your phone?"

"Yeah, uh, this one here," she said as she pointed to the living room phone which had been ripped out of the wall. "Well, it broke. Come upstairs with me. It isn't cordless. Maybe it'll be Jack."

Melanie raced upstairs and answered the phone just before the answering machine was to sound. "Damn salesman," she said as Craig entered her bedroom. Melanie, who had still been holding her beer attentively, now set it down on her white dresser and took a seat on her white fluffy bed. "I swear they always call me at the worst times. Anyways, I'm really sorry for interrupting. Please continue with what you were saying."

"I beat the hell out of him, Melanie," Craig blurted. He sounded just as much afraid as he did angry.

"You what?"

"I'm not even sure he's still alive," Craig said. He was not speaking with pride in what he had done but rather fear. He didn't feel sorry for David in the least, but he had never seriously injured anyone before.

"You killed him?"

"I don't know. I hope so," Craig lied.

"What the hell do you mean you *hope so?*"

"You weren't there Melanie. He was standing over her like—like he was a predator and she was his prey, and he was going to enjoy a delicious meal. The son of a bitch stood there, over her with this devilish smile upon his face—the kind of look as to say that he was never going to stop and there was nothing I could do about it."

"So what did you do?" Melanie asked.

"I did something about it. Melanie, up until the time I was ten, all my mom did was take care of me. I have so many memories of us playing together and her raising me right. Now, I know she's done a lot of wrong these past twelve years, but to me I still got to protect her. To me she's still that woman that was there for me every day. I just couldn't take it anymore. Who did that David think he was to beat *my* mother?"

"You still haven't told me what you did."

"I tackled him and beat him within inches of his life, I'm sure. Terrible fighter; big fucking coward when it comes down to it."

There was a long period of silence.

"I don't know quite what to say," Melanie replied. "I'm sorry."

Craig did not respond but placed his head into his hands and began letting it all out.

Craig wasn't used to crying in front of girls, or anyone for that matter. He couldn't remember the last time he had shed a tear—most likely from a routine beating from David in his teenage years. Craig was now a man's man to say the least. He was the type of guy who felt showing any sign of vulnerability was a serious weakness. But at the present moment, Craig was vulnerable. All guards were down and for the first time his prideful ego could not take over.

Melanie tried her hardest to comfort him. She wrapped him up in her arms, stroking his head through his hair.

"I'll tell you, Melanie, there's nothing like seeing your mom with swollen eyes and a bloody nose. I don't even know what happened to her tonight. Probably at the hospital."

"It's okay, Craig. We don't have to talk about it." Tears were still rolling down his face, but they seemed to be lessening as he took deep breaths.

He looked down at the bed, scared to look into Melanie's eyes before doing something that neither of them had expected. Craig leaned over quickly and planted a soft kiss on her lips. At first Melanie was taken aback and resisted slightly, moving backward but still maintaining contact with Craig's lips. And maybe it was the fight she and Jack had, or maybe it was the way Jack sometimes made Melanie feel like she wasn't good enough for him, but for reasons known only to Melanie she leaned back in and reciprocated the gesture, elevating the passion. Their actions moved to even greater heights of betrayal when they undressed each other slowly and carefully. Melanie scooted herself into the center of the bed and Craig crawled on top of her.

The officer turned the page.

Chapter 12

Jack Gardner Takes the Stand

Jack didn't return home the rest of the day after the appointment. Instead, he drove around New York City, visiting many places that he and Melanie had gone to and imagining the times they had shared. It was all the little things they had done together. He drove past restaurants where they had shared first dates. He drove past movie theaters where they had spent many romantic nights together. He certainly missed all of the times they shared together. He drove around thinking about all these times until the sun had completely disappeared. By this time he figured it was best to return home to Brianne, especially since he hadn't told her where he was all day long and she was sure to be worried.

Jack drove back to his home in Long Island and parked in his driveway. He walked up the many steps to the front door as the house was on a hill and was also elevated off the ground. He took out his keys and opened the big wooden door, leaving him on the tile entrance floor into his house. He walked up the spiral staircase, which was just to the left of the entrance, and walked down the hall leading to the bedrooms of the house.

"Where the hell have you been?" asked Brianne as she came out of the bathroom dressed in her pajamas. She wore silk black pants and a white tank top. Jack walked to the end of the hall and into the master bedroom without saying a word.

The room was extremely spacious with a large white bed dead center in the middle against the far wall. The bed had wooden poles on each corner and on top of each pole was a glass orb that was pointed at the end, making it look like something that would belong inside a king's palace. There was a sliding glass door on the left side of the room which led out onto a balcony. Jack enjoyed going out onto the balcony when he was feeling stressed as it had a magnificent view of the Atlantic Ocean for miles. A large mirror was placed on the wall directly in front of the bed so that if someone were sitting on the bed he or she would be seeing their own reflection. In the right corner of the room was a large wooden dresser. Inside the dresser was a small television in addition to all their clothes in the drawers. Another smaller wooden dresser was along the right wall, where the rest of their clothes went.

An archway in the wall next to the bed led to a hallway that expanded the area of the bedroom. On the left of the hallway was a small room, serving as a walk-in closet for Jack, and similarly on the right was a walk-in closet for another, currently Brianne. Continuing to walk farther would take Jack off the carpet and onto a limestone tiled floor that grounded a room almost the same size as the room with the bed in it. To the left in this room was a sink for Jack and similarly on the right, a sink for another. Both sinks were brown with gold faucets atop three drawer cabinets with limestone countertops to match the floor.

Beyond the left sink was a large white bathtub with jets and golden faucets. A small room with a standard white toilet was to the right and on the left was a large granite walk-in shower with two gold faucets. It was a very luxurious shower, the type where you actually set the temperature of the water you want, not unlike a hot tub. All of this together created the impressive master bedroom.

"Did you not hear me, Jack? Where were you?" Brianne asked again. Jack sat down on the large bed and took off his shoes, kicking back from a long day in the car.

"I'm sorry, Brianne. My mom needed me to help her move some things around the house," Jack said sweetly.

"And that took all day long?" Brianne sounded irritated.

"Well, we went out to lunch and just spent the day together. You know how close I am with my mom, and I haven't got to see her in a long time. You're going to be mad at me for being close to my mother? That's kind of selfish isn't it?"

"I'm sorry. I think it's great you spent the day with your mom. It's just a phone call would have been nice."

"We were just out and about and calling just slipped my mind," Jack replied. "One day away really isn't that much of a crime, is it?"

"All right. You're right," Brianne admitted. Jack always had a way of making her feel like she was doing something wrong to get himself off the hook. Not that he particularly cared if she was angry at him, but he didn't really feel like putting up with a verbal argument tonight. "Why don't we both just get in bed and go to sleep?"

Jack didn't reply but dressed down into just his boxers and climbed under the sheets. He hoped he could get a decent night's rest knowing that the very next morning it would be his turn to testify in court. He had to admit he was nervous.

"Good night, Jack," said Brianne. She cuddled up into his arms and Jack had to admit he was annoyed. He definitely liked having someone like Brianne to share the bed with but still liked his space when he slept. It took him a while, but eventually he fell asleep, painfully dreaming of the next day when he would have to tell his dreadful story.

Jack woke up the next morning with a headache after an uneasy night of sleep. Dreams of Melanie and the trial left him with insomnia as he found himself unable to get much sleep. By the time his alarm finally sounded he wished it hadn't. He knew this was the day that he would have to tell his tale and he didn't know if he would be able to compose himself long enough to tell the whole story. He looked to the left and saw that Brianne was no longer in bed. He rolled out of bed and walked down the spiral staircase to the first floor and into the kitchen. Brianne was already sitting at the kitchen table, still in her pajamas and not appearing to be doing anything. The kitchen television was off and she had not made any breakfast. She was merely staring out the window in thought.

"You're up early," Jack said.

"Yeah, I couldn't sleep," Brianne replied, although she gave no notice to Jack. She continued to stare out of the window.

"I couldn't sleep much either," Jack said.

"You scared me in there Jack," Brianne said, finally looking into his eyes. It looked as though she had perhaps been shedding a few tears.

"What are you talking about?"

"You were doing some strange things in your sleep. It just started to freak me out a little bit."

"What was I doing?"

"You were sweating throughout your whole body, and throwing your body back and forth with a terrified look on your face. I didn't know what to do. You looked so helpless." Brianne started to cry and Jack gave her a hug to comfort her.

"I don't know what it was all about, but everything's fine. I promise."

"All right," said Brianne. She wrapped her arms tightly around her boyfriend and rested her head on his chest.

"I'm sorry, but I need to be getting to court soon," Jack said while looking through the kitchen cabinets for something to eat. "I'm going to go take a shower. Do you think you could whip me up some breakfast?"

"Sure, Jack, no problem."

"Thanks, you're the best." Jack leaned over and gave her a kiss on the lips.

He ran up the stairs and into his bedroom. He took perhaps the quickest shower of his life and ran back downstairs into the kitchen. He could smell the aroma of bacon and eggs from the stairs and sure enough his meal was waiting for him on the table when he arrived. He ate as quickly as possible and gave Brianne another kiss before getting into his car and heading over to the courthouse.

Jack parked his Mercedes along the street near the courthouse and walked a small ways before arriving at the court. He had decided to dress a little nicer than usual having known that he would likely be testifying today. He wore his best black suit with a matching black tie and shiny black shoes. He walked quickly as he was extremely nervous. He never liked talking in front of groups of people to begin with. Surely speaking to a courtroom about a murder in which he was present would not be an easy task.

Jack walked up the many steps leading up to the courthouse. He stopped halfway up the stairs, which were crowded by city people standing and drinking their morning coffee. Jack took a look at the gigantic courthouse. All along each of the four walls of the outer perimeter were huge Roman-like white columns that outlined the court building and held up the roof. Inside of the columns was the inner courthouse, which appeared to be jailed by the columns. The courthouse itself consisted of white bricks and a large entrance of two wooden doors. Along the brim of the roof was an engraving: "The true administration of justice is the firmest pillar of good government." He smiled and hoped with all his heart that this was true. If the judicial branch of the government did its job and brought revenge for Melanie in the name of justice, then perhaps Jack could feel whole again.

He stood outside the courtroom, looking at the doors to the entrance. The nervousness was starting to overwhelm him. There were two doors, both with brown handles. On each handle was a latch to press down to open each individual door. Jack made sure he pushed down each latch on the two doors four times each before opening the entrance. He walked into the courtroom, which was already full of witnesses and others involved in the trial. The prosecution, the defense, and the judge had already taken their places. Jack looked at his gold watch and noticed it took him longer than expected and he was about five minutes late.

"Sorry for the hold up," Jack said to the judge.

"Let's proceed," replied Judge Black insisting that it was quite all right. "Ms. Miller, would you like to call your next witness to the stand?"

Cynthia Miller stood up from the prosecution stand wearing precisely the same pinstripe pants and blazer as she did everyday. Her hair was still pulled back into a bun and she still wore the same glasses on her face. "I would like to call Jack Gardner to the stand, your honor."

Jack stood up from the benches and walked toward the witness stand. He took his seat after being sworn in by the bailiff and Ms. Miller approached him.

"Mr. Gardner, could you please state your full name and occupation for the jury?" she asked him.

"Jack Gardner. I work as an attorney here in New York."

"Could you state your relation to the victim, Melanie Stole Gardner?"

"Melanie was and still is my wife," Jack said somberly.

"And how long had you been married?"

"It had only been about a month."

"Could you describe the kind of relationship you had with the defendant, Craig Sanderson?"

"Craig and I have known each other for a long time," Jack began. "Our parents had been pretty close friends when Craig and I were just little kids. We went to the same school every year of our lives, but we didn't become friends until we were sophomores in college."

"Would you say that you and Craig became good friends?" Ms. Miller asked while pacing back and forth in front of the witness stand. She walked with her arms behind her back and her face tilted upward toward the ceiling in pure confidence.

"Yes, he became like a brother to me. We even lived together our junior and half of our senior years in college," Jack explained.

"Mr. Gardner, you claim that you were an eyewitness to the murder. Is that correct?"

"Yes, I was there."

"Was the defendant a close friend of Melanie as the defense has claimed?"

"Yes, they always appeared to get along well," Jack said. "I wouldn't necessarily say they were great friends. They usually only saw each other through me, but yes, I would consider them friends."

"If they were friends, then how can you explain why this happened?"

"I can't say," Jack replied as he shook his head. "I can't say because it made no sense to me. All I can tell you is what happened on that terrible night." Jack's hands and legs started to shake as he knew he would soon have to tell it. He felt his head becoming damp with sweat and loosened his tie around his neck to get a little more breathing room. He took a quick glance at Craig and just as quick looked away. A millisecond was all it took. His eyes had locked with Craig's and Jack felt his enemy's cold piercing eyes staring back into his. The look was terrifying and sent chills through Jack's spine.

"Please, Jack, in your own words, describe what happened to you on the night in which these terrible events occurred," said Cynthia Miller.

Jack took a deep breath and exhaled slowly.

Chapter 13

A Story Is Told

Ms. Miller loved being a prosecutor and the trial had come to her favorite moment. Her main witness would tell his story, and after the jury heard it there wasn't much chance for Craig Sanderson's life.

Jack prepared himself for what would perhaps be the longest and most uncomfortable story telling experience of his life. He touched each side of the witness stand four times and began to describe in great detail all of the events of his last night with Melanie.

"Are you almost ready?" came Jack's impatient voice over the receiver. He had been waiting for Melanie to finish dolling herself up for over an hour longer than anticipated and he was growing overanxious. Tonight, the couple was to celebrate their one-month-long marriage. Since becoming husband and wife, they made a vow to celebrate their marriage anniversary every month of their lives to remind themselves that no matter what they went through in life, they would always make it through all obstacles and celebrate together.

"Yes, Jack, I'm ready now. Come pick me up."

"Finally," Jack said as he hung up the phone. He walked in front of the full-length mirror in his room to give himself final approval on his appearance. He was wearing his nicest black suit, with a matching black tie and shiny black shoes. His short dark brown hair was groomed nicely and his face was clean-shaven; he definitely looked dressed for the occasion. *Couldn't look any better,* Jack thought.

He picked up his keys off the kitchen table and walked out of the house to his Mercedes. He backed out of the garage and zipped down the street, passing all the other luxurious houses, before his cell phone gave a loud ring. He answered it.

"Hey, Jack. What are you doing buddy?" It was his good friend Craig Sanderson.

"Why? What's up?"

"I think we should hang out tonight," Craig said. "It's been so long since we hung out just the two of us like we used to."

"I'm sorry, Craig, I can't. Mel and I have plans to celebrate our one month marriage."

"Fuck, Jack. You're always with her. What are your special plans? Have sex all night?"

"No, actually I'm taking her to Le Rivage," Jack said.

"Wow, you've got to be kidding," Craig said. "What are you doing after that?"

"Probably take her over to the hill," Jack said. The hill was a place that Craig often took his many dates to seal the deal. Craig had told Jack about the place, but Jack had never really taken advantage of it.

"Yeah, well have fun with that." Craig hung up the phone.

Jack knew that Craig was getting jealous over all the time Jack was hanging out with Melanie. He figured he probably should call back and try to calm Craig down, but he didn't want to deal with his attitude tonight. No, tonight he wanted to make sure everything was perfect for his first anniversary.

By the time he got to Melanie's house he had forgotten all about Craig as his nervousness was getting the better of him. Why he was nervous around his very own wife, he didn't know. Melanie's house was made of dark bricks that had ivy growing on the outer walls. A fire escape came out of the second story window, followed by a staircase leading down the next level. The house was in the middle of a small court with two other quite similar houses. Jack walked up to the front door and knocked. It took Melanie several moments to answer, but when she did it was well worth the wait.

She opened the door and her bright green eyes lit up as Jack handed her the red roses he had gotten her. "Aw, thanks, Jack," she said with a big smile. She looked stunning to Jack. She wore a short white dress that reached to about the height of her knee. It was held up by spaghetti straps around the shoulders. The dress was cut very low around the chest, exposing much of her round breasts. She had matching white high heels on making her almost eye level with Jack. Melanie gave Jack a tight hug and he reciprocated with a kiss on the lips. She walked into the kitchen and placed the roses into a vase while Jack waited in the living room.

"You ready to go?" Jack asked as he took her hand and led her toward the car. He opened the door for his wife before walking back to the driver side to get in himself.

"Where are we going?" Melanie asked anxiously.

"You'll see," Jack replied.

The two of them cruised down the shoreline of the Atlantic Coast with the top down on Jack's car, allowing the air to flow freely onto their faces. They curved back and forth following the road through small hills, looking down at the ocean to the left of them. They drove up a hill to an area with a single restaurant.

"Le Rivage!" Melanie exclaimed. "I can't believe you remembered."

"Well, you told me you always wanted to come here."

Melanie smiled before pausing for a moment. "Are you stupid? How in the hell are we going to afford this?"

"Don't worry, Melanie, we're celebrating."

Le Rivage was perhaps the most expensive and romantic restaurant in all of Long Island. Melanie had mentioned to Jack on several occasions that she had always wanted to go on a special date there, but knew she would never be able to afford it. Only the best came to Le Rivage.

They parked in the parking lot that was below the restaurant. All around them they were surrounded by small green hills and valleys. They both stepped out of the car and shut the doors. A series of cement steps led up to the entrance. They held hands a they walked up the stairs, with perfectly cut green grass on both sides. The restaurant itself was built of cream-colored bricks with solid wood trim around the windows and doors. The entrance door was large and built of dark brown wood. It had elegant lanterns hanging off the wall on both sides of the door, lighting up the entrance.

Once they got inside and were taken to their seats they were surprised to be even more impressed by the beauty of the restaurant. Jack had reserved a private area outside for just the two of them. The inside of the restaurant also consisted of brick and wood. On each table were a couple roses in the center of the table. Dimly lit old-fashioned lanterns hung from the walls to go along with French oil paintings of country sides and impressionist print designs. The waiter walked them out onto the balcony, which was outside along the oceanfront and completely separated from the rest of the restaurant. An old-fashioned candle sat in the middle of the table softly illuminating it, and complimenting the red roses.

Jack pulled out Melanie's chair for her before sitting down himself. "This is amazing Jack. Thank you so much," Melanie said before leaning over the table to give him a soft kiss. She reached over to hold his hand in hers as they both looked out to the beautiful scenery surrounding them. The ocean water was a dark blue and was lit by the now rising moon. The accumulation of all of these factors resulted in perhaps the most romantic setting both Jack and Melanie could imagine.

After a couple hours of sipping expensive wines and feasting on French cuisine, they decided to leave the restaurant. "Thank you so much, Jack," Melanie repeated. "That was the sweetest thing ever." The two got back into Jack's car, and Jack took them to the hill that Craig had been to so many times.

The trip to the hill was longer than Jack expected, but he remembered exactly how to get there from the directions Craig had once given him. When they reached the top of the hill, Jack parked his car near the edge. Once they had approached the edge, they were able to see the most miraculous view of the New York City lights on one side, and the serene ocean view on the other side. "I hope you had a nice night," Jack said after they both unbuckled their seat belts.

"Oh, trust me. I did," Melanie replied. Jack looked into her eyes and carefully stroked her long blonde hair.

"Just think," he said. "We get to do this every month for the rest of our lives."

The passion in the car grew to a much more intense level as the two began touching each other more intimately until, before they knew it, they were both naked from the waist down and Jack was slowly penetrating his wife on the passenger seat. As the car windows fogged up and the car rocked back and forth, they were suddenly struck with fear as they heard police sirens coming their way.

"Shit!" screamed Jack and Melanie at once. Jack immediately jumped off Melanie and back onto the driver's seat. They could only see the red and blue lights flashing in the rearview mirrors through the steamed-up windows.

"Did he get out of the car?" Melanie asked.

"I don't think so," Jack said. "I think he just wants us to leave." Jack started up the engine less than a second before he heard a loud knock on the window. Jack rolled down the window before letting out a big sigh of relief. "Craig, you bastard, you scared us half to death," Jack said with a laugh. "Are you on duty tonight?"

"License and registration," Craig mumbled.

"Funny, Craig," Jack again said. "Why are you here, man? You knew I had a special night planned."

"License and registration," Craig repeated a little louder.

Jack paused in confusion and before he was able to say another word, Craig opened the door and pulled Jack out of it forcefully. "What the fuck are you doing?" Jack yelled.

"You get out of the car too, ma'am," Craig said. Melanie quickly got out of the car without thinking twice. "Come over here and stand next to your husband." Craig seemed to act like he had no idea who the couple was.

"Have you been drinking Craig?" Jack asked.

Craig immediately swung and connected his knuckles into Jack's jaw, throwing him into the car. "Don't worry about it," Craig said. He turned Jack around and pulled his arms behind his back, locking handcuffs around his wrists. Jack did not speak right away as his mouth was now full of blood and he was spitting it out. "You turn around too, Melanie," he said before cuffing her as well.

"What are you arresting us for?" Jack exclaimed.

"It's obvious you've both been drinking," Craig said. "I can't just let you drive away and endanger the citizens of New York." Craig shoved Jack into the back seat of his police car. He told Melanie to get into the front seat and she didn't dare disobey him. She had never seen this side of Craig before. It was as though he was possessed. She knew he must have been under the influence of alcohol, but even drunks didn't forget who their friends were. "You comfy back there, Jack?" Craig said with a smile.

"If this is your idea of a joke, it isn't funny!" Jack said.

Craig didn't respond to Jack.

"I'm sorry, Melanie. Are those cuffs too tight? Let me take them off," Craig said politely. He took off Melanie's cuffs and asked if she was comfortable enough. She simply stared back at him in complete confusion.

"Why are you doing this?" Melanie asked softly as Craig began to drive back down the hill. Craig looked back at Melanie almost completely expressionless but with a hint of sorrow and remorse. He did not say a word though and continued to drive. Before long Craig had driven them straight back to Melanie's house.

"What the hell?" said Jack. "I thought you were arresting us. This doesn't look like a police station to me."

Craig didn't respond. He got out of the car and opened the back seat.

"Get out, Jack," Craig commanded.

"I'm not going anywhere until you tell me what the hell is going on!" Jack demanded.

Craig immediately pulled out a gun from his belt and held it to Jack's head.

"Get the fuck out of the car or I send a bullet through your brain, and I don't think you will enjoy it."

Jack stared at Craig with a mixture of confusion, anger, and frustration as he didn't know what the hell was going on.

Surely this couldn't be happening because I wouldn't hang out with him tonight, Jack thought. Nevertheless he got out of the car with his arms raised in the air.

"Put your fucking hands down and walk toward the door," Craig ordered while lowering his gun. He didn't want to attract any attention from neighbors, although no one was likely to see anyway as the night sky was completely black except for the glimmer from the moon. Craig walked over to the passenger door and told Melanie to get out. "Melanie, would you be a doll and go open the door?" Craig asked so sweetly it was almost as though he was mocking her.

Melanie opened the door and walked in followed by Jack and Craig, who had a gun pointed toward their backs.

"Come on, up the stairs," Craig ordered. Melanie and Jack both paused and looked at one another. "Move it!" Craig ordered again. The two of them walked up the stairs with the terrifying feeling that this may be their last climb up these stairs. "Melanie, into your room and sit on the bed," Craig said. She did as she was ordered. Craig brought Jack into another room across the hall.

The smaller bedroom on the right was white and blue. The walls were white, but the window blinds and bed sheets were white with blue stripes. The carpet in this room was beige to match the rest of the house. There was a sliding mirror closet on the wall adjacent to the door and two different dressers in the far corners of the room. A twin-size bed sat directly in the middle of the small room.

Craig sat Jack on the floor with his back against one of the dressers. Craig pulled some twine from a bag he was carrying and tied Jack to the dresser and pulled out duct tape, which was surely intended to be put over Jack's mouth.

"Why, Craig?" Jack asked. "What are you doing and why? I gave you everything!" Jack began to scream but was shut up when Craig taped his mouth shut in mid sentence. Jack began squirming and screaming under the tape although no words could be understood.

"I'm sorry I had to do this," Craig said while a tear dripped down his eye. "I had to do what was best for me, Jack. I hope some day you will understand. I appreciate everything you've done for me over the years. You were like a brother to me." Craig wiped away several tears that had now dripped down his face and then walked out of the room. Jack remained tied with his eyes now wide open with disbelief. He frantically searched for a way to get out of his predicament. He knew that Melanie often used the smaller bedrooms as storage rooms. At least he was tied to a dresser and could scan the room looking for a means of escape.

Craig was quite foolish as he did not tie down my arms, thought Jack. Instead they lay in his lap, still handcuffed together. Jack reached up over his head and opened one of the dresser drawers. He felt around for something that might feel sharp, but it was very difficult not being able to see what he was doing. Jack hit the jackpot when he came across a small pocketknife. Seconds after he closed the drawer Jack jumped with shock when he saw a strange figure enter the room. He hid the pocketknife in his lap as he studied the new figure.

Jack could not tell at first whether this figure was still Craig. He was around the same height and was wearing his full police uniform. However, he wore a very unusual white and black mask on his face. The main color was white, but the eyes and mouth were both black. The eyes were very large and droopy and the mouth was open but in a large frown. It was pretty creepy to say the least, and reminded Jack of some kind of scary clown. He also had large black gloves covering up both of his hands. Jack felt as though he was a prisoner and the executioner had just arrived. "Craig, is that you?" Jack tried to yell through the tape, but it only came out a mumble.

The figure did not reply. The mask completely covered his face, making it impossible for Jack to know for sure who it was. The figure began to approach him slowly and Jack felt his knees shaking uncontrollably. The figure bent at the knees into a squatted position and stared Jack straight in the eyes. Jack's eyes started to water in fear as he stared back at the figure. For over a minute the figure looked him in the eyes as though sizing him up for what was about to happen. The figure then reached behind his back and pulled out a long knife from inside his belt. The knife was extremely unique. It had a spiraling black ridged handle with a long thick blade. Along both sides of the blade were deep ridges that caused several points along each side.

Jack began to panic as the figure slowly stroked the knife up and down. The figure walked in front of him, pacing back and forth while he played with the blade. After a minute or so the figure stopped with his back to Jack. Jack now had tears flowing profusely from his eyes as he prayed for his life. The tears suddenly stopped when the figure spun around and in one motion viciously jammed the knife into Jack's side. Jack let out a scream of pain, which was blocked by the duct tape around his mouth. His eyes widened to three times the size they were before and they grew bloodshot red with veins.

The figure stared at Jack and watched him squirm in agonizing pain. Without warning, the figure stabbed Jack again in the same spot. Jack bent over as far as the ropes would let him and tried to hold his hands over his wounds. It was no good in stopping the bleeding. He began kicking and screaming as much as he could although the loss in blood was beginning to drain him. A series of stabs in the same location as well as a series of stabs in one other location on his other side followed without hesitation. Jack felt immense pain as he began to feel he was losing consciousness from the torture.

The figure stood over Jack, who was now motionless, as though taking pride in his kill. He seemed to admire his work for a couple of moments more before leaving Jack in the room.

"So, the masked figure then left you in the smaller bedroom bleeding from stab wounds on both sides of your body?" Cynthia Miller emphasized for the jury.

"Yes," replied Jack solemnly.

"What happened next?"

"I heard voices and screams from across the room. Although I could not see Melanie and the masked figure directly, I knew what was occurring."

Ms. Miller forged ahead. "Tell us what happened in Melanie's bedroom next."

"Objection!" interrupted Joseph West. "If Jack did not see what actually occurred in Melanie's bedroom, how can he be allowed to testify about it?"

"Your honor, Jack should be allowed to testify as to what he heard and based on his interpretation of the sounds, what he believed was occurring," countered Ms. Miller.

"Objection overruled," said Judge Black. "I will allow the testimony as long as Mr. Gardner's opinions are clearly indicated as such. The jury should be advised that Mr. Gardner's opinions cannot be taken as fact since he did not actually witness all of the events that he might describe. Some of the events are being interpreted by Mr. Gardner and, while he may believe them to be fact, they may not be entirely accurate."

"Please continue, Jack," said Cynthia Miller.

The masked figure walked across the hall to Melanie's room. He opened the door, entering into a room at least twice the size of the other one. The large white bed covered with perfectly white pillows was directly ahead of the doorway against the far wall, facing the door. Two small white dressers were on both sides of the bed with beautiful bright flowers placed upon them. Behind each dresser was a long window with pearly white blinds. A large mirror hung on the far wall over the head of the bed.

Melanie sat on the bed fearing what would happen to her next. When she saw the figure standing in the doorway she let out a shriek of surprise and fear. "Craig?" She gasped. The figure did not move forward but still carried the knife, which was now covered in blood. Melanie panicked. "Where's Jack? What have you done with him?" She trembled on the bed.

The masked man didn't say anything but walked toward the bed very slowly. He sat down next to Melanie and began to stroke her hair.

"What the hell are you doing, Craig? Stop it!" She pushed him away.

The figure got closer to her and began stroking her thighs.

"Let go of my leg!" demanded Melanie. She continued to resist and moved farther onto the bed until she was completely on it and pushed up against the center of the headrest, exactly where he wanted her. It was as though she had climbed her way up the web toward the spider, and was now going to be the featured dish of a large meal.

He attempted to climb on top of her but was met by a hard slap in the face. Melanie then kicked him and attempted to jump off the bed. However, the figure jammed the knife into her chest. Melanie let out a garbled shriek as blood began to flow from her mouth. She grabbed a hold of the figure's left sleeve and tried to pull him off. The sleeve gave way and ripped open, exposing all of the figure's left bicep and forearm. The figure tore her dress loudly so that the entire front of her body was exposed. He yelled, "I will have you now!" He unbuttoned his pants and forcefully penetrated her, while she resisted and screamed with everything she had left.

She was dead before he was finished.

The figure moved off Melanie and put his pants all of the way back on. He opened the door and walked back into the other room to make sure Jack was completely taken care of. He opened the door to the smaller bedroom and saw Jack still lying motionless in the same position he had been in before. Jack was not dead, however, and squinted his eyes just long enough to see the entire left arm of the figure that may have just killed him. The figure left the room apparently convinced that Jack was dead and walked down the stairs. Jack heard the front door close before crawling out of the ropes, which he had just cut with the pocketknife. He crawled out of the room on his hands and knees across the hall to Melanie's room, blood dripping from his mouth and wounds the whole time. He opened the door to her room and tried to suppress a scream. "No!" He stammered before coughing up a good deal of blood. He let out another shrieking sound of sorrow and pain and tears fell down his cheeks. He crawled out of the room and back to the smaller bedroom where he knew there was a phone. He picked it up and dialed.

"911, what's your emergency?" the operator asked.

Chapter 14

Facts Revealed

Ms. Miller had been looking at Jack the entire time he told the story with a slightly pleased look. "Mr. Gardner," she began. "You say that the defendant took you to your wife's house, is that correct?"

"Yes, that's correct," Jack said definitely.

"The two of you were married but weren't living together?"

"Yes, we lived together. However, Melanie still kept quite a bit of her wardrobe in her other house. She was going to repaint her house and then we were going to sell it to help pay for the new house I just moved into. Melanie thought it would be fun to get ready for our one- month anniversary separately and then treat it like a special date. Her formal clothes were at her old house."

"I see. So next the defendant brought you into the guest room and then left the room?"

"Yes."

"For how long was the defendant gone?" Ms. Miller asked.

"It was probably about five minutes," Jack guessed. "I'm not completely sure."

"And then after five minutes an 'unknown figure' came back into the room?"

"Yes."

"Do you believe this masked figure to be the defendant, Craig Sanderson?"

"Yes, I do," said Jack.

"And how can you be sure that this masked figure that committed the actual murder was none other than the defendant?" Ms. Miller asked curiously even though she knew what Jack would say. After all, it was her witness and they had rehearsed their testimony several times.

"Well," Jack began. "I'm not exactly sure how, but the figure's left sleeve had been torn off his police uniform. *I suppose maybe it was ripped in my wife's struggle to keep her life.*" Jack paused to regain his composure. "Anyway, I've known Craig for a long time, and he's had a tattoo on his left bicep for a while now. I was actually with him when he got the tattoo. When the masked man came into the room to check if I was dead I was able to see his left bicep, and sure enough the figure had the exact same tattoo on his left bicep."

"Were there any other signs that the person under the mask was indeed the defendant?"

"Well, he was the same height and looked to be the same weight as Craig," Jack said. "He had on Craig's police uniform, and well, I've been best friends with him for a long time. Besides all of obvious signs that it was Craig, it was just a feeling where I knew."

"What does the defendant's tattoo look like?"

"It is two black Japanese symbols, one on top and one directly under it," Jack explained.

"Do you happen to know what these symbols mean when interpreted?"

"Yes," Jack replied. "The top symbol represented friendship in the Japanese culture, and the bottom symbol represented loyalty."

"And why did Craig choose to place those specific values on his arm? Did he ever tell you?"

"Yes, he told me he got them to show his respect to me as a matter of fact. Craig never really had much of parents or family growing up, and I guess in a way I sort of became for him what his parents never were. I was really the first real friend he ever had. Because of everything I did for him, he often told me that being loyal and keeping our friendship sacred was the most important thing in the world to him. I suppose I was foolish for believing him," Jack admitted.

"How do you feel now? After everything you did for him?"

"I feel betrayed," Jack said. "I'm still sort of in shock, to be honest. I wouldn't expect this from my worst enemy, not to mention my closest friend. It can never be forgiven." Tears began rolling from his eyes as he asked for a handkerchief.

"If your wife were still alive today, Mr. Gardner, what would she consider the proper punishment?"

"Objection!" yelled Joseph West.

But Jack blurted out, "I believe that she would want complete revenge. An eye for an eye; a life for a life!"

"Your honor, I withdraw the question. And I have no more questions," Ms. Miller said.

"Very well," said Judge Black. "Thank you, Mr. Gardner. Would the defense like to question this witness?"

Joseph West stood up from his bench and approached the witness stand. "Mr. Gardner, you say that the person that killed Melanie was wearing a mask."

"Correct," Jack responded.

"Now if the killer was wearing a mask at the time, then there is at least the slightest possibility that it was not the defendant and that it was someone else, correct?"

"I saw the tattoos," Jack began.

"Is it not possible that two people could have the same tattoos?"

"It seems pretty unlikely to me," Jack said.

"But is it possible?"

"Yeah, sure I guess."

"So then there is a chance that it was not Craig at all, and was instead someone with similar appearance, or maybe someone pretending to be Craig."

Jack looked confused. "Yeah, I guess there is a chance that could have happed, but I …"

"No further questions," West interjected before returning to his bench.

Ms. Miller stood up. "I would like to recall FBI Lieutenant Henry Wilson to the stand." The medium-height, older male with grayish-black hair took the stand once again. "Mr. Wilson, Jack Gardner has surmised that the left sleeve of the figure's uniform must have been torn off in the struggle for Melanie's life, exposing the defendant's tattoo, and ultimately proving the defendant's guilt. Can you describe how you knew Craig was at the airport and what you found when you searched him?"

"Well, we were able to get a hold of Craig's father and he told us that Craig had a flight that night. When we caught up with Craig at the airport and arrested him, we immediately searched his luggage. He was only carrying one bag, and when we searched it we found his police uniform among some other clothes."

"Can you describe what the uniform looked like?"

"Well, it indeed had its entire left sleeve ripped off, just as Jack Gardner had claimed."

"Did you find anything else in the bag?"

The lieutenant hesitated. "Yes, we also found a black and white mask, just as Mr. Gardner had described."

"Ladies and gentlemen of the jury, all of Jack Gardner's testimony is supported by hard facts and evidence. The FBI caught the defendant red-handed, with all of the materials used in killing young Melanie Stole Gardner. The prosecution rests, your honor."

Judge Black wrote down several notes and reviewed papers while the jury took in everything they had just heard. Moments later he declared that court would be adjourned for the rest of the day and that cross examination and Craig Sanderson's defense would begin on the next scheduled court appearance.

Chapter 15

Out of the House

Melanie and Craig rested in her bed, blankets covering their still naked bodies, for only about ten minutes before Melanie rolled over and felt her life come crashing down. She saw a picture of Jack and her together, which was taken in front of her house. It was sitting on the dresser by the bed, and was bordered by a golden frame. "What the hell have I done?" she said to herself. She rolled back over and looked at Craig who was lying on his back, eyes staring straight up to the ceiling. "Craig, you need to leave now," Melanie blurted.

"Huh? Where the hell am I supposed to go?"

"I don't know. Back to your house."

"I can't go there," Craig said. "Jack might be there."

"So? You live together. What do you expect?"

"I can't see him after this." Craig looked frightened, as if this was his last day on earth.

"Well, you're going to have to go home eventually."

"What are we going to do about this?" Craig asked.

"What do you mean? We're not telling Jack if that's what you're thinking. I don't want to ruin our relationship."

Craig turned his head away from Melanie and grew silent.

"We made a mistake, Craig. Let's not ruin your friendship with him either. You know if he finds out he'll never talk to you again. Is it really worth it?"

"A mistake?"

"Of course it was a mistake. Wasn't it for you?"

Craig paused for a moment before agreeing that it was indeed a mistake. He got out of the bed, put his clothes on, and walked out of the house without another word to Melanie. He walked a couple blocks to the nearest bus stop and rode back to his home, praying that Jack would not be there when he arrived.

When he arrived at the small two-bedroom house, he was relieved to see that Jack's car was not in the driveway. He went into the house knowing that it could possibly be the last time ever doing so. How could he possibly live with Jack after what he had done? He couldn't. It was hard enough for Craig to lie to Jack about borrowing a pencil; how could he lie about something as treacherous as this? He packed up some of his small belongings, such as clothes, shoes and some extra cash he had lying around. He put them in a black duffle bag, which he threw over his shoulder as he looked around his room. He knew he would eventually be back for the rest of his belongings, but for now he had to get out of the house.

As he passed by his room on his way out of the house, he was forced to walk by Jack's room. He couldn't help but walk into the room and have a look around. Inside the room, other than an untidy bed, were several pictures, mainly of Melanie and Jack. There were pictures of the two having fun together: at the mall, on a mountain, at the zoo, pretty much everywhere, and Craig couldn't help the image of substituting his face with Jack's.

One picture, the only one hanging on the wall over the bed, was one that particularly disturbed Craig. He had always known the picture was there and it had always honored Craig to look at it, but now it disturbed him. It was a picture of the Gardner family with Chris, Mrs. Gardner, and Mark standing in the front. Standing right behind them were Jack, Mr. Gardner, and Craig. The Gardners occasionally had professional pictures taken and this time they had asked Craig to go with them. It was a big deal to Craig. He had never exactly had a family of his own to take pictures with, and the fact that the Gardners wanted Craig in their memories, as a member of their family, meant the world to him. Looking at the picture made him feel absolutely disgusted with himself as he realized he would no longer have this adopted family anymore. He had spit in their faces despite everything they had done for him.

He walked out of the room just as there was a loud knock on the door. "Jack!" Craig gasped. However, when he opened the door, it was not Jack standing in the doorway.

"Craig Sanderson?" an overweight, bald police officer with a raspy voice asked. He was accompanied by two younger officers.

"Yes, that's me. How can I help you?"

"Are you going somewhere, son?" the officer asked, gesturing to Craig's bags over his shoulder.

"What can I help you with?" Craig repeated.

"Mr. Sanderson, you're under arrest." The cop pulled Craig's arms behind his back and cuffed them tightly. "Mr. Sanderson, you have the right to remain silent. Anything you say can be used against you in court. You have the right to an attorney. If you cannot afford one, one will be provided for you."

"Arrested for what?"

"Battery, Mr. Sanderson. Did you forget about beating David Cooper unconscious?" Craig grew silent. He had almost forgotten about what had happened before he went to Melanie's house. The officer escorted Craig to the police car and guided him to the backseat. Craig watched his house from the backseat as the car drove off.

Should have expected this, Craig thought. To add to his troubles, he was sure to have a heavy lawsuit coming his way.

By the time they had arrived at the police station, Craig wasn't as upset as expected under the circumstances. At least being detained would mean he could be nowhere near Jack. The officer brought him into what looked to be an interrogation room, which seemed weird to Craig since there were really no questions to be asked. He committed the crime. That was obvious. He waited inside the room for someone to greet him for what seemed like the longest time. In reality, it was only about thirty minutes, but with the cemented, unpainted walls surrounding him, there wasn't much to look at. In fact, the only things in the room were a desk and one chair. Eventually, the same officer who had arrested him entered the room.

"Hello, Craig. I'm Officer Peterson." The overweight cop walked his way over to the desk that Craig was now sitting at and rested his hand on it. "You want to tell me what happened?"

"What do you mean? You already know what happened. I'm sure David told you the *whole* story," Craig said sarcastically.

"Then what is the whole story? He says that you attacked him for no reason. Possibly some built up resentment over him dating your mother."

"Yeah, maybe it was that," Craig said. "Or maybe it was the resentment from him beating my mother for the last several years."

"He beats your mother?"

Craig was silent for a moment. "I walked in on it tonight. He was standing over her yelling and she had a black eye and bloody nose. I really thought he might kill her. I had to defend her. I had to do something."

"I'll be back in an hour or so," Officer Peterson said. He walked out of the room and did not return for nearly ninety minutes. Craig rested his forehead against the cool desk surface as he waited. All the talk about his mother was starting to give him a headache and the coolness of the desk helped to sooth it. He knew Officer Peterson was going to talk to his mother or David. He hoped it would be his mother because she would have to tell the truth.

Officer Peterson finally returned. He approached the desk and stood in the same exact position as before. "I talked to your mother," the officer began. "She denied it."

"What! What do you mean she denied it?"

"She said that Mr. Cooper has never caused her any harm in all the time she has known him. She said that you attacked him and she wasn't sure why. She said you were in a rage and were hitting him in the face and wouldn't stop. She got scared and so she called the police."

"Didn't you see her face?"

"Yes, I did," Officer Peterson said. "Indeed she had a black eye and a bloody nose. I also noticed a lot of bruises on her arms."

"Well, I sure as hell didn't give her those."

"I believe you. You know, Craig, sometimes women don't want to turn an abusive partner in. They think they have a good thing going on and that they are in love. They don't want to ruin it."

"So you believe me then?"

"Yes, Craig, I think I do. However, if your mom denies it then I'm afraid there isn't much I can do. I can't force her to turn her boyfriend in and if she continues to go along with David's story then it will be hard for you to claim self defense."

"So what should I do then?" Craig asked.

"Well," Officer Peterson said, stroking his beard. "There's going to be a hearing at some point since Mr. Cooper has decided to press charges. You will be able to have a lawyer represent you. I'm going to try to help you out, Craig. I'm going to do more research and hopefully find some hard evidence linking David Cooper to the abuse you claim he has been giving. However, you're going to have to stay in jail until the hearing. Bail will likely be posted and could be as high as eight thousand dollars based on my past experiences."

"Eight thousand dollars?" Craig said. "I don't know anyone with eight thousand dollars."

"Well, the trial could be months away. You may be in jail for quite some time."

The officer turned the page.

Chapter 16

Truths or Lies?

Joseph West's frustrations grew as he drove home from court. He lived a good half hour away from the courthouse, due to traffic, giving him plenty of contemplation time. Jack Gardner's testimony was well planned out. He had said nearly everything he needed to say in order to get the jury to believe, beyond a reasonable doubt, that Craig committed the murder, except for the fact that there still was no motive. No one had given a reason why his client would do this to two of his good friends. Also, there were some fallacies with Jack's testimony that West wasn't sure the jury picked up on.

West arrived at his small, quaint home just outside New York City about ten minutes later than expected. His home was a single story dwelling. It was not the nicest and surely not what one would expect the lawyer type to live in. West, however, was not by any means one of the more respected or highest paid lawyers in the New York area. His house was surrounded by grass that was beginning to grow somewhat light brown due to a lack of care. The house itself was a dark brown color, which reminded West of bark on a tree. He didn't particularly mind having his not so impressive small home; he was not a materialistic person to say the least.

West walked through his matching wooden door and through the living room. Newspapers were open and all over the floor in the family room, making it somewhat hard to make it through without stepping on something. West apparently didn't mind as he walked on top of it all, past his worn-out sofa and small television set, into the kitchen. The kitchen table and counter were covered with boxes of Chinese food and cereal, bags of chips, and empty cans of beer. He walked through the kitchen and into his study, closing the door behind him.

His office, or study room, was ten times messier than the rest of the house. Papers were spilling out of their files on the table, making it almost impossible to see the top of the mahogany desk sitting in the middle of the tiny room. The room must have been no larger than an eight by ten jail cell and looked just as gray. The walls were made purely of cement with no paint on them whatsoever. Behind the table were stacks of boxes, sitting on shelves, full of files and papers. It was a wonder that West was able to work under such disorganized conditions.

He pulled out the stool that he used to sit on and scooted up to the table. He reviewed his notes that he had taken so far on the case and tried to find any information he could use against Jack Gardner. It wasn't going to be easy to persuade the jury that Jack was telling a lie. After all, West thoroughly believed that Jack's story was true for the most part, or at least that Jack believed it was true. Perhaps even Jack didn't know the whole truth though.

"Rikers Island Prison, how many I help you?"

"Hi, this is Joseph West. I am the attorney for an inmate of yours. Craig Sanderson."

"How may I help you?"

"I was wondering if I might arrange to meet with him today. It's urgent."

"Hold on one moment." The receptionist placed West on hold while she checked with the security officers to determine the next visitation time for West to speak to his client. "You can come in to see him in about an hour," she reported.

"Thank you very much." West hung up the phone. He got into his brown Ford Taurus and drove to the prison. He checked in with the front office and the security guard walked him to the visitors' area. By the time West cleared security, Craig was already waiting, sitting behind the glass windows. West pick up the phone hanging on the wall so that they could hear each other through the glass and Craig picked up his receiver also.

"Hello, Craig," West said.

"Why'd you need to see me?" Craig asked. "Have you proven my innocence yet?" he joked.

"No, not yet," West replied. "Listen, I need you to be completely honest with me because I don't think I've been getting the whole story."

"What are you talking about? I told you, I'm completely innocent."

"But *are* you completely innocent Craig? I understand if you're scared but you need to tell me the truth."

"What the hell do you think I did?" Craig said.

"I don't know for sure. But I do have a guess. I have to be honest with you. I think you were involved in the situation."

"So you think I'm guilty? You think I killed Melanie?" Craig sounded as though he was more hurt than angry.

"No, Craig, I don't think you killed Melanie, but I do think there was truth in Jack's testimony."

"What do you think was true about it?" Craig asked.

"Well, let's be logical. Your handprints were on the newly painted walls, your uniform left sleeve was ripped, just as Jack testified, and you were caught at the airport leaving the state unexpectedly on the night of the murder with both the ripped uniform and the mask in your bag. The knife that was used to kill your mother looks to be the same unique kind of knife that was used to kill Melanie, even though neither knife has yet to have been found. There are too many connections to you."

"I swear I had nothing to do with it!" Craig yelled. "I told you I had to go to my mother's funeral, that's why I was leaving the state."

"Craig there are too many things that don't add up," West interrupted. "Now, Jack says that you brought them to Melanie's house, and then a masked figure, allegedly you, did the actual killing. Well, I believe everything he said up to this point. However, this is where things start to confuse me."

"How so?"

"Well, in order for Jack's story to be true, it would mean that you would have brought them to the house, and then left the room to change into your mask and gloves. Now why would you suddenly decide to cover up your identity after they already knew who you were? The only thing I can think of is that you did in fact bring them there and ..."

"I didn't bring them anywhere!" Craig said.

"Just relax and listen to my theory, Craig, please," West said. Craig grew quiet. "Again, the only thing I can think of is that you did bring them to Melanie's house and you did tie them up. However, I don't believe you were the figure under the mask and here's why. Jack had explained how you held a gun to his head in order to get him into Melanie's house. Now, his story goes that you all of a sudden got a knife to kill them? I don't buy it. Since he said you had a gun, you would have simply used the gun and not the knife if you really wanted to kill them, so I don't think his story is completely true."

"So what are you saying?"

"I think two people were involved in this murder, but I think only one of them knew it was to be a murder, and I don't think that person was you."

"I don't understand," Craig said, feeling bewildered.

"I think you brought Jack and Melanie to the house for someone else, but you didn't know that a murder would take place."

"Why would I bring someone to harm Melanie or Jack?"

"I have no idea who would want to or why you would have brought them to this killer, but I intend to find out."

"So you're trying to prosecute me now!" Craig said.

"Not at all. I'm completely on your side. All I'm saying is that I believe you knew this figure would be at Melanie's house and delivered Melanie and Jack to him, but I think you were lied to by the figure. I don't believe you knew his intensions were to kill them."

"This is bullshit," Craig said. "I had nothing to do with the murders."

"Listen, Craig, I know you're scared. You didn't know that they would be killed. Someone else killed them and now it looks like you did it. When I cross-examine, I will change our position. We can tell the truth. We can tell everyone how you brought them there, but you in no way knew about the murder nor committed it."

"No, we're not doing that," Craig said. "We are doing what I want. We are still saying that I had nothing to do with this murder whatsoever."

"Do you not understand?" West pleaded. "We have no chance of winning this case; you are going to be put to death. If we prove that you only brought Jack and Melanie there and had no knowledge of the magnitude of what you were doing, I can save your life and you can get a much lesser sentence."

"If you attempt to prove that, I will fire you as my lawyer. We are staying with the original story. I had absolutely nothing to do with it!"

"We have no witnesses, no evidence against Jack's story, no anything. You don't have the cleanest criminal record to begin with. We have no chance."

"Lawyers are supposed to fight for justice, am I right?"

"I am fighting for justice."

"What the hell is just about me going to prison for a long time for a crime that I did not commit?"

"It's not just, Craig, you're right." West had grown tired of arguing with his client. If only Craig would listen to him, he could save Craig from having a lethal injection sent throughout this body until he died. Maybe Craig didn't want to be saved. Was this the big secret of his? Perhaps he was in denial. After all, that happened to many people after such a traumatic experience. Perhaps he couldn't live with himself if he admitted he had something to do with the killing of his two best friends. Obviously it was a secret which Craig desperately wanted to protect, but was it a secret that was worth dying for?

West hung up the phone and stood up from his seat. He let the security guard escort him out of the penitentiary and then walked back to his car. West cursed out loud the whole way home about how stupid Craig was being. "Does he not understand his life is at stake?" West knew Craig must be terrified of his punishment and that was the reason he wouldn't admit to contributing to the murder. However, without telling the truth, he was now basically contributing to his own execution.

Chapter 17

A Friend to the Rescue, As Always

Craig Sanderson was in jail for his assault on David Cooper for about a month before he received his first visitor. The loneliness and boredom didn't bother Craig as much as expected. He didn't interact with the inmates all that often. He found that the nights were much shorter than the days so he would stay up during much of the night so that he could sleep away the long boring days of confinement. He didn't have any particular friends and remained to himself while awake. In the time he was awake, however, he earned the respect of the other prisoners. He was a tough kid. Anytime someone gave him trouble he stood up for himself regardless if they were bigger or tougher than he was.

In the last week Craig was in jail, he constantly held a white envelope in his hand. The contents inside were very important to him, and he spent much of his time trying to understand why it had been returned to him. He had sent the letter to Melanie the first week he had been in jail. However, two weeks later he was disappointed to see that she had not written a response to him, but rather sent him back the exact same letter he had sent her. Craig didn't know what to make of this. Did she not want to talk to him anymore? Was this some kind of sign that she didn't want anything to do with him?

Craig reread the letter he sent her time and time again until he had memorized it completely.

Melanie,

I've been thinking about you a lot lately. It helps pass the nights as there isn't much else to do. Jail isn't as bad as they say really. I'm getting along just fine, but I can't say that I don't miss you and Jack a lot. I know we never really had a chance to talk about what happened the night I was arrested. I'm not sure if you even want to talk about it, but I need to.

You told me that what we shared together that night didn't mean anything to you and I need to know if you were telling the truth. I thought it was a mistake at first too, but being in here this past week has made me realize that it wasn't a mistake for me. I have feelings for you Melanie and I can't just deny them. I feel like you must feel something for me too in order for us to do what we did. It could not have happened for no reason. It must mean something.

Perhaps it was destiny that we shared that amazing night together and honestly I must say that I cannot regret it for I wish that we could share every night together. I understand the betrayal we have committed to Jack and I will not tell him what happened for it can cause no good.

Please don't tell Jack that I'm in jail because I don't want him to visit me. I don't think I can handle seeing him after what we've done, but it's worth it to me if you feel the way I hope you do.

Please write back to me and tell me what you are feeling and where you would like to go from here.

Craig

While sleeping one day, he was awakened by a security guard. "Hey, Sanderson, you've got a visitor."

Craig got up quickly and rose to his feet. After all, in prison you were rarely ever fully asleep until you'd completely adjusted. After sleeping in comfortable surroundings it was hard to make the transition into prison life and be able to have an undisturbed sleep.

"Hello, Craig." It was the lawyer that had been appointed to represent Craig. Earl Pitzer was his name. He was completely bald, except for maybe a few white hairs that had managed to stay on his head. He had a small wrinkled up face with very faint white eyebrows. He was sixty-eight in age but looked as though he was ninety-five. He walked very slowly and with a limp as if he was supported by a cane.

"Is this guy even alive?" Craig had asked when he first saw the lawyer that was appointed to him.

"Well, Craig, I've got good news and bad news for you." Earl Pitzer talked very slowly, taking plenty of time to get his sentences out. He breathed heavily and loudly, making it hard for him to get his raspy voice out.

"I look forward to the good news. For the bad … how much worse can it possibly get?"

"The bad news is," Mr. Pitzer panted out, "you're being sued for $15,000 for Mr. Cooper's hospital bills."

"Great. What's the good news?"

"Your trial is in a month."

"A month? That's supposed to be *good* news?"

"The good news is you don't have to wait here for a month. Someone is here to bail you out."

"What?" Craig said. "Who is it? Melanie?"

"Follow me," the security guard said, opening the cell door.

Craig followed the security guard down the prison hall quickly. The two of them completely left Earl Pitzer behind as he limped along trying to keep up with them. The security guard led Craig to a waiting room and Craig was shocked to see who was there waiting.

"Hey, Craig," Jack said in a disappointed voice. "You ready to go home?"

Craig turned to the prison guard. "That's it?" he said. "I'm free to go?"

The guard gave him a nod and led both him and Jack to the exit of the jail. Earl Pitzer must have found another way out because he was nowhere to be found. Craig and Jack had not waited for him anyway; they walked straight out to Jack's car. Craig didn't care much for Earl anyway. From his first meeting with the attorney, he felt that Earl had no idea what he was doing. He lacked a certain convincing presence that was needed to be a lawyer. Craig could tell that Earl's quiet nature would not sway the judge in any way.

"How did you know where I was?" Craig asked Jack when they got into the car.

"Melanie told me yesterday. Why the hell didn't you tell me?"

"Because I don't need your help, Jack. I'll be fine."

"Well, thank my parents. They're the ones that paid for your bail. And being in jail for a month is not fine. I didn't know what the hell happened to you. Melanie said she didn't know where you were for the first three weeks, and then she finally told me. I still don't get why she lied to me at first. Anyway, she told me everything Craig and we need to talk."

"Everything?" Craig asked. "What do you mean *everything?*" Panic filled Craig's body.

"I mean everything that happened the night you got arrested. About you protecting your mom and beating up that asshole David. About Melanie taking you to the police station to turn him in and then those bastard cops arrested you instead. I swear, money will get the police to do anything."

"Oh, yeah. It was terrible." Craig was relieved that Melanie had indeed not told Jack about their intimate experience.

"Why didn't you call me right when you got in there? I would have bailed you out the first day. I've been worried sick about you these past couple weeks," Jack said.

"Look, I don't need your help," Craig said angrily. "Thanks for bailing me out. But I really don't need any help from here."

"What do you mean you don't need any help? What the hell is wrong with you? My parents spend thousands of dollars to bail you out and it's like you don't care at all." The two of them had now made it back to the house they shared together, the house where Craig had been arrested a month ago.

"I'm moving out, Jack. I need some time to be on my own."

Jack grew silent. He truly had no idea what to say to his best friend. For the first time, no advice came to mind. He wanted to tell Craig how stupid he was being, but obviously something else was going on. He hadn't called the whole time in prison, and now he didn't want to live with Jack anymore. "You do whatever you have to do, Craig. I'm not going to try to stop you."

Over the next week, Craig looked through listings of apartments until he found one that he at least had a slight chance to afford. During that week, Craig and Jack barely talked to one another. Craig stayed out of his way despite Jack's efforts to see what was bothering him. However, during that week Craig had not stopped talking to Melanie. He called her often, whenever Jack was at school. School had started up again which meant that Jack was gone the majority of the day. Melanie was also gone at school, but Craig knew when her breaks were and called her accordingly. He remembered the first time he had called her. She didn't seem too happy to hear from him at first.

"Why didn't you write me back? Didn't you get my letter?" Craig had asked.

"Yeah, Craig, I got your damn letter. What did you want me to say? I told you that it was a mistake and that we shouldn't talk about it anymore."

"So you're saying that you have no feelings for me?"

"Maybe I do Craig but that's not the point. The point is that we can't do anything about it. I care about Jack a lot and I don't want to hurt him."

"But you want to hurt me?"

"I don't want to hurt you, Craig, but I love Jack. I have feelings for you but they are mostly physical. It's not the same as what I share with Jack."

Craig hung up the phone immediately after hearing her say that.

It was a sad day for Jack when Craig moved out of the house. He still couldn't understand why Craig would move out of their house and into some low-class apartment for no apparent reason. Indeed he was acting strangely lately. He had not even called Jack's parents to thank them for the bail money, which was extremely odd since Jack's mother had always been like a mother to Craig as well. Maybe this whole situation with his mother had really hit him harder than Jack had expected. Or maybe it was something else, but what? Craig packed up the rest of his belongings and moved along with his new life, a life that would not involve Jack Gardner in any way, but a life that would hopefully involve Melanie Stole.

The officer turned the page.

Chapter 18

A Glimpse of Light for the Defense

Almost a week passed before the next scheduled court appearance. In the meantime, Joseph West had to find something to use against Jack Gardner. Jack's testimony had indeed been preformed nicely, almost flawlessly. West was near positive that Jack wasn't lying on the stand. Perhaps it was just that Jack didn't know the truth himself. But who knew? Perhaps Jack *was* flat-out lying. *But for what reason?*

West decided to drive down to the police station to review some of the facts of the case. When he arrived he was greeted by a now familiar face.

"Hello, Mr. West. What can I do for you?" Travis Denton asked. He was wearing his police uniform, which seemed quite professional compared to West's casual jeans and T-shirt. To make it worse, West's unkempt, wild hair looked as though it had not been washed in a month compared to Denton's nicely groomed appearance.

"Just want to review some of the evidence. Still trying to put it all together, you know?"

"Yeah. You think you have any chance of winning the case?"

"There's always a chance. Won't be easy though."

"You really think Sanderson didn't do it?" Denton asked as he led West down a long corridor. They walked past several doors on their way to a back room that was heavily guarded by locks, bars, and security officers.

"Well, you were the one who came to the rescue," West said. "Do you think he's innocent?"

"Seems to be guilty, but I always give people the benefit of the doubt. Unfortunately, my lieutenant is set against any further investigation. He says Craig's our guy without a doubt. I don't think it's right."

"I really don't know what to believe at this point," West said. "Even if I did it wouldn't do any good at this point."

"And why is that?"

"I have no idea who the hell else could have done it," West said while shaking his head. "Haven't been able to put the pieces of the puzzle together yet."

Denton was granted entrance into the room after he had the security guard open all of the locks. "Well, the room is yours, West. Of course, one of our officers will stay and watch you. Standard procedure," Denton said.

"Of course," West replied matter-of-factly. West gave the officer a nod. The security guard didn't acknowledge West back. He simply stood inside the room in front of the door with his arms folded across his chest. Tattoos filled both of his arms and even part of his neck before his bald head took over. West looked around the room, which was more of a garage really. It was a standard-sized room, but the walls, floor, and ceiling were all made of cement without any paint covering them. On the far wall, away from the door, was a cabinet full of many drawers containing many files, as well as stacks of boxes which held much of the evidence for the case. West could tell that several of these rooms were for different cases being investigated by this precinct.

West searched through Jack Gardner's background files and found out that they were flawless. There were no traces of criminal activity in his adult records. As a matter of fact, there was no criminal activity ever traced to any member of his immediate family, or anywhere up his family tree. Jack had graduated from Hofstra University with honors. He went on to law school before passing the bar exam on his first try and becoming a fine lawyer. He found that Jack's father was a successful businessman, his mother didn't even have a traffic ticket to her name, and both of his brothers were successful. The older one, Mark, was following in his father's footsteps as a CPA. The younger one, Chris, was currently enrolled in a local junior college where he was the basketball star. Both grandparents on each side of the family were also worthy of praise. West didn't look too deeply into their lives other than their occupations, but Jack could describe them in much more detail if he had been asked to do so.

* * * * * * * * * *

Mr. Gardner's parents were just as successful as their son. His father, Grandpa Gardner, and his mother, Grandma Gardner, still lived in Nebraska where the entire family originated from. Mr. Gardner was one of seven; he had two brothers and four sisters, of which he was the second oldest. Many of them had spread their wealth and moved all about the country, settling in Colorado, Pennsylvania, New York, Arkansas, and Nebraska. The Gardner grandparents still lived in Nebraska in a large three-story house. As a matter of fact, the basement alone was much nicer and larger than a lot of houses Jack had seen his friends growing up in when he was a teenager. Part of an eighteen-hole golf course crossed through their never-ending backyard. A pond sat some two hundred yards behind the house and it would freeze over during the cold winters. As much wealth as they enjoyed, they were just as sharing and giving.

Jack's fondest memories of Christmas were when all the relatives on the Gardner side of the family (all seven brothers and sisters and their families) would come from all over the country to stay under the Gardner grandparents' roof. All in all, around twenty-five people lived together under the same roof for about a week. They had been meeting there every single Christmas since before Jack could remember. His memories were full of playing Super Mario Bros. on Nintendo, running around the large house, and playing in the snow with his many cousins. When it came time for opening presents, all the kids knew they would be receiving a generous monetary award from their grandparents, which put quite a smile on their faces. They always gave out a warm sense of family with their hospitality.

Although not quite as wealthy as the Gardner grandparents, Mrs. Gardner's parents, the Sechovec grandparents, were just as successful in Jack's eyes. They two were able to raise four great kids, the youngest being Jack's mother. Mrs. Gardner had an older brother, who had moved to New York from Nebraska along with one of her older sisters. The Sechovec grandparents also lived in Nebraska before they all moved to New York. One of Mrs Gardner's older sisters stayed behind in Nebraska though. She had been born mentally retarded—something that must have been quite difficult for the whole family to deal with, but surely it only made them stronger.

Mrs. Gardner's parents had moved to New York shortly after her parents left Nebraska. This was mostly because they didn't want to be away from their youngest child. Of all the children the Sechovecs bore, Mrs.

Gardner was the one who visited her parents most frequently, and the one who called them daily. Although she was the youngest, she looked out and cared for her now eighty-five-year-old parents the most.

The Sechovec grandparents were not the wealthiest of people, certainly not as wealthy as the Gardner grandparents. Grandpa Sechovec had joined the Navy during World War II, missing any college opportunities. After that, Grandpa Sechovec did a number of jobs, some of which under today's standards might be considered unskilled. He worked as a baker, worked in a meat-packing plant, sold insurance, worked as a handyman, sold fruit from an orchard, and finished out working in a walnut factory before retiring around the age of eighty.

The Sechovec grandparents lived in a small mobile home park. The house itself was very small, but they didn't need much. They were perfectly happy with what they had. Grandma Sechovec in particular had most likely never been upset a day in her life. She always seemed cheerful and full of energy despite her age. They had, and continued to have, a great life together, quite content with the wonderful family they had built. To Jack, it seemed as though they took more pride in Mrs. Gardner and their grandchildren than anything else in this world.

* * * * * * * * * *

West put down all files related to Jack Gardner. Clearly this was not the way to go. Jack Gardner was not leading West any further into solving the case. He looked around the barren room and took a deep breath. Perhaps the answer was to look through the files of his own client. Maybe there was some clue that he had previously over-looked. Some answers must involve Craig. West picked up Craig's files and took a look through them, although he had done so many times already.

Craig had indeed been charged with a couple of felonies, one of which was for battery after beating his mother's boyfriend, David Cooper. There were also a few counts of small-scale robbery, but nothing West didn't already know by now. His mother, as well as David Cooper, was now dead. His father lived in California, but Craig said only recently had they begun to develop any kind of relationship. No leads linked anyone associated with Craig to the murder.

If Craig had indeed led Melanie and Jack into the house and someone else did the killing as West presumed, then a couple of questions needed to be answered. First of all, who would want Jack and Melanie dead? Second, what relation could this person or persons have to Craig to make him sell out his friends? And lastly, did Craig know he was taking them there to be executed?

The biggest flaw with West's theory was that of the tattoo on the murderer. The tattoo, as seen by Jack Gardner, was identical on both Craig Sanderson and on the masked murderer. What possible explanation could there be for that, except if both Craig and the murderer had the same tattoo in the same location. West had heard of gangs and cults having tattoos as a trademark to their group, but he didn't think Craig was involved in anything like that. Nothing in his records had him linked to any type of gang-related activity. Unfortunately, West couldn't see anything Craig was involved in during his teenage years as his juvenile records were not open once he turned eighteen. West didn't think those records would be much help anyway. He had already checked over Mr. Sanderson's and the former Mrs. Sanderson's files to see if there was any mention of Craig from when he was a minor, but there wasn't.

Then it dawned on him. Why was he looking through Mr. Sanderson's files? Craig had not even lived with Mr. Sanderson during his teenage years. He put the Sandersons' files down and picked up one that he had yet to crack open. When he opened this file, he found his first glimpse of light. He found information that could possibly change the entire case. And although he promised Craig that he would not run with his new theory, promised Craig he would stick with the story that stated Craig had absolutely nothing to do with the murder, he had to bring the information out. It was for Craig's own good, even if he didn't know it.

West thanked the officer and walked out of the room. He walked by Denton, who seemed to be walking toward the file room.

"Leaving?" Denton asked.

"Something came up," West said, quickly walking past him. "Thanks for letting me in. I'm sure I'll be seeing you again."

"Good luck," Denton called out after him.

West smiled as he walked down the hall. It seemed he had finally gotten some of that luck.

Chapter 19

A Gang Member Reunited

Craig had been living at his new apartment for a couple of weeks now. His new place made his old house with Jack look like a palace. The apartment complex seemed to be falling apart and Craig thought it was a wonder they were still in business. The walls inside Craig's apartment were a dark brown and the carpet, while once tan, now matched the walls due to the many stains it displayed. There was no real kitchen, just a sink, and the dining table was in the small living room. Some of the lights didn't work which gave the entire apartment a dark gloomy feel.

Craig had been calling Melanie every day since he arrived at his new apartment; however, she had not once answered his calls. Craig was beginning to go crazy. Every day that he didn't get to talk to her made him want her that much more. He needed to hear her voice, just to make sure she was all right. One day he decided to leave a message if she didn't answer. It would be the first message he had ever left her. He was always scared to leave one in case Jack was at her house. He picked up his dirty old phone and dialed the number he was quite familiar with. It rang five times and Craig took a deep breath after every one. He was upset as always when she didn't answer.

"Melanie, this is Craig. You haven't been answering any of my phone calls these past couple weeks and I'm worried about you." There was a long pause before Craig continued. "I miss you, Melanie. I know I shouldn't be saying this on an answering machine, but I can't stop thinking about you and that one night. I don't want that to be the only night we share together. I want to be with you."

"Craig you need to leave me the hell alone!" Craig's message was interrupted by Melanie's voice after she picked up the phone.

"Why? Why haven't you been answering my calls? Have you been sick? Are you okay?"

"I'm fine!" Melanie continued to yell. "The reason I haven't been answering is because I don't want to talk to you!"

"But why? Is Jack starting to suspect something?" Craig sounded confused as if he couldn't understand why she wouldn't want to talk to him anymore.

"No, he isn't suspecting anything; it's just that I don't want anything with you Craig. Just friendship!"

"I know you want to be with me, Melanie. I could tell ever since we shared that special night at your house."

"That was just one night. I made a mistake. We both agreed it was a mistake. That was supposed to be the end of it."

"I know, but I don't want it to be the end. I want us to be together. Maybe we could even live together."

"We're not going to be together. I love Jack and I want to be with him forever. If you can't accept us being just friends, then I suggest that we don't talk anymore, for both our sakes."

"Fine then, Melanie. I hope you have a great life with Jack, but trust me, you're going to regret this." Craig slammed the phone down, hanging up on Melanie who sat speechless on her couch, in shock.

Craig didn't waste anytime. His anger had grown to unbelievable heights as he picked up the phone and made another call. It was time for him to finally go back to the life he had once lived, a life that was full of people who cared about him and showed him loyalty and friendship, a life where he belonged. He didn't belong with a friend who would soon graduate with honors at the top of his class. He belonged with tough people like himself, people who had to stick together to survive.

"Hello," came a low voice on the other side of the phone.

"Is this Daniel Cooper?"

"It is. Who is this?"

"Craig. Craig Sanderson."

"Craig Sanderson? It's been a long time, Craig. What can I do for you?" Daniel Cooper spoke in a low tone, but still with authority.

"I um ..." Craig hesitated for a moment. "I want to come back."

"I see," said Daniel Cooper. "How long has it been since you were with us?"

"I was seventeen."

"You left us, Craig. After everything we did for you, you still left us. Not to mention you almost killed my father. Why should I let you back in?"

"I was young then. I'm almost twenty-three now. I'm not the little boy that I was. I could be very valuable to the group this time around."

"And what about my father?"

"You can't blame me, Daniel. You know how he is. You experienced it too before you were sent to live with your mother. I couldn't just sit back and let him hurt my mother and not do anything about it."

"I see. Well, I suppose that can be forgiven. I understand how his rages get. But still I am unclear. Why do you wish to come back now?"

"Because I have nothing anymore, Daniel. I have no friends. I have no family. I have no money. I have nowhere to turn. I need you and the others to be what you once were to me. I promise I will make it worth your while. I will do whatever you want."

"All right, Craig. I believe you. You can come back."

"Thank you so much. You won't regret it."

"Of course you will need to be branded this time. No running away like last time."

"Yes, I figured."

"Call me tomorrow. We will need to meet to discuss your loyalty further."

Daniel Cooper hung up the phone and Craig Sanderson sat down on his sofa and leaned back with a content smile on his face.

The officer turned the page.

Chapter 20

An Unlikely Partnership Formed

Joseph West walked into the courtroom the very next day with a new positive frame of mind. For the first time he felt that a piece of the puzzle had now gone his way. Perhaps it didn't prove Craig's innocence, but it did raise some serious issues concerning his guilt. Today he would raise those issues, and bring some light to the jurors who had been shadowed by the overwhelming proof of Craig's guilt. However, when he opened the large courtroom doors and walked down the aisle to his bench, he was stopped by something that he did not expect. Someone was sitting in his seat on the defense bench. He was a very old man, who was wearing a brown suit and matching tie. West was confused until Judge Black notified him of what was going on.

"We are sorry we didn't inform you earlier Mr. West, but we will no longer be needing your services. The defendant, Craig Sanderson, has requested a change of his lawyer, and has asked that Earl Pitzer continue from this point on."

West was shocked. If this had been months ago he wouldn't have cared, but he had put too much effort into the case at this point to just back off. He was fully dedicated to proving Craig's innocence, if indeed he *was* innocent. Recently he had almost come to believe that he and Craig were becoming somewhat of friends. He felt hurt and even betrayed that Craig didn't feel the same way. He gave Craig a look as if to say, "What is this all about?"

"Sorry, West," Craig said. "But I just couldn't trust you anymore. You weren't going to stick to my story and I know it. Earl here will let me tell it the way it truly is. The way that shows me having nothing to do with any of the murders linked to this case. I want the world to know that I am innocent. I'm sorry."

West looked at his former client for a couple moments before turning his back on the bench and walking out of the courtroom. He didn't stop walking until he reached his car, and then he sped off on his way to the police station.

"Can I please speak to Officer Denton?" West said to the officer at the front desk.

"Just a moment," The officer replied. Sooner than expected Denton greeted West.

"Mr. West, what can I do for you?" he said with a smile.

"I don't have a lot of time, Denton. I need to get back into the file room." It would have been almost disrespectful that West called an officer simply by his last name with no title in front, but Denton was only a young man and he was used to it. For this reason, Denton never seemed to mind, even if West wasn't but a half decade older.

"Wait a minute, aren't you supposed to be in court right now?"

"That doesn't matter. Look Denton, I like you. You seem like the kind of guy that would want an innocent man to be saved. I need access to all the files and I need to make copies of certain documents."

"So what's the problem?"

"I'll level with you Denton. I've been fired as Craig's attorney."

"Then what the hell are you doing here?"

"I can't let the case go. He has no chance of winning it without me. I've found evidence that may help to prove his innocence and I need to further research it. Now, here's where I need you to come in. I can't have the security guard in the room while I photocopy. I can't have anyone see me make copies. Since I'm not on the case officially anymore, the court won't allow me to have the files."

"I don't know about this West. I've only been on the force a year or so. I'm not really in the position to be granting favors."

"A man's life is at stake, Denton! Does that mean nothing to you?"

"How do I know he's even innocent?"

"How do you know he isn't? Do you really want that hanging over your conscience if he's put to death?"

"What do you want me to do?"

"Get rid of the other officer for fifteen minutes, that's all I need."

"Follow me." Denton took West down the long corridor which led to the room that held the files of the case. Another was waiting for them when they reached the end of the hallway. "Want to unlock the doors for this gentleman, Steve?" Denton asked the other officer.

"No problem," the officer said in a polite voice. He sounded much friendlier than his looks would suggest.

"Hey, Steve, payroll wants to see you. Said something about a check. They said to come right away. I'll watch this man for you while you go check it out."

"It's about damn time they write me my check," the other officer said as he walked down the hall murmuring under his breath the whole time.

"He's been complaining about a paycheck that he claims he didn't receive a while back. Never shuts up about it," Denton said.

"Good thinking," West replied. They shut the doors behind them and Denton leaned back against the wall and watched as West searched through file after file.

"You know none of the actual work leaves this room right?" Denton reminded him.

"Yes, yes, I know. I just need to make a few copies."

West must have copied nearly one hundred papers by the time he was done. Not to mention all the notes he took down regarding the concrete evidence and artifacts pertaining to the trial. He went into great detail describing the mask, knife, police uniform, and everything else that pertained to what the masked killer was wearing that night.

"Are you ready yet?" Denton asked impatiently.

"Yeah, thanks a lot." West picked up all the new papers he had gathered and put them into a briefcase that he had been carrying. They walked out of the room quickly, but there was still no sign of the other officer.

"Guess I have to wait here until Steve comes back," Denton said. "You can show yourself out. Again, good luck."

"You did the right thing," West said as he shook Denton's hand. He showed himself out of the police station as Denton had suggested.

* * * * * * * * * *

Back in the courtroom, Craig's new attorney, Earl Pitzer, took the floor. He had to walk with a cane and sported large glasses on his squinted eyes. He cleared his throat before speaking. "Your honor." Mr. Pitzer cleared his throat once again. "Your honor, I would like to recall Jack Gardner to the stand." Mr. Pitzer spoke in a very low tone, as though if he spoke louder he would collapse and die.

"Very well," Judge Black said. "Mr. Gardner, if you would please take the stand and remember you are still under oath."

Jack arose from his seat and took the stand for the second time. He wasn't surprised he had been called for cross-examination. He was the main witness for both sides. If the defense could discredit him, they would at least have a chance. He had provided the prosecution with the testimony they needed: the eyewitness account of a victim.

"Mr. Gardner," Earl Pitzer began, "you claim that my client was the one that killed and raped your wife, is that correct?"

"Yes. I know it was him."

"Why would he have killed your wife on the same night he was flying across the country? If someone was to be committing a murder that they intended to get away with, obviously they would not incriminate themselves by leaving the state. Am I right?"

"Well, Craig has never been the smartest individual I've known. I can't answer that question. I can only suggest that it was a foolish move on the defendant's part."

This isn't helping at all, Craig thought. *Jack's going to make me look like an idiot.* After only one question he could see his attorney's incompetence and decided to stop it.

"Your honor?" Craig interrupted his attorney's examination. "No more questions please." The judge looked confused, as did Mr. Pitzer. "I would like to take the stand myself if that's okay."

"Very well, you have that right," Judge Black said. "Craig Sanderson please take the stand."

Craig got up from his seat and walked by his attorney. "Just let me talk. Don't ask too many questions."

"What?" Mr. Pitzer said, holding his hand up to his hear.

"No questions," Craig said a little more loudly. "Just let me tell my side of the story."

"If that's what you want," Mr. Pitzer said.

Craig took the stand. His attorney looked confused, as if he didn't know exactly where to start. "Please, Craig, tell your side of the story."

"Very well," Craig began. "The beginning of Jack's testimony was true. Well, at least the first part that involved me. I did call him and ask if he wanted to get together to hang out, and yes, honestly I was a bit upset when he told me that he was going to spend yet another night with

Melanie. For whatever reason, I was getting tired of them hanging out all the time. Well, after I found out he was busy, I sat at my house for a while doing nothing but being bored. By the time I thought Melanie and Jack might be home from their date, I went over to Melanie's house. I wanted to talk to Jack and apologize for getting upset with him earlier and tell him that I understood that he had to spend time with his wife. But when I got there and rang the doorbell, no one answered the door. I waited, but still they didn't come. I would've waited longer, but I had a flight to catch and had to pack. Like I've said, I had to fly to Colorado to go to my mother's and her boyfriend's funerals. I drove back to my house, and then later I called Jack to pick me up to take me to the airport. I was stopped in the airport and thrown to the ground by police as they handcuffed my hands behind my back. They made outrageous accusations concerning me being responsible for murder. At first, I didn't even think about the arrest. The only words I could hear were that Melanie was murdered. I can't explain to you enough how I felt at that moment. I loved that girl so much. As a friend, I mean." Craig corrected himself. "She was like a sister to me and I still to this day cannot come to grips with her death. Losing my mother was hard enough, but then to go through this. I don't even know how to describe it. All I can ask is that you, as the jury, don't condemn me for my friend's death that someone else committed."

Everyone in the courtroom was silent. The jury, as well as everyone else in the courtroom, had been hanging onto his every word. It was the very first time they had been able to hear the accused speak.

"Is that all?" Judge Black asked.

Mr. Pitzer looked at Craig and Craig gave him a nod. "No further questions," Pitzer said before wobbling back to his seat.

"Would the prosecution like to cross-examine?" Judge Black asked.

Cynthia Miller stood up from her bench. "Yes, I very much would like that." She paced back and forth in her arrogant strut before asking Craig a few questions.

"So Mr. Sanderson … You agree with what Jack said … that you were upset with him the night of the murder … that you were tired of Jack and Melanie spending so much time together because you were feeling left out."

"Well, yes, I was upset."

"I see. Mr. Sanderson, did you ever have any romantic feelings for Melanie Gardner?"

"No! Never," Craig blurted out. "She was married to my best friend. How could I possibly have any feelings for her?"

"I see. Then what made you so mad about them spending so much time together?"

"I don't know. I guess I was just in a vulnerable state. My mother had been killed, and I was flying to her funeral. I just thought Jack would want to see me before I left. I ended up seeing him before I left anyway. In fact, he drove me to the airport."

Ms. Miller laughed. "Mr. Sanderson, Jack was lying on a floor bleeding at the time. How could he have also driven you to the airport?"

"Listen," Craig stammered. "Me and Jack were the best of friends. I wouldn't have done anything like this!"

"That makes sense," Ms. Miller said honestly. "If you two were such great friends, then naturally you would want to see him before such a terrible experience. However, where things get a little strange for me is how you were all of a sudden found at the airport carrying a duffle bag that contained the apparel used at the crime scene. Would you care to explain that interesting coincidence?"

"I wish I could. Honestly, I had packed my bags right before I left to go to the airport; simply had clothes in it. Somehow my bag must have been switched, I guess."

"What items were in the bag when the police opened them?"

"I didn't actually get a look at them when the police were handcuffing me on the ground," Craig said. "But I was told that my police uniform and a mask were in there."

"And was it indeed your uniform?"

"Unless someone made an exact replica."

"Do you have any clue how your uniform could have ended up in this duffle bag that you claim wasn't yours?"

"No, I don't."

"Now, the knife that was used was never found, just as the knife used to kill your mother was never found. But, the autopsy stab wounds were very unique. Well, the interesting thing about this," Ms. Miller said with a smile, "is that it appears to be the same kind of stab wound that appeared on your mother. Seems to have been the same knife."

"So I've been told."

"Well, that makes for another nice little coincidence, now doesn't it? Would I be accurate in saying that whoever killed your mother most likely killed Melanie?"

"Yeah, I suppose so … if it was the same knife."

"Hmmm. Did you ever have any reason to not like David Cooper or your mother?"

"I hated David Cooper. I won't deny that. But I loved my mother very much. We had our fair share of problems, but every family does."

"Mr. Sanderson, assuming the likely—that the murderer was the same person in both cases—who is the only person with a strong connection to both?"

Judge Black looked at Mr. Pitzer, expecting an objection to this line of questioning, but Earl Pitzer seemed too interested in the answers he was hearing.

"I know what you're getting at, ma'am," Craig said. "But I didn't kill either one."

"Ladies and gentlemen," Ms. Miller preached. "These two deaths were from two different worlds. The couple killed in Colorado had no connection to the young woman killed in New York—no connection at all—other than Craig Sanderson. He is the only one who was deeply connected to both. He was the only one with at least the slightest motive to kill both of them. He is without a doubt, the only one who could have committed all of these murders."

"Objection!" Earl Pitzer finally stammered.

"No further questions," retorted Ms. Miller.

* * * * * * * * * *

After trial that day, Jack Gardner went back to his home. When he opened the door and walked inside, he saw his girlfriend Brianne sitting on the couch. He couldn't see anyone else, but he could hear the voice of another.

"Jack, come in here. There's a visitor for you," Brianne said.

"Hello, Jack. My name is Joseph West. I used to be Craig Sanderson's attorney."

"Yes, I know who you are," Jack said, shaking West's hand.

"I was hoping I might have a few moments of your time. I know I'm no longer on the case, but I have some information that I think you might find interesting."

"Please follow me. We can talk in private. I'll be back in a couple minutes, Brianne. Thanks for inviting him in."

Jack led West into a private guest bedroom and shut the door behind them. "My girlfriend Brianne doesn't know anything about the case. I'd like to keep it that way."

"That's your girlfriend? Wow, she's gorgeous."

"What can I do for you?" Jack asked, changing the subject.

"It's about the case."

"You were fired. What could you possibly want to know about the case?"

"Well, I still need some help in solving it."

"What the hell are you doing still trying to solve it? Let it go. The police have already done their job. We know who the culprit is."

"Yes, you think you do. But what if I revealed information that might change that?"

"What kind of information?"

"Well, you know how you identified Craig as the killer by seeing his tattoo?"

"Yeah. So?"

"I did some research. First, I searched through his files and his parents' files, but couldn't really come up with much. Then it hit me. Maybe there would be something regarding Craig in David Cooper's files."

"And?"

"And I found some information about Craig from when he was a teenager, just seventeen years old. I don't know if you knew this, but David Cooper was a very successful doctor."

"Yes, I knew that."

"I figured you would, but this you may not know. Craig was arrested when he was seventeen. He had been caught selling drugs with a gang that he had been running with. They were known primarily for selling cocaine and marijuana. Well, it turns out that David Cooper kept marijuana at his house. He claimed to have a condition where he needed medical marijuana for personal use. Whether that is true or not is of no relevance. Bottom line, Craig stole the weed from David Cooper and gave it to his gang to sell. When Craig was arrested, negligence charges were put on David Cooper, as he had left the drugs easily accessible. Also, Craig was a minor, so eventually it was taken off his records."

"Craig? In a gang?" Jack was truly shocked. "He never even told me anything about that. So what does that have to do with the case?"

"It has everything to do with the case," West said. "Here's why: in the description of the gang members in the police report, it identified all of them as having two tattoos on their left bicep. All of the tattoos were similar on every member. They all had the same Japanese symbols on their arm that you identified on the killer. Well, all of them except Craig that is. But, like you said, he eventually got the tattoos later."

"So bottom line, what does it all mean?"

"It means the killer may not have been Craig. It could have been anyone who was ever in that gang."

Jack thought for a moment. It still didn't make any sense. Far too much evidence led to Craig. "Well, how do you explain him being caught with the evidence at the airport?" Jack asked.

"Naturally I haven't figured everything out yet. But I intend to."

"Well, I'd really like to help you out, West. Really, I would. No one wants to catch the criminal more than I do. If there's anything I can do to help, I will, but I really don't see what else I can do."

"You were the only one who truly knew him, Jack. You lived with him for a while, didn't you?"

"Yeah, we lived together for about a year. Then he left."

"Why did he leave?"

"I'm not really sure. It was rather unexpected. He never did give me a good reason. But listen, I've had a long day and I'd really rather just relax with my girlfriend. If there's anything else I can help you with, don't hesitate to call."

Joseph West followed Jack out of the room and out to the front door. "Thank you very much for your time, Jack. You can be sure I will be talking with you shortly."

Jack shut the door and went upstairs where Brianne was waiting for him. He took off his suit and tie, getting into an undershirt and shorts, and relaxed on the bed.

"So who was that?" Brianne asked.

"One of the attorneys for the case I've been involved in."

"I still can't understand why such a small crime like robbery is taking so long to come to a conclusion. It seems like it will never end!" Brianne said.

"I know, Brianne. It'll be over soon."

Chapter 21

Jack and Melanie

It was nearing one o'clock in the morning as Craig waited in the dark alley way for whoever it was that was supposed to be coming. The night was dark and cold, just like his life was now. He had not spoken to Jack or Melanie in over half a year. Instead, he was busy trying to work his way up the ladder so that he could ask Daniel Cooper for a favor. So far things were not going well for him. He had been a member of his old gang for the last six months but it wasn't getting him anywhere. The gang struggled to get the drugs they needed to sell, and Craig was paid the least , being at the bottom of the totem pole.

He was waiting now for someone who was supposed to be buying eight ounces of cocaine—most likely some desperate fool who had nothing better to do than get high. It was getting cold on the New York City streets, and Craig wished the drug addict would hurry up so that he could go home. Over an hour he waited, but still no one came. Daniel would certainly be livid about another lost profit, but Craig gave up hope.

When Craig got back to his apartment, he got his mail key and went to the mailbox, as he had not checked it yet today. Two letters waited for him, and neither was pleasing to see. The first was an eviction notice. Craig had failed to pay his rent for a couple months in a row now, and the letter stated that he would have to be out of the apartment in a week. *Great,* Craig thought. *Where am I going to go now?* Craig knew the letter would be coming eventually, he just hoped that maybe he could stay for another month before getting kicked out.

The second letter he received was even more painful to read. He stared at the invitation and honestly felt sick to his stomach.

COME JOIN THE CELEBRATION!
Melanie and Jack are Getting Married!

The heading alone was almost too much for Craig to take. He did not want to read the rest of the message, but he did anyway. It was written by Jack personally to Craig.

> *Craig,*
> *As you can tell, Melanie and I are getting married. I know we haven't spoken for a while, but I still really want you to come. After everything we've been through and how close we were, I don't think my wedding would be complete without you. Please give it some consideration and take the time to celebrate with us.*
> *Forever your friend,*
> *Jack Gardner*

Craig stared at the invitation for a few moments. "That bastard really thinks I would show up to his damn wedding?" Craig threw the invitation in the trash.

By this time it was nearing three o'clock in the morning, but Craig wasn't tired. The information he had just received had him riled up, and he knew that even if he tried, he wouldn't be able to sleep. He called Daniel so that he wouldn't have to deal with him in the morning.

"Hello," Daniel answered.

"Daniel, it's Craig."

"You'd better have a good reason for waking my ass up at three in the morning."

"Unfortunately I don't. Your guy didn't show tonight. Waited for an hour, but he never came."

"Don't ever wake me up to tell me that shit again. You'd better find a way to make some money on your own." Daniel hung up the phone.

The officer turned the page.

Chapter 22

A Less Pleasant Gardner Reunion

"Are you ready to go yet, Jack?" Brianne said. "I don't want to be late. I want to make a good first impression."

"All right, all right, I'm ready," Jack said, walking down the stairs. "What time were we supposed to get there anyway?'

"Ten minutes ago. Can you hurry up?" Brianne was truly nervous to meet Jack's family for the first time—his mother in particular. Jack had told Brianne how Mrs. Gardner was not that fond of any of Jack's girlfriends, especially Melanie. Brianne would have to overcome her nervousness as they now sped down the highway in Jack's Mercedes toward the Gardner house.

When they arrived, several other cars were already there. Jack recognized them to be his brother Mark's, his brother Chris', his parents' , and his grandparents'. Jack opened the door and walked into the kitchen where he saw everyone sitting in the family room. "Hey, everyone, we're here," Jack announced.

"Jack!" Mrs. Gardner cried out gleefully. "How are you?" She gave Jack a big hug, ignoring Brianne to begin with.

"Mom, this is my girlfriend Brianne," Jack said.

"Well, it's nice to meet you, Brianne."

"You too, Mrs. Gardner. Jack's told me so much about you."

"Well, I can't say the same about you. Jack hasn't been calling me lately. Makes me want to cry." In fact Mrs. Gardner had cried several times from missing her son.

"Oh, Mom, stop." Jack gave her another hug. "So how has everyone else been?" Jack addressed the rest of the house.

Chris was sitting on one couch, petting the pretty family cat, which Jack had rescued from the pound on his twelfth birthday. That cat meant a lot to Jack; he paid more attention to the cat than anyone else in the house. He was an orange color with swirl designs of tan with the softest fur you could ever feel. Mark and Dianne were sitting arm and arm on the opposite couch. Grandpa Sechovec, Mrs. Gardner's dad, was sitting on the family room chair watching television, and Grandma Sechovec was washing her hands in the sink. Jack went around the room, saying hello to everyone, giving each of them a hug, and introducing Brianne.

"Where's Dad?" Jack asked.

"He's out barbequing the steak," Mrs. Gardner answered.

Jack looked through the back window and saw his father working away on the steaks.

"Jack, could you show me where the bathroom is?" Brianne asked.

"Sure. It's just right down there on the right," Jack pointed out.

"Thanks."

"Come here, Jack. I need you to help me with something in my room," Mrs. Gardner said. She walked out of the kitchen and down the long hallway to her bedroom, and Jack followed.

"Brianne seems nice," Mrs. Gardner said. "Much nicer than Melanie."

"Don't insult my wife, mom. But yes, she is very nice. That's not why you brought me back here, is it?" Mrs. Gardner shut the door behind them after they entered the room. She sat down on her king-size bed and told Jack to sit next to her.

"No, that's not why I brought you back here. We haven't talked in a long time, Jack. You know I worry about you."

"When have you not worried, Mom?"

"Well, it doesn't help when you don't call. Are you still taking your medication?"

"No, Mom, not anymore. Doctor told me it's all in my head. That the pills aren't really helping. He wants me to try to come up with answers to why I have these problems. Wants me to find out what I'm afraid of or something."

"I see. Has it been getting worse?"

"Yeah, it's been pretty bad lately." Jack touched both sides of the bed next to him four times at the sound of it.

"Well, it's understandable with everything you've been going through. How is the case coming? Getting close to the end, isn't it?"

"Yeah, it's almost there. Just have closing statements and the final decision left."

"Are you holding up all right?"

"Yeah. It's tough, you know, but I'll be fine. The sooner this thing gets over with, the sooner I can move on with my life. Perhaps my OCD will decline."

"I just can't believe it," Mrs. Gardner said. "Why would Craig do such a thing?" Mrs. Gardner shed a couple of tears, and Jack wrapped her in his arms.

"Don't cry, Mom. You know that's the one thing I can't stand to see."

"I just can't help it. We did so much for him!" Mrs. Gardner cried. "He tried to kill you!"

"I want to see justice served just as badly as you do. We just have to be patient. It'll all be over soon enough," Jack assured her. Mrs. Gardner sniffed her nose and wiped away the few tears that had dropped. "Why don't we go back to the family room? I'm sure everyone is waiting for us," Jack said.

"All right," Mrs. Gardner agreed. "Just give me one more hug." Mrs. Gardner hugged him tight and didn't let him go for several moments. When she finally did, the two of them walked back into the kitchen.

By this time Mr. Gardner had returned from the backyard with a plate of steaks ready to be eaten. The dining room table was set with dishes and silverware. "Hey, there, Jack," Mr. Gardner said. "You ready for dinner?"

"Yeah, I'm starved," Jack replied. "Did you get a chance to meet my girlfriend?"

"Yes, I did. She said she's ready to eat down one of these fine steaks. Come on, everyone, time to eat."

Brianne, as well as everyone else in the family room, stood up and took their seats in the dining room.

"Looks really good," Brianne said, and everyone else agreed.

After saying grace, everyone dug in, helping themselves to steak, salad, and corn.

"How have things been going for you, Jack?" Grandpa Sechovec asked. "Big-time lawyer and all." Grandpa Sechovec was darker skinned, resembling Mrs. Gardner and Jack. He was about Jack's height and slightly overweight. Back in his younger days, he had been a fit, and somewhat decorated, basketball player.

"It's going well. I'm ready to start working again."

"You start soon then?" Grandpa Sechovec adjusted his baseball hat before taking a bite of his steak.

"As soon as the case is over I get to start again."

"Oh, yeah," Jack's little brother Chris chimed in. "How is that case going?"

"Perhaps we shouldn't talk about that over the dinner table," Mr. Gardner ordered.

"Yeah, I agree," Jack said. "You don't want to hear about that stuff, Chris." Jack was interrupted by a ringing of his cell phone. "Please excuse me, everyone; I have to go answer this." Jack got up from the table and walked down the hallway to his old bedroom. "Hello," Jack answered.

"Jack Gardner? Joseph West. How are you doing?"

"Is there a reason you're calling, West? How did you get this number? I'm with my family."

"We need to meet up, Jack."

"And why is that?"

"As you know, the case is coming to a close, Jack. There isn't much time left. Craig is going to be sentenced to death and you're not doing anything to stop it! It's like you don't even care!"

"Listen, West. You can do all the research you want, but the fact remains: Craig Sanderson killed my wife. He tried to kill me. Craig deserves everything he has coming to him. I've gotten over it and moved on. I suggest you do the same."

"Yeah, well you're not going to be over it once you cause your best friend to be wrongly executed!"

"How dare you talk to me like that!" Jack hung up the phone. *This man is never going to give up,* Jack thought. Jack took a few moments to calm himself down before returning to the dinner table.

"Who was that?" Brianne asked.

"Just someone from the firm," Jack said. "Told me about a case he wants me to take on as soon as I can."

"What is it again that you do?" Mr. Gardner asked Brianne.

"I'm not exactly sure yet. I'm still weighing some of my options, but I definitely would love to do something in the medical field. Maybe nursing, but I'm not sure yet."

Chris interrupted her. "Jack, I really want to hear about the case. What's been happening? Is he going to die?"

Brianne looked at Jack with a concerned look on her face.

"Ha ha. They don't give robbers the death penalty, Chris," Jack chimed in. "Anyway, I told you we're not going to talk about this at the table. How's work been going, Mark? Is Dad treating you right?" Jack changed the subject as fast as possible.

"Well, at the rate I'm going, Dad will be working for me in a year or two. Isn't that right, Dad?" Mark gave Mr. Gardner a playful nudge in the shoulder.

"Yeah, we'll see about that. You just keep bringing me my coffee. Maybe I'll promote you to ironing my pants if things keep going well," Mr. Gardner joked.

"What about you, Chris?" Grandpa Sechovec asked. "Are you going to work for your father too?"

"No," Mr. Gardner said. "I already made the mistake of hiring one son. There's no way I'm letting any more of them near my work!"

"So you're just going to keep chasing the girls then?" Grandpa asked Chris.

"That's what I plan on," Chris replied, and Grandpa chuckled.

Grandma Sechovec interrupted him. "An early grave is what you're going to be chasing if you don't start taking your pills," she said to her husband. "Did you forget again?"

"Oh, relax. She's always on my back, isn't she, Jack?" Jack didn't want to make his grandmother upset, so he simply smiled back without saying anything. "I'll take them later."

"The doctor said you were to take them before dinner." Grandma seemed annoyed. "I tell him to wash his hands, he doesn't do it. I tell him to take his vitamins, he doesn't do it. I tell him to take his pills, he doesn't do it," she said to everyone. "The doctor said he has to take these pills to help with his cholesterol, but he just won't listen to me."

"Dad, you have to listen to your doctor. Do you want to leave Mom all alone?" Mrs. Gardner said.

"I know, I know. I'll take them right after dinner. Let's just talk about something else. All this talk about death is depressing." Grandpa Sechovec spoke as though he didn't have a care in the world despite his age. Everyone grew silent but continued to eat away at the dinner Mr. and Mrs. Gardner had prepared.

After dinner, everyone sat around the family room except for Chris, who was most likely in his room talking to one of his friends on his cell phone. Grandpa sat on the living room chair and turned on the television. "Damn Yankees are losing. What the hell is wrong with them? Most money in the league, best players in the league, and they still can't win a damn World Series."

"Calm down," Grandma said. She took a seat on the couch and Mr. and Mrs. Gardner sat down next to her. Mark and Dianne sat down on the love seat and Jack pulled up two chairs from the kitchen table for him and Brianne to sit on.

A loud noise came from Grandpa, which the others could only guess was a cough. No one said anything, as everyone was used to him coughing loudly.

"Is he okay?" Brianne whispered to Jack.

"Yeah, he's fine. He coughs like that a lot."

However, the coughing didn't stop. He continued to cough as his face grew red and his veins became more apparent.

"Dad, are you okay?" Mrs. Gardner asked with serious concern. Grandpa Sechovec did not respond. Instead he fell off the chair onto one knee. "Dad?" Mrs. Gardner cried.

"Grandpa?" Jack called out, jumping up from his chair and going to his grandfather's side.

"I think I'm all right," Grandpa panted out although he didn't look like he was all right.

"Jack, go get the car running," Mrs. Gardner ordered. "We need to take him to the hospital."

When they reached the hospital, Grandpa Sechovec was taken to an emergency room to be observed by the doctor. The rest of the Gardners waited in the lobby. Mrs. Gardner got up from her seat, walking away from the others to be alone with her thoughts. She paced back and forth, never stopping, and continually bit at her fingernails. Jack got up from his seat and went after his mother.

"It's going to be okay, Mom," he said.

Mrs. Gardner buried her head into her son's shoulder and wrapped her arms around him. "I know," she sobbed. "I just hope there's nothing wrong. I don't think I could stand it if there was."

The two of them sat down in chairs far away from the others. Jack hated to see his mother cry more than anything in the world. His stomach clenched up, and his heart fell into a million pieces. He didn't know what else to say to his mother, so he just stayed silent with his arms around her. "I love you, Mom," he whispered. He touched both sides of his waiting room chair four times, relieving him of some of his stress. "Everything will be all right," he told himself.

Immediately after Jack spoke, a short Chinese man with a bald head, except for some black hair around the sides, dressed in a white coat, came over to Mrs. Gardner. "Excuse me, Mrs. Gardner?"

She nodded.

"I'm Dr. Chan, your father's doctor. I have some news that I thought you should become aware of immediately. Mr. Sechovec felt that you were the one I should tell."

"What is it? Is there anything wrong with him?" Mrs. Gardner was so anxious it seemed she would soon explode.

"I'm sorry to have to tell you this. But with everything you told us about his frequent coughing and occasional chest pain, we decided to run a couple X-rays."

"And?" Mrs. Gardner interrupted.

"Did your father ever smoke at all?"

"Yeah, he did, but he stopped long ago, when he was in his fifties or so."

"I'm sorry to say that we've detected that your father has lung cancer."

"He has what?" Mrs. Gardner gasped. "Is he going to be okay? How has this not been detected earlier?"

"Well, it's often hard to spot without an X-ray. And yes, we think that we have caught the cancer in time. If we put your father on the right treatment, it could save him, or at least prolong his life greatly."

"So you're saying there's a chance I could lose my father?" Mrs. Gardner cried.

"Unfortunately, it's hard to say. Lung cancer is one of the most dangerous types of cancers, and full recovery from the disease is difficult."

Mrs. Gardner was silent. She simply stared at the floor, not able to look the doctor directly in his eyes.

"I'm sorry, Mrs. Gardner. You can go see your father now if you would like." Dr. Chan walked away.

"I can't go see him right now," Mrs. Gardner told Jack. "I can't let him see me like this." She wiped away a tear from her eye. "Can you please go tell the others to visit him now?"

"Sure, Mom," Jack replied before walking back to where everyone was sitting.

Mrs. Gardner, however, went to the restroom and cried her eyes out in a stall until she felt there were no tears left in her eyes. *What if he doesn't make it?* Mrs. Gardner thought. *What am I going to do without him?* She wiped away more tears from her eyes and walked out of the bathroom.

Chapter 23

An Old Friend

Jack parked his car along the street before getting out and entering the Eastside Bar. When he walked in, he noticed that not many people were in the bar. There were just a couple of people sitting on bar stools and sipping away at their drinks. However, the one person he was expecting to meet there, the reason he had gone out so late at night, was there sitting at a table toward the back. He had brown, thick-rimmed glasses on which matched his short brown hair and brown eyes. He was wearing a long, tan coat and blue jeans. He wasn't severely overweight, but had a bit of a gut. Jack walked over to greet him.

"Mr. Sanderson," Jack said. "It's been a long time."

"Indeed it has, my son." Mr. Sanderson stood up and gave Jack a big hug. "How have you been?"

"Actually I'm getting married," Jack said. "Not sure when though."

"Are you serious?" Mr. Sanderson sounded shocked. "Well, look at that. Little Jack is all grown up now, isn't he?"

"I wish I could say your son will be at the wedding."

"What? You don't think he'll show? Why not?"

"I don't know. He's been acting very strange lately. I haven't talked to him in the longest time."

"Well, I hate to say it, but he's been in a very bad place lately, Jack."

"What do you mean? Is he okay?"

"No, my son. He isn't. He's been out of luck lately." Mr. Sanderson took a sip from his beer mug.

"Have you talked to him lately?"

"I talked to him less than a month ago as a matter of fact. It turns out he's been struggling to even keep a place to live."

"He was living with me for a year, as I'm sure you know. But, then he just decided it was time to leave. No explanation. No nothing. Did he ever tell you why he left?"

"No, he didn't mention it. But, then again, he never even mentioned you were getting married, so maybe he didn't want to talk about you. I'll ask him about it next time I speak with him."

"So what *did* you and Craig talk about, then?"

"Well, if you can believe it, I told him why me and his mother split up."

"You told him the *real* story?" Jack Gardner sounded shocked. "Why?"

"I didn't want him to hate his mother, but I felt that he had a right to know the truth about it all. Don't you think he deserved to know?"

"Yes, I guess so. How did he take it?"

"He wasn't that upset actually," Mr. Sanderson said. "He said he didn't think too highly of her anymore anyway so it didn't make much of a difference. I told him how I felt though, when it all happened. I told him that it was the worst day of my life and that nothing she could do would ever make up for it. I told him that if he ever did that to another man—have sexual relations with his wife that is—then I don't think I could ever consider him my son again."

No one spoke during a long pause. Jack could tell that Mr. Sanderson was replaying the events of that day, the awful day in which he had been betrayed, over and over in his head while they spoke.

"Did you tell him about me? That I was there and all? Did you tell him about the knife?" asked Jack.

"No, no. I didn't tell him any of that. Good thing you were there, though, that day. I honestly can say I would have killed both of them." Mr. Sanderson laughed. "It's crazy what love will make you do, isn't it?"

"Yeah, well, listen," Jack said. "I better get back to my soon-to-be-wife Melanie. I told her I was only going to be out for an hour or so."

"You didn't tell her that you were meeting me, did you?"

"No, I just told her I had to run to my mom's house really quickly."

"Okay, good."

"Listen, don't tell Craig about our meetings either. I don't think he would like it much knowing that you see me a lot more than you see him," Jack said.

"You don't need to worry about me, Jack. We've been meeting on and off for years without Craig knowing, and every time we meet you tell me not to tell him. But don't worry. I never have, and I never will. By the way, how are your parents doing? Are they all right?"

"Yeah, they're doing great. Never better."

"Yeah, well that must be nice," Mr. Sanderson said with a smile. "Tell them I said hello and that I'm doing just fine."

"I will," Jack replied. "And please remember to talk to Craig. Find out, if you can, why he doesn't want to live with me anymore. I really miss the kid. I need to know what's going on with him."

"No problem." Mr. Sanderson stood up and gave Jack another hug before the two parted ways. Jack walked out of the bar and back out onto the street. It was getting late, and he hoped that by the time he got back, he would find his lovely fiancé waiting for him anxiously in bed.

The officer turned the page.

Chapter 24

A Case Coming to a Close

Three weeks had gone by since the incident at the Gardner house with Grandpa Sechovec. He had recently been discharged from the hospital and now was back to normal life at his home. However, it wasn't completely normal as Mrs. Gardner was at the Sechovec house almost every day worrying about him and his condition. Jack was concerned also. He had spent a lot of time at the Gardner house to make sure Mrs. Gardner was doing all right and Brianne had often gone with him.

Joseph West was worried about other things, however. With the court decision expected soon, he found his time dwindling and began to grow even more frantic. When he walked through the police station doors, he had only one thing on his mind: find Denton.

"Hello," West said to the front desk officer. "I was hoping I could speak with Travis Denton. Is he in?"

"Let me check," was the reply from a young woman.

Moments later Travis Denton walked out to greet Joseph West. "How's it going, West?" Denton said, extending his hand. West took it and replied back.

"There's no time for small talk. What time are you off work today?"

"I'll be off at six thirty. Why?"

"We need to meet somewhere private. Can you meet me at the café on Market Street as soon as you get off?"

"Sure," Denton said. "Am I allowed to eat there or do we not have time?" Denton joked.

"It's really not a laughing matter. I have important news to discuss and I think you're the only one who can help me."

"All right, well, I'll see what I can do."

"See you tonight," West said. He turned around and walked back out the door.

* * * * * * * * * *

At the courtroom, it was time for closing statements. "Ms. Miller, would you please?" Judge Black ordered.

Ms. Miller stood up from her bench wearing precisely the same outfit as she had worn everyday in court. She adjusted her glasses and walked over to where the jury was sitting to address them.

"Ladies and gentlemen of the jury," she began. "As this case has progressed, it has sickened me more and more every day. How could anyone in their right mind kill and rape a young woman? This young woman had her whole life ahead of her, but it was brutally and mercilessly taken from her.

"The defendant was a police officer, someone who was supposed to uphold the law. He was given the trust of his citizens, and abused that trust in the worst way possible. Someone who was supposed to be the citizens' hero turned out to be their worst villain. We don't know why he did this exactly. Perhaps, he had romantic feelings for Melanie which she did not reciprocate. But this we cannot be sure of. One thing we can be sure of, however, is that Craig Sanderson committed this crime.

"His fingerprints were on the walls of Melanie's room, despite the fact that the room had recently been painted. The defendant claimed he had not been to Melanie's house long before the room had been painted, obviously a lie. The wedding ring that Melanie was wearing was taken off her finger and placed on the dresser near the bed, another sign that Craig had feelings for this woman.

"Jack Gardner was an eyewitness to his attack. He placed Craig Sanderson at the scene and clearly identified the materials Mr. Sanderson used to commit the murder. And in fact, Craig Sanderson was caught trying to flee the state on the same night, with precisely all the tools Jack Gardner had described hidden in a duffle bag that he was carrying. All of the tools besides the knife, which has not been found. Perhaps the defendant disposed of it. I'll remind you that the police found the mask and the ripped uniform just as Jack had described. And might I add, ladies and gentlemen, that the defendant's semen was found on Melanie's bed. The very same bed where the murder and rape occurred!

"Young men in the jury, picture your wife or girlfriend if you have one. I want you to picture your best friend. And now picture your best friend killing the woman you love, and then raping her after she was dead. That is the situation we have here. Ladies and gentlemen of the jury, picture your daughter if you have one. Imagine your daughter being raped and murdered by a vicious man. Your daughter, your little girl, someone that you care for more than anyone, was helplessly overpowered by a hardened criminal. That is also the situation we have here. In each of these situations, imagine what you would want to do to the man that did these things to the woman you loved, no matter what relation you were to her. Imagine what you would want to happen to this man. Would you want justice to be served?

"What possible justifiable reason would there be for a man like this to live? When a criminal is sentenced to life in prison, parole is eventually available. If this criminal gets free, there is a good chance he will strike again. Perhaps this time, it *will* be your wife, daughter, or friend. Think about these things when you make your decision. We trust you to do what's right for the good of the victims, the citizens, and the state of New York."

Ms. Miller walked back over to her bench, took a sip of water, and sat back in her chair.

The jury looked as though they had just been hit with some awful truth. It was as though they didn't quite realize the complete severity of the situation until Ms. Miller had personalized it for them.

"Mr. Pitzer, it's your turn," Judge Black said.

"Of course, your honor," Mr. Pitzer grunted out.

He stood up, picked up his cane, and wobbled over to where Ms. Miller had been just moments before. He cleared his throat, which had become customary, and then delivered his closing statement. It was much shorter than the prosecution's statement, and extremely less effective. It was worthy of no praise whatsoever and did little to help Craig's hopes of acquittal and survival. After Earl Pitzer gave his closing argument, he took a seat and Craig rested his head against the table. He knew it looked unprofessional, but he didn't care. It was all over for him.

"Very well," Judge Black said. "Ladies and gentlemen, you have heard all of the facts, all of the witnesses, and seen all of the evidence. It now comes to the time where the jury must reach a verdict."

The judge gave the jury instructions for their deliberations before announcing that court was dismissed for the day.

* * * * * * * * * *

Joseph West sat at the café for thirty minutes before Denton showed. He was sitting with several files that he had been looking over nonstop since he was fired from the case.

"Would you like another cup of coffee?" the waiter asked him.

"No thanks, I'm fine," West replied. He was really thinking, *I'd rather have a beer.* He had not even taken a sip from his first cup of coffee yet. He didn't care too much for it to begin with but wanted to buy something since he was sitting at the café table. "Denton! Glad you came," West said before getting up and shaking the officer's hand. "Want some coffee?"

"No, let's just get this over with. What can I help you with?" Denton was still wearing his police uniform and West could tell that he had come directly from work.

"Are you done with work for the day?"

"No," Denton sighed. "This is just my break. Boss needs me to go back in tonight. It sucks being a rookie on the force."

"I'm sure," West said. "Anyway Denton, I think I've found our man."

"Our man?"

"Yes, our man," West replied. "The man who is responsible for the death of Melanie Gardner."

"So you're certain that Craig kid didn't do it, huh?"

"Yeah, I'm certain."

"Then talk to Ms. Miller. Tell her you know he's innocent. Tell her to back off the case until the facts come out."

"Tried," West said. "Turns out Ms. Miller is more heartless than whoever killed that Melanie girl. She said, 'I don't care whether he did it or not. I have a job and I'm going to do it.'"

"Oh, so what do you think happened anyway?"

"Well, you see, what happened was Craig owed someone a favor—a big favor. I'm not sure why, but I'm certain he did. For this reason he drove Melanie and Jack to the set up place where a killer was waiting. Now, Craig was involved with a gang when he was younger. Got busted selling drugs with them.

"I don't have all day. Are you going to tell me who this killer is?"

"Daniel Cooper."

"Cooper? That name sounds familiar."

"David Cooper was the boyfriend of Craig's mother."

"Oh, right," Denton said. "The man who was most likely killed by the same person as Melanie."

"That's correct. Now that's David Cooper. Daniel Cooper is his twenty-eight year old son."

"And he is involved in this how?"

"Daniel was, possibly still is, the leader of this gang that Craig belonged to. He was arrested on two different occasions for trafficking drugs, and a couple of the members in the gang sold him out. Told the police that he was the brains behind the whole operation."

"I still don't see how this has anything to do with the Melanie Gardner case," Denton said.

"Well, I believe that Daniel Cooper probably had a lot of influence with the members in the gang—Craig in particular."

"And how do you come to that conclusion?"

"Craig was just seventeen when he first joined the gang. He probably looked up to Daniel as the leader. Plus Craig never sold out Daniel. The police report said that Craig wouldn't talk. So …" West paused. "If Daniel wanted a big favor, Craig just might do that for him. Plus, Jack Gardner talked about the figure in the mask as being physically similar to Craig. Daniel Cooper is about the same height as Craig. He fits the profile."

"Okay, it sounds like a stretch, but perhaps you have a point," Denton said. "But still, what do you want me to help you with?"

"Well, Denton, I was hoping you might have some connections that I do not."

"Connections?"

"In order for my theory to make sense, Daniel Cooper must have had some reason to harm Jack or Melanie Gardner. What other reason would he want to kill them?"

"I have no idea. I don't even see any connection between the Coopers and Jack or Melanie," Denton said.

"Well, there might not be a direct connection, but maybe there is a middleman?"

"The Sandersons?"

"Of course the Sandersons. Craig's mother was living with David Cooper and so was Craig. Obviously Craig had a strong connection with the Coopers."

"Did Daniel Cooper live there too?"

"No. Daniel's mother divorced David at a young age and he had ended up living with his mother. I'm sure Daniel and Craig had met on more than one occasion. Now, as we all know, the Gardners and the Sandersons were once very close. We also all know that Craig's mother and David Cooper were killed. Now, wouldn't you be upset if your father was killed?"

"Yeah, so?"

"What if, for whatever reason, Daniel blamed Jack Gardner for the death of his father? Don't you think he would want revenge?"

"Yeah, I suppose so."

"And don't you think he would seek out the one person who could lead him straight to Jack Gardner? The same one person who had the authority to place handcuffs on Jack and tie him down for Daniel."

"But why would Jack Gardner kill David Cooper?" Denton asked.

"For that I have no answer." West took a sip of his coffee. "Gross," he grunted. "But that's not of huge significance right now. Now, for your job Denton, I need a large favor and I hope you can help me."

"Explain."

"For our theory to have any merit, we have to show some direct connection between Jack Gardner and Craig's mother. Some connection that shows that Jack Gardner and her were in communication. Maybe he killed them, maybe he didn't. Doesn't matter."

"And how do you plan on coming up with that?"

"I need you to gain access to phone records. I want you to look for any call ever made from Jack Gardner's household to Cooper's house. If we can find calls that were made, then we can at least show that my theory is a good possibility. There will be a connection that shows that Jack and Craig's mom had spoken, and had some sort of relation. With more investigation maybe we can find some reason why Jack would kill her."

"So now you think Jack killed them?" Denton seemed confused. "Doesn't really seem like the killer type to me."

"Well, you never know. Maybe he killed them, maybe he didn't. All we need is for you to provide the records. Once we show some connection, perhaps we can get the police to look further into what we are saying. You must act fast though. The decision for Craig's case is coming soon. We have no time to waste."

"I can't get those records," replied Denton. "I am not involved with the Gardner case anymore."

"Damn it, Denton, do you want an innocent man's blood on your hands? I am only asking for a few phone records. You don't have to do anything else. This is a small task. There is no harm to anyone to see some old phone records."

"Okay. I guess there is no real harm in me getting you some phone records. Anything more though needs to go through the detectives. I think I can get the records tonight," Denton assured him.

"Then waste no time. Go now and please come back with good news."

Denton got up from the table and walked back to his police car. He turned around before opening the door.

"Hey, West," he said. "What if no calls were ever made?"

"Then," West paused, "we have no evidence, and perhaps we just have to accept the fact that Craig's life will soon be over, whether he is guilty or innocent."

Denton didn't reply, but got into his car and drove away.

Maybe West was right, Denton thought as he drove back to the police station. Even if West wasn't right, he didn't want to have the guilt of a man being executed because of a lack of effort on his part. Now, he had a task ahead of him. How to get into the phone records? He was only a rookie on the force and didn't exactly have access to all such records. He may need a warrant for such a search, but there was no time for that now. Besides, he had been ordered to stop investigating this case. No, he would have to do this task quietly. He didn't know for sure if he could give West the answers he was looking for, but one thing was for sure: he had to try.

Chapter 25

Another Midnight Meeting

Less than a week after Jack had met with Mr. Sanderson, he made a similar trip to the Eastside Bar. He walked into the bar and sat at the same table as he had the other night, but this time no one was waiting for him. *Must be running late,* Jack thought. He headed over to the bar and ordered himself a beer before returning to his table. It didn't take long until his friend arrived.

"Jack! Great to see you again, my son," Mr. Sanderson said. He gave Jack a hug as always and took a seat at the table.

"So did you talk to Craig?" Jack asked.

"I did. Afraid I have some bad news for you though. I don't really know how to break it to you."

"I'm a big boy," Jack said. "Plus I'm engaged to be married. What could possibly be wrong?"

"Well, I was asking Craig why he hasn't been talking to you lately," Mr. Sanderson began. "Wanted to see what was wrong with him, you know? He was on the right path when he was hanging out with you and I'm afraid he's lost sight of the road without you. Anyway, he told me that it's hard to be around you now. Told me that there is a secret he has been hiding from you and that if he told you, you would kill him."

"A secret?" Jack was shocked. "What kind of secret? I don't believe that. Craig and I didn't keep secrets from each other."

"Trust me, he did," Mr. Sanderson replied.

"Well, are you going to tell me or not?" Jack was growing severely impatient.

"You know about—oh, I don't know—maybe a year ago, when Craig was going through problems with his mother?"

"Yes, I was there with him through it all. Why?"

"Are you sure you were *always* there for him, because he feels quite differently."

"What do you mean? What did he say?"

"Well, he told me that you wouldn't listen to his problems. Told me that you just yelled at him to stay in school. But believe me, no matter what you did, there is no justification for his betrayal."

"Tell me what the hell he did!" Jack pleaded, causing a few people in the bar to turn in their chairs to take a look at their table.

"I will, Jack. But just know that I am on your side. When he told me this, I was so angry, so ashamed, that I told him I couldn't consider him my son anymore. You are my only son, Jack."

"Certainly it can't be that bad," Jack insisted.

"Melanie cheated on you with him," Mr. Sanderson blurted out. "I'm so sorry."

"She what?" Jack exclaimed. "What the hell do you mean she *cheated on me with him?* There's no way."

"I heard it straight from his mouth. He said that's why he couldn't live with you anymore. He couldn't stand the thought of what he had done to you."

Jack's hands began to shake uncontrollably and he dropped his glass of beer on the floor so that it shattered into a million pieces.

"Please, Jack. Stay calm."

Jack did not answer for several moments. He touched both sides of his chair four times. "This all happened during the time he was fighting with his mother?"

"You remember the night that Craig beat up that son of a bitch David? That's the same night."

"Where? My house?"

"No, he told me it was at Melanie's house."

"That bastard!" Jack said and clenched his fists tight. "I was at her house that very same night."

"It gets worse," Mr. Sanderson said.

"What the hell could possibly be worse? The two closest people in the world to me betrayed me."

"I asked him if it was just a one time thing. He told me he's in love with her! He's been sending her letters he tells me. You might want to check

Melanie's house for them. I started screaming at him. I told him I knew how it felt to be betrayed and that I couldn't believe he could do that to another man, especially a friend like you. He said I couldn't understand and that love took him over. If I were you I would never talk to him again." Mr. Sanderson was breathing frantically. It was almost as though he was more hurt by the news than Jack was.

"That bastard! But, I can't believe that he actually is in love with her. It must have just been a one-time thing. Maybe they made a mistake. Some mistakes can be forgiven."

"I don't know. All I know is what he told me. Perhaps you're right. Perhaps he doesn't really love her. It could have just been an excuse, you know? Maybe he just wanted to give a good explanation to why he did it. Just be on the lookout."

"I can't listen to this anymore," Jack said as he stood up from the table. "I have to get home. I have to talk to Melanie."

"Please understand why I had to tell you. I could not just let Craig get away with something this terrible."

Jack didn't say a word but gave Mr. Sanderson a hug and rushed out of the bar making sure to touch each side of the door frame four times before walking out.

He sped to Melanie's house and parked along the curb on the street. He clicked the lock button on his key chain four times and checked the door handle four times to make sure it was locked. *I can't believe this,* he thought before taking a deep breath and walking toward the front door.

"It's about time my man came back to me," Melanie said as she attempted to give him a kiss. She was denied however, as Jack turned his head. "What's wrong?" she asked him.

"Listen Melanie," he began. "We need to talk and I need you to be completely honest with me."

"What's wrong?"

"I just got back from talking with Mr. Sanderson."

"Mr. Sanderson? What the hell? Why did you talk to him?"

"That's not the point Melanie. He told me something terrible. Something that I thought would never happen to me."

"Please tell me, Jack." By this time the two of them had migrated to the living room couch and were sitting next to each other. "What did Mr. Sanderson tell you?"

"He talked to Craig. Turns out you haven't been entirely honest with me now, have you?"

Melanie felt her knees begin to shake and her heart pounding. She prayed that this wasn't going where she thought it was. "Jack, I don't know what you're talking ..."

"Don't act stupid, Melanie," Jack interrupted. "You cheated on me with Craig. I know everything."

Melanie grew completely silent. She covered her face with her hands and dropped her head to her knees. She began to cry uncontrollably.

"I don't know what to say," she cried.

"So it's true then. I can't fucking believe this shit! After everything we shared!" Jack stood up from the couch and walked over to the kitchen table. Melanie got up and followed him.

"I'm sorry, Jack. I don't know what to say," she repeated although he could barely understand her through the tears. "I don't deserve you."

"You did that to me and you were still going to marry me? Why would you agree to that special bond if you had committed such an act?" Jack couldn't believe it. He paced back and forth in front of Melanie as if he was about to make a kill.

"I didn't want to lose you. You know how much I love you." Jack didn't respond to this. "Jack ... are you saying you don't want to marry me now?" Jack paused for a few moments and thought it over before answering.

"Do you love him?"

"Love him? Jack, that's ridiculous! I only love *you!*"

"Was it just a one-time thing?"

"Yes, Jack I promise! Well, for me at least."

"What the hell do you mean by that?"

"Well," Melanie hesitated. "I think Craig may have feelings for me. He wanted to keep seeing each other and told me he couldn't be without me. That's why I stopped talking to him. I think he's over it now though. Hasn't tried to talk to me in months."

"I don't want to call off the wedding Melanie. I love you. I want this to work, but it's going to take time. As you well know, I don't believe in divorces. Over half of married people get divorces these days. Makes me sick. Maybe with time we can work this out."

Melanie nodded to say that she agreed and hoped that would happen.

"Do me a favor though," said Jack.

"Anything," Melanie replied.

"Don't tell Craig that I know. It won't do anyone any good, especially if he still loves you like you say he does."

"I don't even want to talk to him. He scares me in a way."

"Good."

"What about you, Jack? Are you going to still try to be friends with him?" Melanie wiped away some tears from her eyes.

"We'll see. We need some more time apart. Maybe some months down the road we will all be able to put this behind us and be friends like we once were."

"Those were the days," Melanie replied.

"Listen, Melanie," Jack said. "I love you, and maybe we can work through anything together. Just promise me that you will be honest with me from this point on."

"I promise," Melanie said and Jack gave her a hug and a kiss. "Still, you never told me that you talk to Mr. Sanderson. How did you end up talking to him?"

"We've been meeting from time to time for many years. We always enjoyed each other's company when I was young. Then I ran into him several years back and we have developed quite a relationship. I love that man, but tonight he scared me. He was talking about you and Craig's affair with such fire and hatred. His hands were shaking and his forehead sweating the whole time. It was almost as though it was once again him who had been cheated."

The officer turned the page.

Chapter 26

Verdict!

Joseph West sat alone in his small home, helplessly thinking about what was going on just miles from his house. He had been informed that the jury had reached a decision. A bailiff he had been friendly with had kept him informed of big events in the trial. Today was the day, the awful day where a man would likely be convicted and sentenced to death, possibly for something he didn't do. Oh, sure, the formal sentencing by the judge could be weeks from now, but once the jury delivered its conviction, death was almost a sure thing.

The fact that West could do nothing to stop it sickened him in a way that he had never felt before. Denton had not come through yet with the phone records. It turned out he didn't have as good of connections as West hoped for, and it would take more time before Denton would be able to access the records. But, what if Denton couldn't come through in time? Would the answer to the case remain a mystery? Would everyone just accept that Craig was a murderer and deserved the punishment he received?

* * * * * * * * * *

In the courtroom, everyone was filled with anticipation. It seemed that everyone was on edge. No one spoke, but the silence made everything seem even more dramatic and eerie. After all, in a matter of moments a man's life would be decided by twelve other people just like himself. Everyone in the court looked around at one another, wondering when the judge would come in and the process would begin.

The defendant sat at the defense bench with intense anticipation. He looked like he hadn't gotten a wink of sleep, and who could blame him? Late yesterday, Earl Pitzer had told him that the jury would announce its decision in the morning.

Jack was more nervous than anyone. It had taken months and months for this day to come. Now that it was here, all Jack wanted was for it to be over. He didn't possess the same kind of strong resentment that he held for Craig as he did when the trial began, although he would never fully forgive him. Brianne had helped greatly with this. At times, she almost made Jack forget about Melanie completely, although Jack hated to admit it. Now, once Craig was convicted and if he was sentenced to death, Jack would be able to leave that part of his life completely behind. He could move forward to a new life, perhaps settle down, get married, and have kids. Who knew?

Judge Black walked in, and the room got even more deathly silent. The sounds of people squirming around in their seats could be heard. He took a seat, and soon after the jurors walked in and took their positions. "Has the jury reached a verdict?"

A man who appeared to be the oldest of the jurors stood up. He wore thick glasses and had no visible hair whatsoever. "We have, your honor."

Judge Black had the bailiff collect the slip of paper from the jury foreman with the decision written on it. The judge began to silently read. He returned the slip of paper to the jury foreman. "Would you please read the verdict?" Judge Black ordered.

"We, the jury, find the defendant, Craig Sanderson, guilty of the charge of first-degree murder."

Craig dropped his head and covered his eyes so that no one would see them tearing up. It was all over for him now.

"What does the jury recommend as its sentence?" Judge Black asked.
"Death!"

Everyone in the crowd murmured among themselves as if they were surprised, although Jack doubted if anyone didn't know it was coming. Jack leaned back and relaxed in his chair. It was all over now. No more death. No more betrayal; hopefully, he would find happiness instead.

Craig was escorted out of the courtroom by the bailiff. He looked at his feet while he walked, careful not to make any eye contact with anyone until he reached the exit. However, suddenly he turned around and looked directly into Jack's eyes.

Jack felt time stop during this moment. All of the time they had spent together flashed in his mind and left just as quickly, for it was gone now. They would not share those moments ever again, and it was all because of selfishness. Craig wanted something he couldn't have and couldn't leave Melanie and Jack alone, despite Jack's feelings. Jack knew he would never see Craig again, and if he had another chance to speak to him, he would tell Craig that he hoped she was worth all of this.

Craig turned around and walked out of the courtroom. If he could have answered Jack, he would have said that he made a mistake and that nothing, especially a girl, could possibly be worth this.

Chapter 27

You're Coming Home with Me

Six months had passed since Jack had found out about the secret relations of his fiancée, Melanie Stole, and his old best friend, Craig Sanderson. Jack had recently bought a new house. It was extremely large compared to his old house. The two-story house stood atop a hill overlooking the Atlantic Ocean and the powdery sand of Dillon's Beach that led up to it. It was a house that as a law student Jack could not afford. However, Jack was one who believed in being highly leveraged and investing in real estate for future income growth. Even so, Jack could never have bought this house if Mr. Gardner had not guaranteed the loan.

Although Melanie often stayed at the new house with Jack, she still had her house. The new house wasn't finished yet. With little furniture yet, it was hard to stay there at all times. Also, Melanie was planning on repainting her old house so that she could hopefully make some money on it—a project which Jack and Melanie had planned to do since becoming engaged but had failed to get around to it.

Jack wasn't happy yet, however. Since the discovery of Melanie and Craig's affair, Jack and Melanie had agreed on a long engagement and had not set a definite wedding date. It was taking some time for memories of this betrayal to fade in Jack's head and heart. He wanted things to go back to the way they once were—when he, Craig, and Melanie were friends and things weren't complicated. Fortunately enough, best friends were given a chance to reunite.

One day as Jack was walking down the street toward where he had parked his car, ready to go back home from a routine trip to the grocery store, something caught his eye in the alley to his left. A man, a desperate man, clearly clean out of luck, sat with his back to a dumpster. The man had a scruffy beard, with shaggy hair and old raggedy clothes. Jack didn't like to be judgmental, but the man clearly fit the standard homeless profile.

Jack continued to stand in the middle of the sidewalk, looking down the alleyway, until the man tilted his head up and stared back at him. Jack was stunned for several moments, but the other man was too tired and hungry to show any shock or surprise.

"Craig? What the hell are you doing?" Jack rushed over to him. "Get up, Craig. This is pathetic." Craig stumbled up to his feet, using the dumpster for support. "What the hell happened to you? Come home with me."

Jack grabbed Craig by the arm, but Craig resisted and shrugged Jack's hands off.

"You want to help me? Buy some weed from me, then." Craig reached into his coat pocket and pulled out an empty zip-locked plastic bag. "Oh, I guess I finished it all myself."

"Let's go," Jack commanded. He grabbed Craig by the arm, this time more firmly, and Craig surrendered. Jack threw him in the car and drove back to his house on the hill.

"Wow, someone's moved up a little bit in the world," Craig said. "Guess law school is paying off. Maybe I should have stayed in school after all, huh, Jack?"

Jack didn't respond to this. "Come on, Craig." Jack helped Craig out of the car, up the path to the front door, and into the large home. Jack gave Craig a seat on the living room sofa and walked out of the kitchen. Within moments he came out with a glass of water and a peanut butter and jelly sandwich. "You know I was never much of a cook, but this will have to do."

"Why are you doing this for me?" Craig asked.

"What do you mean? You're my best friend. It doesn't matter what happened in the past. Now, eat up." Craig consumed the food and water as quickly as possible, making sure to finish every crumb and every last drop of water. "Now I want you to take a shower," said Jack. "No, offense, but you smell worse than that dumpster you were sitting against."

Jack showed him where the shower was and turned on the water for him. "I'll be right back." Jack came back moments later with an armful of clothes. "Here, these old sweat clothes are a little big for me; they may be small for you, but they'll do. Put these on once you get out of the shower. And please, throw those clothes you have on straight into the trash where they belong."

Jack walked out of the room as Craig enjoyed the most refreshing shower of his life.

When Craig walked back down the stairs from his shower and entered the living room where Jack was sitting on the couch watching television, he seemed to be in a different state of mind and body. He looked much cleaner and more refreshed and his good looks were once again visible.

"Come sit down," Jack said to him. "I'm sure we have a lot to talk about."

"We don't need to talk about anything. Just give me a couple minutes and I'll be out of your way."

"Where are you going to go? Back to your dumpster?" Craig didn't reply. "What happened to your apartment?"

"Which one? Been kicked out of a couple now. Don't exactly have one at the moment, but so what? I'll be fine."

"You have no place to live? Well, now you do. You're staying here whether you like it or not."

"No!"

"Enough! This is getting ridiculous. I mean, I'll bet you weren't even planning on coming to my damn wedding were you?" Craig hung down his head and didn't speak. No one spoke for several moments. "Why wouldn't you come, Craig?" Jack asked. "I really thought you would want to see me on such a big day in my life. Well, don't worry about it right now. The wedding has been delayed for a while now."

"I'm sorry. I've been living out of a dumpster though. Please forgive me if I didn't think I would fit in at a wedding. I didn't even have enough money for a suit or a tie … or even shoes for that matter."

"You do now," Jack said. "You're going to stay here. Things are going to go back to the way they used to be."

For the next couple of hours, Jack and Craig talked about anything they could think of, which was a lot since they had so much to catch up on. Not a single word was ever mentioned of Melanie as they chatted. At least not until the knob on the front door turned and Melanie walked through the front door. She walked into the living room and stopped dead in her tracks once she saw who Jack was talking with.

"Melanie, look who's here," Jack said.

"Yes, I noticed," Melanie said in a not-so-friendly tone. "I'm going to go upstairs to change. Nice to see you, Craig."

"Listen, Jack, do you think you could drive me back into town?"

"You promised that you would live here at least until you got back onto your feet," Jack pleaded.

"I know, I know. I just need to go visit a friend. I want to tell him where I'll be in case he needs me."

Jack was hesitant but eventually agreed. "All right. How long will you need to be there?"

"Just give me an hour or two," Craig said. "Don't worry about me. I'll find my own ride back."

Jack and Craig got into the car and drove back to Manhattan where Jack dropped him off.

"Remember, you're staying the night at my place tonight," Jack reminded him.

Craig laughed. "I know, Jack. I'll be there."

Jack sped off back to his house where he knew Melanie would be waiting for him. When he opened the door and walked into the living room, Melanie was sitting on the living room couch with one leg crossed over the other to match her crossed arms.

"Hey, Mel," Jack said.

"I don't want him staying here," Melanie said. "It's too awkward for me to handle after everything that's happened."

"You don't think it's awkward for me?" Jack said. "Of course it is. But he's my best friend and he needs our help. I'm not going to abandon him no matter what."

"What if he's still in love with me? What if he tries to make a move on me or something? I don't want anything to do with him!"

"Will you please relax?" Jack pleaded.

"I just don't think it's a good idea. Nothing good can come from it."

"Hey, if he does anything … you tell me. You're going to be my wife. If he harms you in any way, you tell me and he will be out."

"All right, if that's the way you want it. He can live here, but I can't guarantee that I'll be staying over here much while he does. And, well, I guess we'll just see what happens."

"That's fine. You can stay at your house if that makes you feel more comfortable. Just please, give Craig a chance. I know you wouldn't deceive me again and I don't think he would after I've taken him in off the streets. Everything will be fine, Melanie, I promise you."

"All right. I hope you're right," she repeated as she got up from the couch and walked out the room.

The officer turned the page.

Chapter 28

Will You?

Travis Denton parked his police car outside the Market Street Café and walked into the restaurant, looking around from table to table. "Ah, there you are," he said. "Hello, West. How did it go?" Denton asked.

"How did it go? Well, it went all right. Right out of the courtroom."

Denton sat down at the table in which West had been waiting for him. "What do you mean? I got you the records. What could have gone wrong?"

"You know, I didn't think anything could have gone wrong either. Just as I suspected, Jack Gardner had called the Cooper house many times before she was killed. Maybe Jack Gardner killed her."

"But why?" Denton said.

"Well I don't know if you know this or not, but the former Mrs. Sanderson had an affair about sixteen years ago. Mr. Sanderson ended up coming home and catching them in bed together, almost killed them both. The police were called and a report was filed. Do you happen to know who called the police?"

"No idea," Denton replied.

"A little boy, a little boy just ten years old, with a thick scar under his left eye. The little boy saw the whole thing. He actually prevented Mr. Sanderson from committing any murders that day. He hid some knives that were in the Sanderson's kitchen. Do you happen to have any idea who that little boy was?"

"Jack Gardner?" Denton said surely.

"That's correct. You know what else the phone records showed that we didn't know? Jack Gardner was making frequent calls to Mr. Sanderson. I mean, the calls were daily, like clockwork. Turns out they were much better friends than anyone knew. I don't think Craig even had any idea."

"So you think that's enough to show Jack killed them both?" asked Denton

"Well, I'm sure Jack hated Craig's mom for everything she did to his friend, Mr. Sanderson. Maybe Jack killed her as a favor to Mr. Sanderson; either that, or just plain disgust as to how terrible of a person she was. It would make perfect sense as to why Daniel Cooper would want revenge and tried to kill Jack in return."

"Yeah, I guess when you look at it like that it makes some sense," Denton admitted. "Anyway, you still haven't told me. What happened when you brought the evidence to Judge Black?"

"Ah, Judge Black." West laughed. "The most under-qualified judge in the world. The son of a bitch threw out the evidence. He said we couldn't use it. Said that it was obtained unlawfully and couldn't be used in the court of law."

"You have to be kidding," Denton said. "Sounds like my lieutenant. No one seems to give a damn about the truth, just as long as they get some type of answer."

"Yes, well, apparently our justice system would rather follow technical procedures than save an innocent man's life. Obviously preserving our citizens' rights to privacy is more important than executing a man with a lethal shot. Unbelievable."

"So there's nothing we can do? Just sit back and let Craig be executed?" Denton said.

"It's back to the drawing board," West said. "At least there will be an appeal of the verdict. That will give us some time. However, Craig doesn't seem that interested in assisting in his defense."

"Why?"

"Maybe he's just tired of it all," West said. "Months of being accused of murder by his best friend is enough to make a man go crazy. Besides he doesn't have much to live for in this world anymore. I guess he's just giving up," West repeated. "He could be dead in a few years if he didn't have appeals. Well, anyway, I've got to be going. I think I'll go see if I can track down Jack Gardner and question him. Maybe I'll be able to get something out of him. Call me if you think of anything, all right Denton?"

"Got it," Denton replied.

West gave him a nod and left a few dollars on the table to pay for the coffee he had bought, and then he got up from his seat and went off to search for Jack Gardner.

* * * * * * * * * *

Just miles away, Jack Gardner left the courthouse in New York City and got back into his car, which was parked on the street where Brianne was waiting for him. "What were you doing in there?" Brianne asked.

"I told you, Judge Black needed the witnesses to come in and sign some papers and stuff. Just to close out the case. But now that it's over, no more talking about it."

"You must be excited, to start work again and all. I can't believe you were off for that long. We have to start paying the bills you know!" Brianne laughed.

"Yeah, well, I'm more excited about my life out of work. Now with the case over I can put all my thoughts on you." Jack leaned over and gave her a kiss. "And now with that said, let's go home. We need to get ready for our date tonight."

"You still haven't told me what we're doing," Brianne said, sounding extremely excited. She loved surprises and lately Jack found himself enjoying the thought of supplying her with those treats. "Come on, Jack. You have to at least give me a clue."

"No. You're just going to have to wait." Jack smiled at her and continued on home.

By the time the darkness of night had come, the two of them were nearly ready to leave.

"Do I need to dress up?" Brianne asked.

"No, just wear something casual. Jeans and a sweatshirt will do," Jack replied.

By the time the two of them were completely ready and in the car, it was nearly nine o'clock.

"Can you tell me where we're going now?" Brianne begged.

"You'll see soon enough."

Jack drove down the hill on his way down to the beach. When they got there, Brianne was elated. "Dillon's Beach!" she said. The beach was always Brianne's favorite place.

"Come on, let's go." Jack parked the car and the two of them walked out onto the powdery sand. The night was nearly perfect. The stars were shining bright, and the moon was nearly full. The sky was clear of all clouds and the air was crisp and cool. The breeze was just a little too strong, blowing Brianne's hair back and forth wildly. The surface of the water shined in the moonlight's reflection. It was nearly perfect.

"Follow me, Brianne," Jack said. He led her down the beach until they reached the rocks at which they had once shared a day together. They climbed up the rocks and rested for a moment when they had reached the top of them. A sand hill behind them led even higher. Once they had caught their breath, Jack led Brianne up the hill farther. The hill flattened out at this point and several feet of sand surrounded them on all sides. It was a deserted area, not generally meant for anyone to enter. There Jack laid a blanket down on the sand so that the two of them could look out onto the ocean from above.

"Jack!" Brianne gasped. "It's so beautiful."

Jack smiled back at her and put his arm around her shoulder once they had sat down. He looked at her, and for the first time he felt as though he truly loved Brianne. *I suppose love comes and goes,* Jack thought. He had always thought that he had loved Melanie. But now, that didn't matter anymore. He knew he loved Brianne, and that was all that mattered at this point.

Jack picked up a picnic basket that he had brought along and placed it on his lap. He opened it up and pulled out two glasses that he filled with champagne.

"A drink, my lady?" Jack said politely.

"Please," Brianne said sweetly.

"A toast," Jack said lifting his glass of wine into the air.

"To us," Brianne said, lifting her glass up to Jack's so that they touched. The couple held each other for a long time, both very content with the life they were sharing together. "Do you think we'll be together forever?" Brianne asked all of a sudden.

Jack chuckled. "What? Do you mean like marriage?"

Brianne nodded but did not laugh back. She was dead serious. "I know you've been married once before and that it didn't work out, but not everyone is the same, Jack."

"Would you ever cheat on me?" Jack asked.

"Cheat on you? Jack, I would never. Do you know how crazy I am about you? I've been yours since the moment we met."

"Good answer," Jack said with a smile. After that, neither of them knew quite what to say. While Jack continued to stare at his girlfriend, Brianne continued to stare out into the serene waters.

No one spoke for at least thirty minutes, but when someone did it was Brianne. "This really is beautiful Jack. Thank you so much for bringing me here."

Jack didn't respond, but continued to stare at her. She truly looked beautiful with her long brown hair flying wildly in the wind so that it exposed her gorgeous face in its entirety: her big gorgeous eyes, her sensual lips, and her perfect smile. At that moment, something came over Jack. He was overwhelmed by a feeling he rarely had experienced. "Brianne," Jack took her hand. "I have something I want to ask you."

"Ask me? What is it?"

"Well, it's kind of hard to say really. There's something I want you to do for me."

"I would do anything for you, Jack. You know that."

"Anything? Are you sure about that?"

"Yes, Jack, I'm sure. So what do you want?"

"I want you to spend the rest of your life with me. Brianne," he knelt on one knee. "Will you marry me?"

Brianne covered her mouth with her hand to hide her gasp. "You want to marry me?" she cried out with joy.

"Yes. I love you more than anything."

"Oh, I love you too! Of course I'll marry you." Brianne jumped on Jack and kissed him sweetly.

"I don't want to wait though. Let's do it this week," Jack said.

"This week? Why so soon?"

"What is the point in waiting? I want to start my new life with you as soon as possible."

"All right," Brianne agreed with a big smile. "This week it is. Are you sure you can make it happen?"

"I would do anything for you too, Brianne. I'll make it happen."

Chapter 29

Justice Is Served

"I guess we just have to accept it," Denton said while they were sitting at their usual table. "Just sit back, have a drink, and realize that there is nothing we can do about it."

Just accept it? West thought. How could he just accept it? A man's life was at stake. He didn't think he could do it. "Can't do that, Denton," West finally said. "Even if he's put to death, I'm not going to stop my investigation. I don't care if I'm looking through these files and records for the rest of my life, you got that?"

"I'm here with you all the way," Denton said. "You got me chasing your wild theories and I guess now I'm hooked. I just want to know the truth. However, right now I gotta go to that wedding I was telling you about."

"Maybe you can ask him some questions while you're there. Maybe you'll get something out of him," West mused.

Denton laughed. "Come on now, I can't ruin the man's wedding day. And I for sure can't ruin hers."

"Yeah, well, it doesn't matter. Our time has run out. Craig has already been sentenced, so what's the hurry? Guess we have the rest of our lives to find the answers to these riddles," West said.

"Yeah, all right, well I'm off. Give me a call tomorrow and we'll get back on it." Denton got up from his chair and got back into his car on the way to the wedding. He thought about Craig being sentenced to death. Here he was on his way to a wedding, a day that symbolized new beginnings and life, and yet somewhere else Craig was awaiting his inevitable ending.

* * * * * * * * * *

Down the road several miles, on Dillon's Beach, three rows of white chairs filled with family and friends sat on both sides of a sandy aisle way that led the groom and bride to the altar. Red roses and daisies were sprinkled about the path. At the end, where the altar in a church would be, a white wooden arch covered in magnificent bright flowers of yellows, reds, and oranges stood with the priest under it. Three groomsmen stood on one side with black tuxedos and three bridesmaids stood on the other side adjourned in white dresses. Scattered lights illuminated the aisle as well as the entire area.

The weather was perfect with a light, cool, and refreshing breeze from the beautiful blue ocean. There were no clouds and darkness was softly starting to appear. The faintest trace of stars could be seen in the sky, as well as the circular shape of the perfectly full moon. The sand was perfectly white beneath everyone's feet, and the water seemed unusually crystal-clear for the Atlantic.

As soft music could faintly be heard in the background over the light crashing of the waves into rocks, Jack Gardner walked down the sandy aisle way with his mother on his arm, just as she always wished.

"Jack, are you sure about this? You have only been seeing Brianne a short time," Mrs. Gardner whispered to Jack.

"You just want me to always stay your little boy, don't you, Mom?" teased Jack.

"If I have to lose you to someone else, at least I have this special walk with you," said Mrs. Gardner as she squeezed Jack's arm tightly.

He looked at her and smiled when he saw a tear fall from her eyes.

Moments later his lovely bride Brianne walked down the same path, guided arm and arm by her father.

Over the next hour they exchanged their vows, put on rings, and promised to always be there for each other through it all. The most important of these to Jack was the rings; the small symbol of love that showed the rest of the world that the person who wore it was permanently joined to another for life. When Jack slipped it on her finger, he knew that things would be different this time around.

At the end of the service, Jack and Brianne walked around and visited with the guests that had come. "Hey, Grandma. Hey, Grandpa," Jack called out to his grandparents.

"Oh, Jack. We're so proud of you," Grandma Sechovec said with a smile. She gave him a big hug.

"Well, I'm glad you could be here," Jack said.

"You're going to be glad once you get the honeymoon started," Grandpa Sechovec joked.

Jack was extremely glad that his grandfather had been able to make the wedding. With his lung cancer, things weren't always as pleasant for him as possible. However, Grandpa was doing better than the doctors had expected and they thought he might even possibly recover.

Then Jack saw someone in the distance whom he recognized but had not expected to be there. He was wearing his police uniform still, but stood in the back, not talking to anyone. *Denton,* Jack thought. *That son of a bitch. What the hell is he doing at my wedding?* Jack couldn't believe the nerve of him. If he wanted to question Jack some more, did he really have to do it on the most important day in Jack's life? *I wonder where his buddy West is,* Jack thought. They were hardly seen without each other lately. *When are they going to let it go?*

"Grandma, Grandpa," Jack said. "I'll be right back, all right?" Jack walked away from them and went toward the direction where Denton was standing. However, he was nowhere to be seen now. *Where did that bastard go?* Jack thought. *Oh, well.* He went back over to where his grandparents were but they now were gone too.

"Hey, son," someone came up from behind Jack and placed hands on his shoulder. "How's the newlywed doing?"

"Good, Dad. How'd you like the service?"

"It was nice," Mr. Gardner said. "You set up quite a ceremony. Hope you have a good honeymoon too."

"Yeah, if I can afford it. This wedding almost wiped me clean," Jack said. "You think you could let me borrow twenty bucks for old time's sake?" he joked.

Mr. Gardner laughed. "I think once you get married the handouts have to stop, don't you?"

"Yeah, I guess so."

"Hello, husband." Brianne came from behind Jack and gave him a hug.

"Congratulations, Brianne," Mr. Gardner said and gave her a hug.

"Thank you so much," she replied. Jack was hoping that she hadn't seen Officer Denton. She would surely be suspicious as to why a police officer was still following him around. And he didn't want her to know what happened to his ex-wife, because that would be enough to scare any girl.

After they had thanked all the guests and visited for a while, Brianne and Jack went back home to their house. There they celebrated their wedding, watching the waves of the ocean, drinking champagne, and spending countless hours under the sheets of the large bed.

* * * * * * * * * *

Up the Hudson River from New York City, inside Sing Sing Correctional Facility, Craig Sanderson was led into a dark and eerie chamber that would be the stage for the last moments of his life. He walked down cement steps into the chamber with his arms and legs both chained together by shackles. The orange convict suit he wore did little to make the scene livelier and why should it? After all, the only thing to come out of this chamber was death itself.

Craig was strapped down on a cold gurney and could feel the lifelessness of all the souls who had died in that very place before him. He wondered how many of them were innocent just as he was. One of the attendants who escorted him to the room picked up a hypodermic needle from one of the drawers of a table, which was in the middle of the room. Four prison guards stood on all sides of the room. The escort, or executioner as he was to Craig, filled the needle with the fluid that would soon cause Craig's heart to slow down until it was finally stunned and stopped all together.

Craig realized he had little time left to live. At this point, half of him wanted nothing more than to stay alive, to see his friends again, and perhaps to see his father. He wanted another chance to live more productively, more fulfilling. He had gotten that opportunity before. Jack Gardner had given it to him, but it was taken away. However, the other half of him wanted this life of his to be over. The sooner this injection was in him the sooner he would be able to forget all of these problems. Perhaps, he would even have a chance to see his mother. Maybe she wouldn't be drugged up this time around. Maybe in heaven she wouldn't know who David Cooper was and maybe she would be beautiful just as she once was.

As he thought, he closed his eyes to picture his mother one last time in case there was no afterlife. (This might have been what scared him the most). As he thought, the executioner raised his arm in the air with his hand holding the injection. He placed it to Craig's arm, and Craig swallowed for the last time and clenched his whole body. The executioner pushed the shot into Craig's arm and his body shook a little. Nothing happened at first, but within moments he found it hard to breathe. Perhaps it was the shot, or perhaps it was just his imagination, but his heart stopped and his hands unclenched as he sat there lifeless with his eyes wide open.

At that moment, Craig awoke in a cold sweat and began to cry.

Chapter 30

180 Degrees for Craig

Craig lived at Jack's house for nearly eighteen months. Jack and Melanie had just got married and Craig was the best man just as Jack had always thought he would be. About a year and a half was all it took for Craig to change his life around.

"I'm in!" Craig came rushing through the door to meet Melanie and Jack in the living room. "I got the job."

"You're kidding," Jack said.

"Nope," Craig said with a smile before showing them the paperwork.

"Well, how do you like that? Craig, a police officer, working for the law. It almost seems like an oxymoron," Jack replied.

"Well, I would have never gotten it if it weren't for you. Once you gave me that crazy idea a year ago to put my aggressions into a job where I could help people. Never thought I would be working on the right side of the law though." Craig smiled.

"Yeah, well I didn't get you through the police academy. You did all that work on your own. You really should be proud of yourself. I can't tell you how proud I am. Melanie too, right Mel?"

"Yes, very proud," Melanie answered.

"Yeah, well she's your wife. She has to agree with you," Craig said. Craig and Melanie had become much more comfortable with each other. They still didn't talk all that frequently, but at least no uncomfortable feelings came between the two anymore—at least none that Jack could see anyway.

"Yeah, well, listen," Melanie said while standing up from the living room couch before grabbing her purse and keys off the glass table in front of them. "I have to get back to my house. Still trying to repaint it, you know?"

"What was wrong with the first coat?" Craig asked.

"Didn't look good," Melanie said. "I *am* trying to make some money when it sells." She walked out of the room and out the door without another word.

"Want a drink, Craig?" Jack asked walking into the kitchen.

"Just water would be good. I'm law enforcement now. Have to set a good example for you citizens," Craig joked, although he talked about his new job with a certain amount of pride. Jack came back into the living room, sat down on the sofa, and turned on the television. Craig took the love seat and began sipping at his water while Jack drank his beer.

"So tell me more about this job, Craig. How did you get it? When do you start?"

"Don't ask me how I got it 'cus I have no idea. My boss, Frank Peterson, said he saw something in me or something like that. I don't really remember."

"Yeah, well, I guess it doesn't matter," Jack said. "I always knew you were going to do something with that life of yours. I'm proud of you," Jack said once more.

"I know you are. Anyway, I start next week." Craig wasn't much for all that sentimental crap.

"A week, huh?"

"That's right … Jack … that's kind of what I wanted to talk to you about. I think it's about time I move out on my own. I appreciate everything you've done for me, but this just seems right. I'm a grown man."

"I couldn't agree more. I think that's a good idea. So what's the problem?"

"Well, I don't exactly have enough."

Jack interrupted Craig. "Say no more my friend. I'll give you whatever you need."

"All I need is the money for the deposit," Craig promised.

"Once I start getting my paycheck I'll be able to pay the monthly rent and pay you back. I promise."

"Don't worry about it. Consider the deposit a new house warming gift," Jack said. "Hell, we gotta drink to this." Jack went into the kitchen and came back with a beer for Craig.

"Yeah, what the hell," Craig said. "Bottoms up."

Craig and Jack celebrated together for most of the day.

"Tomorrow we're going apartment shopping. But until then, we party it up," Jack said bringing out more and more beers.

Later on in the night, Jack and Craig went down to one of the local bars, Eastside Bar. "You sure Melanie's all right with you coming to the bars?" Craig asked. "After all, she's got you on a leash."

"Lord knows that's a lie," Jack said. "I think it'll be fine." The two of them both had much more alcohol than they should have. By the time it got to midnight, Jack recognized what appeared to be a familiar face. He wanted to ask Craig if he was seeing things, but didn't want Craig to see the face if indeed his eyes weren't failing him. "Craig, I'll be right back. I need to go to the bathroom."

"Sure Jack, whatever you say!" Craig hollered. Jack walked to the back of the bar. The closer he came to the man, the easier it was to recognize him. The man also seemed to have been drinking more than he should have. He was leaned over the table at which he was sitting with a couple empty glasses of beer.

"Well, well, well, Mr. Sanderson," Jack said. "What are you doing here?"

"Well, actually I was hoping to see you, my son." Mr. Sanderson didn't seem too drunk, but Jack could definitely smell the alcohol on his breath. "Didn't know you would be with Craig though. Quick, come outside with me behind the building. I don't want Craig to see us."

The officer turned the page.

Chapter 31

Came in a Dream

With one year passing, a lot can happen. Jack and Brianne Gardner experienced their greatest joy with the birth of their first child, Michael. Jack had gone back to work and was experiencing more success with every case he took. Brianne had begun to study nursing, something she had always wanted to do. The Gardner family was doing just fine. Mr. and Mrs. Gardner spent a lot of time at the Sechovec house. In fact, Mrs. Gardner would hardly let Grandpa Sechovec out of her sight. The thought of losing her father was too much for her to take. Meanwhile, not much had happened in Joseph West's or Travis Denton's lives. Hope that the case was going to be solved had been growing even slimmer.

However, around this time, while Travis Denton was peacefully sleeping in his apartment, he was suddenly awakened by an awful thought. He sat up in his bed and pulled the sheets off him. He wiped his brow as he noticed he had been sweating a bit. It was a hot night and he rarely used the air conditioning, but he didn't think that was what the sweat was about. He quickly put on a white shirt and gym shorts and made a call to Joseph West.

Ring … Ring … Ring …

No one answered. *Where the hell could he be?* Denton thought. He didn't know, however, this couldn't wait.

He jumped inside his car and made the fifteen-minute drive over to where West lived. He walked up the path that led through the grass to the front door. Denton noticed that the grass, if he could even call it that, was almost completely dead on both sides. A once green lawn had been turned to an ugly brown. *Guess he doesn't care much for lawn work,* Denton thought.

He knocked on the door and wasn't surprised when there was no answer. "Well, it was worth a shot." He turned the knob of the door just in case, and to his surprise, the door opened. Denton could see lights on in the back rooms as he entered the home and walked through the living room and kitchen. Trash covered the entire floor, dirty dishes covered the counters and filled the sink, and bags of trash seemed to have been there for weeks. The place smelled of rotten food and garbage. Denton was appalled as he tiptoed past the rooms. As he walked closer to the lighted rooms, he could hear that a television set was on, but still he didn't see anyone. "West," he called out. "Are you in here?" Still no answer.

He walked down a small hallway, toward the lights, which was just as dirty as the living room and kitchen had been. He could see that a door was open at the end of the hallway, the room in which the light was on and the television sounds were coming from. Papers seemed to be spilling out of this room to the hallways. No pictures of West or anyone else were hanging on the wall, and Denton had to think for a minute to make sure he was in the right house. As he got yet even closer to the room, he could finally hear someone laugh. Denton stood upright and relaxed a little at the sound of it. He didn't realize that he was tiptoeing through the house, hunched over in suspicion. "West? Is that you? Say something." He heard someone laugh again, but no one answered his call.

Finally, Denton arrived at and decided to enter the room. What he saw was Joseph West sitting on the floor, leaning back in an awkward position against the bed. There were papers spread all about the room. Denton was now standing inside the room, but West didn't notice him. He continued to watch some cartoon on television and laughed once in a while at some ridiculous scene.

"What the hell is wrong with you?" Denton finally said.

"Hey! Denton! When'd you get here?" West called out louder than necessary.

"Just walked in actually. Are you all right?"

"Oh, I'm just great, Denton. My client will soon be dead and guess what? I still can't find any leads after all this time! I did a great job didn't I?" he said.

"Are you drunk?"

"Well, I might have had a sip or two," West said. He pulled out a bottle of Jack Daniels that had been at West's side so that Denton had not been able to see it. He took another big swig of the whiskey and stumbled up to his feet. "Really, Denton. I'm fine."

"I think I might have something."

"Have something? What do you mean? Are you sick? I'm confused."

"Something regarding the case," Denton corrected him.

"Case? Case of what? You got more alcohol?" West looked like a puppy who had just been told he was going for a walk.

"Maybe we should talk about this in the morning," Denton said.

"No, no, no. I'm perfectly fine. Tell me what it is." West walked over and sat at the desk chair in the corner of his room. Denton walked over to him.

"All right, well I was thinking about it and ..." Denton paused as West's eyes rolled back into his head and he fell off his chair and into a slumber on the floor. "Guess it'll have to wait till tomorrow," Denton said. He picked West up off the floor which was not too difficult. Denton was quite muscular and West was fairly thin. He laid him on the bed, and took a seat on the chair that West had fallen from moments before.

Denton sat on that chair as he watched West sleep and hoped that in the morning he would be of a clearer mind.

Denton was only awake for about an hour, however, before he fell into sleep himself. When he awakened, West was still asleep. West had not switched positions the entire night it seemed. Denton wasn't sure exactly what time it was, but he could tell that it was past sunrise by the light gleaming through the window.

"Come on, West," Denton said. "Time to wake up." Denton nudged him a couple times and West rolled over onto his back before opening his eyes. "How you feeling there?"

West grunted. "Oh, yeah," he said. "I forgot you were here. Did I fall asleep on you last night?"

"Yeah, I guess you could say that. Some might say you more of passed out than fell asleep, but same difference."

"What are you doing over here anyway?"

"I wanted to talk to you about something. West, are you doing all right? Your place is a mess."

"I'm fine."

"I think this case is starting to drive you crazy."

"Starting? I've been crazy over it for well over a year. It's hopeless though. Craig will die."

"What happened to following this case until the day you die?" mused Denton.

"It's no use. We'll never find the true culprit." West spoke with a defeated attitude and Denton figured the alcohol was responsible. "You know how we thought it was Daniel Cooper? We couldn't have been more wrong. You know how we linked Jack Gardner to phone calls to Craig's mom. Well, guess what? Craig Sanderson was staying at Jack Gardner's house. All we found was Craig calling his mother to say hello." West shook his head. "How could we be so wrong? No, Denton, we'll never find the one responsible."

"Oh, we'll find him all right," Denton said. "We were just looking in the wrong direction."

"What do you mean?"

"I know this sounds strange, but what if Mr. Sanderson killed her?"

"Why the hell would Mr. Sanderson kill Melanie Gardner?" West asked. "That doesn't make any sense at all."

"Is there somewhere else we could talk about this? Maybe a table or something?" said Denton.

"Yeah, sure. Follow me," West said and walked out of the room, down the hallway, and into the kitchen. He pushed several papers and files that were on the table down onto the floor so that it became ever messier. "There we go," West said. "So why do you think Mr. Sanderson killed Melanie? What possible evidence could there be for that?"

"Let's think about it. You must at least acknowledge that he had the motive to kill both his ex-wife and David Cooper. They had an affair behind his back."

"Well, yeah, obviously he had a motive for that. But where's the connection with the Melanie girl?" West asked.

"Well, what do we know about Melanie? We know that she was a newlywed, right?"

"Yes. She had only been married a month."

"All right, well why would Mr. Sanderson kill his ex-wife fifteen years after the affair?" Denton asked.

"No idea. Maybe the jealousy finally got too much to take."

"No, no, no," Denton said. "What if after fifteen years of living together, Craig's mother and David Cooper had finally decided to tie the knot?"

"Who gets married after fifteen years? What's the point?"

"I don't know," Denton said. "But just suppose they did. Maybe Mr. Sanderson found out about it. Maybe there's something about marriage that pisses this guy off."

"I don't see what you're talking about."

"Well, just suppose the thought of Mr. Sanderson's ex-wife marrying another man made him so mad that he decided to kill them."

"Maybe you have something. Maybe that connects him to the couple, but what is the connection to Melanie Gardner?"

"I don't know," said Denton. "But I think something has to connect these two cases. The same people are involved to some degree in each."

"There's one thing I never told you," said West. "When I was still working for Craig, he told me something. Something that I thought wouldn't help his case at all. Actually, I knew it would be detrimental, which is why I told him to never tell anyone about it again."

"And what is that?" asked Denton.

"Craig and Melanie had a love affair. The two of them had gone behind Jack Gardner's back and had romance themselves. I figured this would make it look like Craig killed Melanie because he was so in love with her, so I made sure he stayed quiet about it. What if Mr. Sanderson killed Melanie as a favor for his son?"

"A favor to his son? They weren't even close. I remember that from questioning him in the Stole case. He said he hadn't seen his father in fifteen years," said Denton.

"Fifteen years? I like Craig a lot, but I'm not sure we can believe him on this one. I think they've been in more contact than we think."

"So what do you think we should do?"

"Well, maybe Craig and Mr. Sanderson were in on this together," said West. "Obviously two people were involved. One person could not have done this alone."

"How can we show that Mr. Sanderson and Craig did this together though?" Denton asked.

"They didn't do it together. Craig may have led them to Melanie's house, but he didn't know that his father would kill the couple. He didn't know what would happen. Maybe he wanted his dad to just scare them as some sort of revenge. Trust me; Craig couldn't have done this on purpose. The way he spoke to me about Melanie and Jack … there's no way he would have tried to kill them. Anyway, what we need to do is go to Craig's apartment. Dust the place for fingerprints, any sign that Mr. Sanderson might have been there. It could still be vacant. Accused murderer's former homes don't re-rent quickly."

"What about Melanie's house?" Denton asked. "Do you know if it's been vacant for the past year?"

"I'm not sure," West replied. "Sometimes they leave crime scenes open for a while. Check it out. If it's been vacant then we should dust down her place as well. Maybe the police missed it in their investigation."

"If Mr. Sanderson did kill Melanie Gardner then perhaps his fingerprints would be in her house also," Denton said.

"Exactly. You take care of the police work. I'm going to go through Craig's mother's files. See if there is anything that shows they were intending on getting married. Maybe the Denver Police overlooked something."

Chapter 32

A Flawless Murder

Three weeks on the force, just over three weeks was all it took before Craig was hit with something beyond his control. Craig, Jack, and Melanie were all sitting at the apartment Craig had recently moved into. They were sitting in the living room, peacefully talking about Craig's new job. The television was playing in the background, but none of them were paying much attention to it. They were all interested to hear how Craig's job was coming along. It was extremely unusual for them to see Craig with a police uniform hanging in his closet.

"So how are they treating you over there, anyway?" Jack asked.

"It's all right," Craig said. "They don't have me doing too much important work. Just been riding around with this partner they have me working with."

"Anything exciting happen?" Melanie asked.

"Oh, yeah. Exciting stuff happens all the time. Just the other day I got to watch my partner give someone a speeding ticket," Craig joked and the others laughed. "I doubt anything exciting will ever happen. Can't complain, though. It's a hell of a job."

Just as Craig stopped speaking he heard a knock at the door. Craig looked confused. "That's odd," Craig said. "I wonder who that could be." He got up from the couch and went to answer the door. When he did, he was surprised to see his boss, Frank Peterson, standing outside his door. He was accompanied by a younger officer who couldn't have been any older than Craig. "Am I in trouble, boss?" Craig said.

"No, I'm afraid not. Can I come in?"

"Um … sure, of course." Craig opened the door further and motioned Officer Peterson to come inside.

"Craig, this is another rookie on the force."

Craig gave him a nod. "So what do you need?" Craig asked as he led them into the living room.

"Maybe we better do this alone," Officer Peterson replied.

"No, no. It's fine. These people are like my family," Craig said. "Wait a minute … I'm not getting fired, am I? What did I do wrong? I told you I was sorry for dropping your coffee that day."

"It's nothing like that," Officer Peterson said. He scratched his fat neck, which was mostly hidden, and gathered up the courage for what he was about to tell Craig.

"Then what is it?" Craig asked anxiously.

"It's about your mother," Officer Peterson said.

"My mother?" Craig seemed shock. "Oh, no!" he gasped. "Did she overdose again? Did David do something to her? That son of a bitch!"

"Craig!" Officer Peterson yelled. "Calm down."

"Did David do something to her?"

"Well, yes, possibly. That seems to be how it started anyway."

"Started? What do you mean that's how it started. How did it end, then?" Craig demanded.

"Your mother is dead, Craig. So is Mr. Cooper. I'm so sorry." Officer Peterson said it in a soft but steady voice.

"She's what?" Craig gasped, although he only mouthed the words because his voice would not quite come out. His eyes welled up with water, and he didn't speak for several moments. Jack and Melanie exchanged glances but did not say anything. Jack didn't know what to say. He knew there was nothing he could say to comfort his friend. All he wanted to know was how. How did she die? He was waiting for Craig to ask the question, but it seemed to take an eternity.

"Just answer one question," Craig said. "Did *he* do it? Did David kill her?"

"We're not sure. He's dead too." This news was even more shocking than the news of his mother's death.

How the hell did David die? Jack thought.

"Can you please tell me something you *do* know?" Craig asked impatiently.

"All I know is what the Denver Police told me, but I'll be happy to tell you that," Officer Peterson said sympathetically, as though he knew what Craig must be going through. "Your mother was killed, Craig. We're not sure how. She was stabbed in the heart." Craig cringed at the thought of it. "She had fight marks on her. The Denver Police think that a fight broke out between the two of them, perhaps David was beating her. They don't really know. But, what they do know is that she died from a stab wound to the heart, and that David Cooper was found with a knife in his dead hand. However, it wasn't the knife that killed your mother. The knife didn't fit the stab wound on her. They're not sure what happened to the actual knife. Anyway, she was huddled up in a corner. Apparently, no one was around to save her."

"And what about David? What happened to that bastard?" Craig asked.

"Well, the way it looks is that your mother killed him. But again, the police aren't exactly sure."

"My mother would never," Craig protested. "Why would they think she did?"

"Well, they think it was self defense. They found your mom with one of David's guns in her hand. Sure enough David was killed by a bullet from the gun she was holding. They think she shot him after she was stabbed and they both died together. They were also both drunk. Listen, Craig, I know this is a lot to take. We don't have to talk about this now if you don't want to. I can come back another time."

"Come back? For what?" Craig asked.

"Just to ask some questions. You know, standard procedure."

"You think I did it?" Craig asked. "I've been here. How could I possibly?"

"No one is suspecting you," Officer Peterson assured him. "I told you, it's just standard procedure."

"Ask your questions now, then. I really don't want to discuss this again. Once is enough, don't you think?"

"Well, what I think is that if you didn't have anything to do with this, you would want to help your mom and be as cooperative as possible."

Craig grew silent. "Ask away," he said.

"Please don't get upset with me for saying this," Officer Peterson said, "but as you must expect, your father is our prime suspect at this point."

"My father? What possible reason would he have to kill them?"

"Well, the Denver police have learned that they had an affair when your dad was still married to your mom. Maybe it was revenge."

"That was fifteen years ago. Who goes for revenge fifteen years later?" Craig cried out.

"Yes, we are quite aware of this. That's why it doesn't make any sense, but you have to understand that there really isn't anyone else they suspect."

"Did you ever think that maybe it was someone from David's life? The guy is a piece of shit. I'm sure lots of people hated him."

"Craig, have you spoken with your father lately?"

"Not recently."

"Did he ever mention any malice toward your mother?"

"I talk to him once a year if I'm lucky," Craig said. "We didn't have much of a relationship. When we finally spoke it sure as hell wasn't about my mother. He never even mentioned her."

"All right, all right," the officer said.

"Listen, boss," Craig said. "I really don't know anything, and I don't think I will be any help. If you have any further questions, you can call me tomorrow."

"All right. Thanks for all your help, Craig. Once again, I'm terribly sorry for your loss."

Craig led his boss and the younger officer out of the front door, and Jack followed his friend. Craig was about to shut it when Officer Peterson turned around.

"Have you seen your father in the last fifteen years?" he asked.

"Nope, never," Craig replied. "He's lived in California the past fifteen years. Hardly ever even talk to him on the phone."

"I see," Officer Peterson responded. "Good evening." He turned around and walked back toward his car.

If only Craig knew that his father had another house besides the one in California ... A house just miles away, here in New York, Jack thought.

The officer turned the page.

Chapter 33

He Would Never!

Jack and Brianne Gardner were playing with their four-month-old son, Michael, when someone knocked on the door. They must have had a lucky honeymoon, because the child came nine months after the wedding. Although he was small, Jack could see so much of himself in the child. Each day Jack couldn't wait to wake up in the morning as the child began to look more and more like his father.

"Can you go answer that, Jack?"

"Yeah, no problem." Jack picked up little Michael and carried him over to the front door. He opened it and saw Officer Peterson and Officer Denton standing outside the front door. "Hello, officers," Jack said. "Is there something I can help you with?"

"We have some news for you," Officer Peterson said. "Could we come in, please?"

Jack seemed annoyed. "Is this about the Melanie case still? Listen gentlemen, I really don't want to think about the case anymore. It's been over a year, and I've put it behind me. Why can't you just let it go?"

"It's important, Jack. Trust me," Officer Peterson said.

"All right then. Come on in." Jack moved out of the way so that the officers could enter the house.

"Quite a house you got here," Officer Peterson said. "Business must be going well, huh?"

"I'm certain you're not here to talk about my job, officer," Jack said. "So how about we get to the point?" Jack led them into the living room where

Brianne was sitting on the couch. "Brianne, I need to talk to these officers for a moment. Could you take Michael upstairs and put him to sleep?"

"Yeah, sure," Brianne said. "It's time to feed him anyway. Good day, Officers." She gave Denton an unusually dirty glare before she left the room and walked up the long spiral staircase to the second floor of the house.

"So?" Jack said, growing impatient.

"This isn't easy for us to admit Jack … We may have made a mistake. A big one."

"What kind of mistake? What do you want from me?"

"Jack," Officer Peterson began. "Craig didn't kill Melanie." The officer shook his head and looked at the floor.

"Of course he did," Jack protested. "I was right there. I saw him do it. He tried to kill me too, remember?"

"No, Mr. Gardner," Denton chimed in. "You said you saw someone that looked like Craig. Someone that had a mask on. Maybe you thought it was Craig. You were in a frantic state. But, what if it wasn't him?"

"Jack, did you have a close relationship with Craig's father, Mr. Sanderson?" Officer Peterson asked.

"I used to see him when I was very young, just as I told the court," Jack said. "What does he have to do with this?"

"Have you ever seen him since that one day? The day he was cheated on by his wife?"

"How do you know I was there?" Jack asked.

"We're cops. It's kind of our job to research."

"No, I haven't," Jack said. "That was the last time I ever saw him. He lives in California, you know? Anyway, what does he have to do with my ex-wife?"

"Well, nothing," Officer Peterson said. "Except for the fact that he may have killed her."

Jack nearly spit out the water he was sipping on. "Mr. Sanderson? He would never do that!"

"Whoa there, Jack. Calm down," Officer Peterson said. "I thought you haven't seen him in seventeen years."

Jack hesitated. "Well," he paused again, "I haven't. But I used to know him. And he was always the nicest guy. Wouldn't even harm a fly if he could."

"You remember that from when you were ten?" Denton asked.

"Sure do."

"That was a long time ago," Officer Peterson said. "Things change, and whether you want to accept it or not, Mr. Sanderson killed your ex-wife."

"Do you have any evidence of this?"

"Sure do. There's no doubt about it this time."

"Tell me about this so-called evidence."

"You probably didn't know this, but Mr. Sanderson was actually living in a home here in New York. For whatever reason, Craig must not have wanted us to know," Officer Peterson began.

"And how do you know that?"

"We were able to find his fingerprints at Craig's apartment," the officer said. "Also found his prints at Melanie's home, where the murder took place. Now why else would his fingerprints be at the murder scene? What other possible reason could there be for Mr. Sanderson to be at Melanie's home? He didn't even know the poor girl."

Jack was silent for a few moments. "Why would he kill her if he didn't even know her? What sense does that make?"

"Well, we know it doesn't make much sense. But there's something you might not know Jack ... Melanie and Craig had once been romantic with each other."

"What?" Jack said. "But ... There's no way. I had no idea. How did you find that out?"

"You know Craig's old attorney, Joseph West? Well, Craig had told West all about their affair and then West mentioned it to Denton one night when he had had too much to drink. Anyway, West also brought to our attention that in the police report for Craig's mom's murder, the description of her included that she had a diamond ring on her finger. We had completely overlooked the fact. David Cooper and Craig's mom were engaged."

"But why would he kill Melanie?" asked Jack.

"Maybe he has something against marriage now because of what happened to him all those years ago. We're not really sure. Maybe Craig couldn't stand seeing you and Melanie together so he had his father kill her. The motive doesn't really matter at this point," Officer Peterson said.

"That's all the evidence you have? You're condemning a man based off that?"

"I'm afraid there's more. After we found some of these clues, we found out where Mr. Sanderson was staying in New York. We busted into his place and guess what we found?"

"How about you just tell me?" Jack said, growing impatient.

"The knife that was used to kill the former Mrs. Sanderson," Officer Peterson revealed. "He hadn't even cleaned it off. Her blood was still on it. It was hanging up on his wall like it was some type of goddamn trophy. Made me sick. Guessing it's the same knife he used to kill Melanie. Funny thing is, her blood was nowhere on the knife. We think maybe he used a different but similar one to kill Melanie. Don't know where it is, though. Still, it's a relief to know that we caught that bastard and most questions are now answered."

"Wow!" Jack said.

"What is it?" Officer Peterson said.

"Nothing. I just can't believe we got the wrong man. I thought it was Craig for sure. What will happen now?"

"We will have to go to the district attorney and try to get the case reopened," said Officer Peterson. "It will take time, though."

"Anyway," Officer Peterson continued, "we just wanted to stop by and tell you the news. Sorry for any inconvenience we caused you."

"No problem," Jack said. He stood up and led the officers out of the living room and to the front door. "If you find out anything else, be sure to call me."

"Will do," Officer Peterson said. "Good day."

Jack turned around and walked back to the living room. Brianne came down shortly, no longer carrying little Michael.

"What was that all about?" she asked.

"Turns out the wrong man got convicted," Jack replied.

"Really? Someone else robbed the store?"

"Huh?" Jack said. "Oh, yeah … um … someone else robbed the store. Damn jury can never get it right. Is Michael sleeping?"

"Yes, finally. Took me that whole time you were talking to the officers before he even blinked."

"I'm going to go upstairs and watch him sleep."

"Is everything okay? Do you want some company?" Brianne sounded overly concerned, as she always did.

"I'm fine, thank you. But right now I would rather just be alone."

"All right," Brianne replied.

Jack walked up the spiral staircase and down the hall into the master bedroom where Michael's crib was. He walked into the room and pulled up a chair so that he could sit next to the crib. He looked into the crib where he saw his little boy sleeping. He got up for a minute to lock the door, ensuring that he would not be interrupted. He then watched his son sleep for hours. As he watched, a tear fell from his eye as he thought about how happy he was. He never knew that he could be this happy after everything that happened with his former wife. He thought about how lucky he was to have so many special people in his life, and at that moment he promised his little boy that he would never leave him.

Chapter 34

A Tear from Mrs. Gardner

Only a month from the time Jack learned of the police's decision to arrest Mr. Sanderson, he was awakened by a phone call in the middle of the night. He didn't know what time it was, and frankly, he was too tired to care.

"What do you want?" he answered. He could unmistakably hear his mother's voice on the other line but couldn't understand quite what she was saying. "Mom, is that you? Mom, I can't understand you. What's wrong?" Jack could hear that she was sobbing uncontrollably. However, he was sure he heard the words, "Grandpa," "hospital," "go," and "now."

"I'll meet you there, Mom."

Jack hung up the phone.

"Is everything okay?" Brianne asked from the other side of the bed.

"I'm not sure," Jack said. "Sometimes my mom freaks out about nothing, but I need to go to the hospital to be sure. Can you stay up and watch Michael until I get home?"

"He'll be fine, Jack."

"I know, but I would just feel a lot more comfortable if you were watching him while I am gone."

"All right. Whatever makes you happy." Jack gave her a kiss on the lips and quickly got dressed. He raced out of the room, but not before he looked into his son's crib to make sure that he was still there and sleeping soundly.

"I'll be right back," Jack whispered to his boy.

He raced over to the hospital, and when he got there he found his mom and dad and his brother, Mark, in the waiting room. Mrs. Gardner was sitting by herself, however. She didn't seem to want to talk to anyone else as she sat there biting her fingernails. Before approaching her, he decided to see what the problem was.

"Hi, Dad," he said, going up to his father, who was talking to Mark. "What's going on?"

"Grandpa called. He was having some trouble breathing."

"Is everything going to be all right?" Jack asked. "Mom doesn't look so good."

"You know your mother. She's scared to death right now. Then again, she would be scared to death if Grandpa called in the middle of the night just to say hello. I think everything will be fine."

"Has anyone spoken with a doctor yet?"

"No, we're still waiting for one to come out and tell us what's going on. I'm not sure what's taking so long."

"Where's Grandma?" Jack asked, looking around the waiting room lobby. "Why isn't she here?"

"Oh, she's just in the bathroom. She'll be right out."

Just then Grandma Sechovec emerged from the bathroom. She had taken off her glasses and was wiping her eyes with a paper towel. Jack couldn't tell whether she was crying or if she was just cleaning off her glasses. Either way, she walked over to Jack and gave him a hug.

"I'm happy you came, Jack," she said. "Your grandpa isn't doing too well."

"I'm sure he'll be all right, Grandma. Grandpa is a fighter."

"You don't need to comfort me," she said, shaking her head. "Go comfort your mother. We both know she needs it the most."

Jack nodded. However, he didn't know quite what to say to his mother. He knew he had to be careful. Any wrong word could easily throw Mrs. Gardner into an ocean of tears. The key was to make sure he didn't mention any bad possible outcomes. For example, he shouldn't say, "Don't worry Mom, he will live," because right away she would think of the possibility of him not living. Most likely it didn't matter though. Jack was sure she was already thinking that very thought.

Jack sat next to his mother, but decided not to say anything at first. The lobby couches they sat on were fairly comfortable. Jack figured they must count on visitors staying for long periods of time. Mrs. Gardner was not looking at Jack. She had her head turned in the opposite direction so that it faced the wall and did not make eye contact with anyone. Jack was hesitant to even make physical contact with her, but eventually he put his arms around her and gave her a big hug. She still didn't face him, however, but she did hold onto his hand, gripping it very tightly.

"Everything's going to be okay, Mom," Jack finally whispered, as he started to rub his hand on her back. "Everything will be fine," he repeated.

Mrs. Gardner turned her head toward him and Jack could see that tears were lightly falling from her eyes. Jack immediately turned his head to the other side away from his mother's sight. He took a deep breath before looking back in her direction. "It was probably nothing," he said. "Grandpa just had a little trouble breathing. You know you worry too much about everything, Mom." Jack tried to stay positive and laugh a bit to ease Mrs. Gardner's mind and keep her optimistic, something that was by no means an easy task.

"I'm really scared," Mrs. Gardner whispered. "What if he doesn't make it? I can't picture my life without my parents. Who's going to be excited to see me at all times?" Mrs. Gardner shook her head and shed some more tears.

"You can't think like that. I told you everything will be fine," Jack responded.

Just then, a doctor came out that Jack recognized. Mrs. Gardner immediately rose to her feet and went to greet the doctor.

"Hello, Mrs. Gardner. I'm Dr. Chan."

"Is he all right?" Mrs. Gardner blurted out. She looked like she was about to burst as she waited on the answer which would determine much of the rest of her life.

"Well, we're not sure yet." Not the answer Mrs. Gardner was looking for.

"What do you mean you're not sure? Aren't you a doctor? Is he all right or is there something wrong?" she continued to ask.

"He's still having some difficulty breathing." Mrs. Gardner cringed. "But we think he's going to be just fine."

"Can we go in and see him?" Mrs. Gardner asked.

"Not yet, but I'll be sure to come out and tell you as soon as you can." The doctor turned around and walked away from the Gardner family.

"I knew something was wrong," Mrs. Gardner muttered. "Or else they would let us see him now." She went back to sit at her couch and stared at the wall. Jack went back to the other family members to see how they were doing.

"We're fine," Mr. Gardner said. "Maybe you should get home Jack. There's nothing much for you to do tonight."

"I can't leave with Mom like this," Jack said. "Let me just call home and make sure everything's all right."

Jack took out his cell phone and went to an empty area of the lobby.

Ring … Ring … Ring.

No answer. *Why the hell isn't she answering?* Jack thought. He called again.

Ring … Ring …

"Hello," Brianne said.

"Are you sleeping?" Jack said angrily.

"I was just resting my eyes. Calm down."

"Is Michael all right?"

"Yes, Jack. I told you everything is fine. You don't need to worry about him."

"All right. I'm sorry Brianne. Can you please stay awake until I get back though? I just want to know everything's okay."

"You're in a hospital, yet you're still worrying about what's going on at home. How ironic is that?"

"I'm worrying about home to make sure that I don't have to be in a hospital visiting one of you two," Jack said.

"How is everything going down there?" his wife asked.

"I don't know. The doctor still won't let us see my grandpa. Kind of makes me suspect something might be more wrong than the doctors are letting on. I don't want my mom to know I think that though. I'm trying to assure her that nothing is wrong."

"That's good. Keep her positive. I'm sure everything will work out fine. Do you think you will be home tonight?"

"Yeah, I'm sure I'll be back within an hour or so. It doesn't look like much is going to happen tonight."

"All right, well I'll see you when you get home. I love you."

"Love you too. Bye."

Jack hung up the phone, but instead of going back to the others, he stayed by himself for a moment. He sat down in a nearby chair and prayed that everything would work out for the best, prayed for his grandfather's safety and health. He prayed that nothing was seriously wrong, and most importantly, that there would be no deaths tonight. He also prayed for his mother, prayed that she stayed optimistic and didn't worry herself to death. Just then, Jack saw Dr. Chan come back out to greet the Gardners.

"Good news," he said. "Your father is breathing normally again. You can all go see him now if you'd like."

"Thank, God," Mrs. Gardner gasped.

She followed the doctor to the room where her father was being examined. She was in a rush and almost ran down the hall. The others followed her but in a calmer manner.

When they got inside the room, Jack saw his grandfather hooked up to machines and cords linked to his nose and arms. It reminded Jack of how Craig must have felt when he saw his mother hooked up to the machines the night she had overdosed. The room itself was very cheerful, quite opposite from the feelings that usually were present in a hospital room. Some assorted plants were sitting on the window ledges to compliment the perfectly white walls.

"How are you feeling, Dad?" Mrs. Gardner asked.

"I'm all right," Grandpa Sechovec whispered, although he did not sound completely all right. He spoke slowly and in a lower tone than usual.

Mrs. Gardner looked at her father with such joy at the fact that he was all right. She had a certain twinkle in her eye when she looked at him that symbolized just how much she cared for her parents. She gave her father a hug and didn't let go for several moments.

"Well, everyone decided to come, eh?" Grandpa Sechovec said as he noticed everyone who had entered the room. "You didn't all have to get out of bed for me. I'll be just fine." he assured them.

"I called them, Dad," Mrs. Gardner said. "You know how worried I get."

"Yeah, well, you all should get back to sleep now. Like I said, I'll be fine."

Mr. Gardner said, "Yeah, Jack and Mark, why don't you both go back home? You have wives waiting for you, and you both have work tomorrow."

"Yeah, we should probably be getting back," Mark said.

"Are you sure you're all right, Grandpa?" Jack said.

Grandpa laughed a little, although his voice was still low and a little raspy. "I'll be fine. Don't worry about me."

"All right, well I'm sure I'll see you soon."

Jack and Mark walked out of their room before saying goodbye to each other and going back to their own lives.

When Jack got home, Brianne was still waiting up for him in bed. She wasn't watching television and no lights were on. She was simply sitting up in bed waiting for him to come home.

"Are you all right?" Jack asked.

"Yeah, I'm fine. Just waiting for you to get back like you asked."

"How's my Michael doing? Still sleeping away?" Jack walked over to the crib and took another look at his son who was still sleeping peacefully. Jack smiled at him and got into bed.

"Was everything all right at the hospital?" she asked.

"Yeah, everything's fine. Grandpa just had a little trouble breathing but he's all right now. I think my parents and Grandma are going to stay the night there. My mom would be too worried to sleep anyway."

"All right. Well, come in bed with me. Let's get some sleep. I've got school in the morning, you know?"

Jack got undressed, down to his underwear, and climbed into bed. He kissed his wife goodnight before turning over and trying to find sleep. It was difficult though, not because he was worried about his grandfather—Jack was sure he was fine—but he was more worried about his mother. He hoped she would relax and just know that everything would be all right.

Jack waited an hour, but sleep would not come to him. It was no use. Brianne had fallen asleep within seconds it seemed and he didn't feel like lying awake in bed all alone. He went downstairs to the living room where he filled a glass of water, lay down on the couch, and turned on the television. He couldn't remember when, or what he was watching on television, but eventually he fell asleep on the couch. It wasn't for long, however.

He was awakened by a ringing sound, which he realized was his cell phone once he came to his senses. "Not again," he said once he saw that it was his father calling. "Yeah, Dad, what's up?"

"Jack, I need you to come over to the house now," Mr. Gardner said.

"Why? Is there something wrong?"

"Just come over Jack and hurry. We'll be waiting for you." Mr. Gardner hung up the phone.

"I wonder what the hell that was about." Jack looked at the time: 5:30 am. He walked up the spiral staircase, back to his room where his wife was still sleeping. He wondered if he should wake her up or not. He decided against it. After all, she had already been kept up much of the night due to him, and Michael was sure to be waking up soon. He wanted to let her sleep the rest of the morning until her alarm sounded. He checked on Michael one more time and whispered goodbye to the both of them before getting in his car and driving over to his parents' house.

When he got there, he saw his brother Mark's car already there along with his grandparents' car. He used his key to unlock the door before walking into the living room. The lights were all off in the house, but since the time was nearing 6:00 am, the house was dimly lit by the sun. Mr. Gardner and Mark sat on the couch and Grandma Sechovec was sitting on the love seat. Jack was sure his younger brother Chris was sleeping in his room, but he wasn't sure where his mother was. Grandma Sechovec's eyes were red, as if she had recently been crying a great deal.

"Hey, everyone," Jack said. He noticed that no one was sitting in the living room chair that Grandpa Sechovec usually occupied.

"Come in here, Jack," Mr. Gardner commanded. Jack went into the living room and took the chair that his grandfather had always sat in at family gatherings.

"What's going on?" he asked.

"Jack … your grandfather … he … he had some complications in the hospital." Mr. Gardner was having trouble speaking, something which Jack was not used to seeing. "He was having trouble breathing … and … before long he couldn't breathe at all … and … his heart gave out Jack."

Grandma started crying again at Mr. Gardner's words.

Seconds later Mr. Gardner gave the news that was the reason they were all up at six in the morning. "Grandpa is dead."

Grandma continued to cry a bit, but no one else spoke. Mark continued to sit on the couch, merely looking at the carpeted floor.

Jack didn't know quite what to say. "Dead?" he mouthed, although the words would not come out. Jack's eyes began to well with water and his hands and knees began to shake a bit. *How could he be dead?* Jack thought. "I just saw him. He told me himself that everything would be fine!" Jack thought a lot about why God had not answered his prayers. But, even more than that, he thought about why God brought his hopes up just to send them crashing down. Why did he make everyone believe that Grandpa would be fine and then take his life away from him?

"Where's Mom?" Jack finally asked.

"She's in her bedroom," Mr. Gardner replied. "She's locked the door and won't come out. It's no use. She's been in there for about an hour. I'm starting to get worried about her."

Jack wiped away a couple tears from his eyes. "I'm going to go talk to her now," Jack said.

"She won't unlock the door," Mr. Gardner replied. "I already tried a couple times."

"I know how to get in."

Jack left the living room, walking through the kitchen and toward the hallway. He walked halfway down the hallway before turning into the bathroom. He opened one of the drawers under the sink and pulled out a Q-tip. He broke the Q-tip in half so that he had two little sticks. He threw one away, but took the other one and walked out of the bathroom and down the hallway to the master bedroom. Jack knocked on the door a couple times, just in case she would change her mind and answer.

"Mom, it's me. Please open up," he insisted. However, no one answered.

The door handle had a small hole in it. The hole led to the lock and when Jack pushed the Q-tip into the hole, it popped the lock out. Jack had learned the trick at a young age when his little brother used to run away from him to avoid physical harm, running into his mother's room and locking the door behind him.

When Jack walked into the room, he saw his mother sprawled out on the bed. Her legs and arms were both spread wide and her face was buried in the many pillows on the bed.

"Mom?" Jack said. There was no answer. Jack was worried that she might not have been breathing until he walked closer to her. He heard her deep breathing and the sniffing of her nose trying to hold back some of the tears. She still did not acknowledge Jack, however. Jack sat down on the bed next to her and began to rub her back. As he did this, his mother began breathing harder and crying much more profusely than before. This, in turn, caused more tears to roll down Jack's cheeks.

Then his mother turned to him. She looked up at him with her brown eyes full of tears. Her lips were quivering as she tried to hold the tears back. As his mother looked at him, Jack had a terrible feeling, one that he had never experienced before. He couldn't believe how badly his heart hurt. He was truly in pain as his mother looked at him helplessly. At the same time, he was so angry he felt as though he could kill someone. Only one other time in Jack's life had he seen his mother cry like that, a time in which she felt she had almost lost one of her sons.

"What am I going to do?" she cried out. "My father is gone. What will my mother do? She is all alone now."

"I know, Mom. But he's in a better place now. He won't have to live with any more pain. He can just be happy."

"There is no heaven. You think he's happy in the ground?" Mrs. Gardner retorted.

"Don't say that. He's watching over us right now and you know it."

Mrs. Gardner shook her head. "No, Jack. No," was all she said.

Jack put his arms around her and tried to comfort her, although he needed to be comforted as well. He was only holding onto her for seconds before he knew that he couldn't do it anymore. He let go of his mother and looked at her one more time. He couldn't stand to see her this way. Nothing in the world could break him down like seeing his mother cry.

It hit a certain point where Jack was so angry he couldn't even stand to be in the house anymore—so angry at life, so angry at everything. He stormed out of the house without saying goodbye to anyone. He got into his car and raced down the street. Only one thing was on his mind: "I need to talk to Dr. Slovano." He called up his psychologist as he drove.

Ring ... Ring ...

"Hello?" Dr. Slovano answered.

"Charles, I need to see you." Jack was still crying as he said this.

"Who is this?"

"Jack Gardner. Please, Charles, I need to see you now."

"I'm not open for another four hours."

"It can't wait. Meet me down at your office in fifteen minutes ... Please ... I'm begging you."

"Begging me? What the hell is wrong?"

"Nothing." Jack took a deep breath. "Can you please meet me there?"

"Can't it wait? I'll be open at ten. We can talk about anything you want to then. All right?"

"Damn it, Charles! It's an emergency. I don't have time to waste. I'm going crazy. Fifteen minutes. Meet me there, *please!*"

"All right, Jack. Fifteen minutes."

Jack hung up the phone and sped toward Dr. Slovano's office. He tried to take a deep breath but it was no use. He broke down again. He tried to hold the tears back, but was unsuccessful. He thought about what he would do if one of his own parents died. The thought alone was much too painful. He closed his eyes tightly and shook his head back and forth to get the awful image out.

Chapter 35

A Possible Danger

Dr. Slovano arrived in fifteen minutes, just as he said he would. Jack had been waiting for him in the parking lot. When he saw Dr. Slovano's car, he jumped out of his car. He pressed the lock on his key chain four times and jiggled the handle four times before walking over to Dr. Slovano. Jack still had tears in his eyes and his hands were still shaking. Dr. Slovano got out of the car and took a long look at his client. Jack looked as though something was terribly wrong and it frightened Dr. Slovano a little.

"Thank you for coming," Jack said, shaking his hand.

"Of course," Dr. Slovano said. "Come on, let's go inside." Jack followed Dr. Slovano into his office. "I'm a little worried about you Jack. Are you sure everything is okay?"

"Of course everything's not okay," Jack said. "We both know that. Otherwise I wouldn't have called you at 6 am." Jack sat down on his usual seat, which was the couch, and Dr. Slovano pulled up his usual chair.

"Do you need a tissue, Jack?"

Jack nodded. "Thank you." He wiped his nose and eyes and took a deep breath.

"You know, you haven't been coming in for your appointments for quite some time," Dr. Slovano said. "I have to admit, it made me happy. I figured it meant that everything was going well with you now that you were off the medication."

"Well, you're right," Jack said. "Everything was going perfect. I actually got married again."

"Well, congratulations. Have you been able to control your OCD lately?"

"Yes. Hardly even thought about it anymore. Like I said, everything was going great. There was nothing to worry about."

"And now?"

"I need the medications back."

"I thought it was working better without them," Charles said.

"Yeah, but this morning something terrible happened. It was awful." Tears began to roll down Jack's cheeks again.

"It's all right. Tell me what happened." Jack was breathing very heavily and it caused even more concern for Dr. Slovano.

"My grandfather died this morning," Jack finally said.

"I see," Dr. Slovano said, adjusting his glasses. He was a little taken aback by the information but supposed he shouldn't have been. Something was obviously greatly wrong here. "Were you close to him?"

Jack thought about it a moment. The whole time he did not look his psychologist in the eye, but rather stared at the floor in a seated position. "Yeah, I guess. I mean, I saw him a lot. We lived pretty close to each other. He was a great guy."

"You know, as people get older, death happens, Jack. It's just a part of life."

"It wasn't the death that killed me," Jack said. "It was the pain I saw in my mother's eyes. It was knowing that the woman who had cared for me all of her life would now have to live with that hurt. I wondered if I would ever see her happy again, like she always used to be. I just can't stand to see my mother cry. I just can't. It makes me feel as though there is nothing good in this world."

"You said she was usually a happy person? So you didn't see her cry often then?"

"No. Hardly ever. There's very few times that I can remember, and trust me I remember every time it has happened. There were a couple times that weren't that bad. I remember she cried the first year I moved to college. She was sad because I guess I hadn't called her very often. When I came home for the weekend one time, I remember her coming into my room and saying how much she missed me and crying a bit. There was another time she had gotten in a fight with my father and she came to me and cried a little. I was too young to remember what it was about exactly. She probably didn't tell me what it was about at the time anyway. But there has only been one other time besides tonight where I saw her cry the way she did."

"What happened? Tell me about it."

"Eh ... I don't know," Jack muttered. "Haven't really told anyone. I'm not too comfortable talking about it. Kind of embarrassing."

"Everything you say is confidential. I won't tell anyone. Besides, it might be important. Maybe I can help you."

"You sure it's confidential?"

"Every word, Jack."

Jack took a deep breath. He was still breathing irregularly and Dr. Slovano knew that whatever Jack was going to talk about was a touchy subject with him. He was used to talking to disturbed clients, some of them crazy. He wasn't sure if Jack was one of these patients, but he knew he may be calling the police straight after Jack left if he thought there was any danger to worry about.

"I was at my girlfriend's house at the time. This girl named Elizabeth. I was only seventeen I think. Anyway, for some reason I had been acting very differently back then. Actually I do know why. You see, I had met this girl named Sarah. She was just a friend to me, but she made me look at everything differently. She made me feel like being ordinary was a crime. She said that normal people were boring, and that being different or weird was what makes people and life interesting. She was a nice girl, very pretty, very smart. She made me think about things differently than I had ever done before."

"So she had a big influence on you then?"

"Yeah, definitely. And one day she told me that she cuts herself."

"Cuts herself? Like how?"

"With a knife. Just some cuts along her wrist and under forearm and stuff. At first, I was really concerned about her. I had never heard of anyone doing that to themselves before. Only saw it on the movies or maybe heard about it, you know?"

"It is a big deal, Jack. It's a very big deal."

"Anyway, she talked to me about it. Made me see things the way she did in a way. She told me that it was no big deal. She told me a couple different things. She told me that it helped her get out her frustrations and it made her feel better. One time she also told me that she felt it was necessary to punish herself sometimes. For some reason it made sense to me at the time."

"Did you do something to yourself?"

"You know, at first it just started out pretty simple. I would cut myself with a steak knife or something. The cuts were like Sarah's. They weren't anything deep or anything. I think I wanted to feel the way that Sarah did. That it made her feel better. I remember going through some rough times and I wanted to feel better. It didn't make me feel better but it did something else for me."

"Explain," Dr. Slovano said. He adjusted his glasses that he had been doing quite regularly.

"People noticed the cuts and red marks on my wrists, especially my girlfriend Elizabeth. She was always so worried about me and begged me to stop. I liked the attention she gave me because of it. When she worried about me, it made me feel good that someone out there cared about me that much. I wanted more of that special feeling and so the cutting continued. I wanted people to feel bad for me, although there was nothing really to feel bad about. Maybe I just wanted them to think there were things going on in my life that they didn't know about; that my life was mysterious or something. I wanted to be different. Just as Sarah had told me to do."

"I see. So what happened at your girlfriend's house that day? It's okay, you can tell me."

"Elizabeth's parents weren't home that day. We were upstairs in her bedroom. She was remodeling her bedroom a bit. There were carpenter tools on her dresser, such as box cutters and paintbrushes, and a lot of other things. I don't remember how it happened, but I saw a razor blade sitting on the dresser. You know, one of those real sharp ones that can cut through pretty much anything? Yeah, well, a spinning fan was hanging on the ceiling of her room. You know the kind with beaded strings that hang down from the fan, where you pull them and they make the fan spin or the light go on? Yeah, well, there was one of those on it, except I think Elizabeth had just put the fan in because the beads were much too long. They hung down all the way on the bed. As a matter of fact, they would have reached the floor if the bed wasn't in the way. She picked up the razor blade and asked if I could cut the beads for her so that they only hung down a foot or so. I picked up the razor blade and cut it for her. It wasn't easy cutting it. I had to struggle and cut hard before it cut through the cord. Almost made contact with my wrist when it finally went through. Kind of gave me an idea. I started fooling around and told Elizabeth I was going to cut myself again. I held it up to my wrist and she pleaded for me to stop. I wasn't really planning on doing it; I just wanted to see how much she cared for me. I wanted her to tell me not to do it because I meant too much to her to risk hurting myself."

"Did you want to hurt yourself?"

"You know I didn't really care. If I did, it wasn't going to be a big deal to me. I didn't want to kill myself or anything either. I wasn't seriously depressed. I put the razor blade back down and we just hung out for a while. Talked on her bed I think. It's hard to remember now, it was so long ago."

"That's not important. What happened?"

"Somehow she made me mad. I'm not sure what it was about now, probably because we were fighting about something stupid. Anyway, I wanted to make her feel bad. I asked her if she could go get me a glass of water and she did. When she got back she was standing in the doorway and noticed that I had picked up the razor blade from the dresser." Jack paused for a moment before continuing. "I told her that I was going to cut myself. She begged me to stop but this time I didn't listen. You know I was used to cutting myself with those steak knives. I could slash myself with those, and honestly it didn't really hurt. It would hardly even puncture the skin. But when I held that razor blade up high above my head, and I slashed it down onto my wrist, I immediately saw blood spurting out. I mean it was dripping down my arm like it was a river. I was so shocked at first. I didn't really know what to do, and I still didn't realize how bad it was. Elizabeth had run to get a towel. She applied pressure on it and wiped off the blood from the cut. When she did this I could see that I had split open the right part of my wrist. I could actually see the spongy insides, and I still remember exactly how it looked. The thought hadn't occurred to me at first, but Elizabeth immediately told me that I needed stitches. I drove home but when I got there my mother wasn't home. When she got back I told her that I accidentally cut myself trying to cut through the beads. I knew right away she didn't believe me. She drove me to the doctor's, where I again told my lie of how it happened. He stitched me and everything seemed fine until the ride home. That's when my mother cried and that's when I felt a terrible pain."

"She cried because she was worried about losing you I assume?" Dr. Slovano said surely. "Worried that you might kill yourself?"

"That's what I thought at first," Jack said. "The doctor said that if my careless slash would have been an inch to the left, it would have cut straight through those two giant veins everyone has in their wrist. So obviously I thought she was worried for my life. I thought maybe she would take pity. Maybe she would think it was something she was doing wrong and feel sorry for me."

"And?" Dr. Slovano said. He was getting very interested in Jack's story.

"And I couldn't have been more wrong. Where I thought she was going to feel bad, she completely turned it around on me. She made me feel as though I was the worst person in the world. Somehow she knew that the cut wasn't an accident. She always did know everything. Anyway, I remember her asking how selfish I could be. She said that I was so selfish to only think about myself. She said if I killed myself, who would be the one that would have to deal with it everyday for the rest of her life? Obviously I knew she was talking about herself. She didn't feel bad that I would be dead and she was right. It is a selfish act to commit suicide. You leave the world and all your problems behind, and leave all those problems and sorrows on the ones that love you most."

"But you said she knew you weren't trying to kill yourself."

"She did, but she still wanted me to feel bad for pretending like I was going to. She cried so hard and spoke with such a tone that I was ashamed of myself. She said, 'Do you think it's normal to be cutting yourself?' I took Sarah's words straight from her mouth. I said, 'Why would I want to be normal? Being normal is boring. Being different is interesting.' This enraged her even more, or perhaps I should say it disappointed her more. She almost went crazy. 'How would you like it if I started cutting myself?' she asked me. 'How would you like it if you came home one day and found me with my wrist cut open just because I wanted to be different?'"

"She has a good point, Jack. You have to think about every one you're hurting when you do something dangerous."

"I never wanted to do anything that would make my mom cry after that day so I guess she did her job."

"Did you ever do anything else that you think would have made her cry?"

"There might be a couple things; if there were I could never tell her though. I'd rather die than have to see that look in her eye ever again."

"What you did back then was very dangerous. Do you ever have urges to do anything like that again?"

"Tonight makes me want to," Jack said. "No one close to me has ever died. I just can't believe such an awful thing can happen to people. One second he was fine, and the next he was gone. It definitely makes me want to take out my aggressions in some way, find some way to ease the pain."

"You can harness those aggressions. You can talk about them with your friends and family. That's where you should be right now, grieving with your family. That's what is important."

"I can't stand to see them right now. I just can't do it. I feel like I should punish myself for my grandpa's death. It must have been my fault. I prayed, but maybe I didn't pray hard enough. I could have prayed harder, my grandfather's life was on the line. How selfish could I have been?" Jack was breathing heavily, almost to an extreme at this point. He was having difficulty even getting out the words. He got up from the couch and paced back and forth in front of the psychologist.

"Jack, please, calm down!" Dr. Slovano pleaded.

But Jack was not listening. He continued to pace back and forth and talk to himself rapidly.

"Maybe if I would have followed the rituals more closely," Jack said frantically. "Maybe he wouldn't have died. It's all my fault. Why didn't I?"

Jack was interrupted by Dr. Slovano. "Jack, I mean it. Calm down or I'm going to ask you to leave."

"I could've helped him," Jack continued to say. He looked hysterical. "I let my grandfather down. I'm so sorry, Grandpa."

"That's it," Dr. Slovano said. "Jack you need to leave my office immediately!" Jack stared at his psychologist as though he had been betrayed.

"Fine," he said. "If you don't want to help me then I'll just be out of your way!"

Jack stormed out of the office and slammed the door on his way out.

Dr. Slovano did not waste anytime. He quickly walked over to his office telephone and dialed the police station.

"Hello, Officer Travis Denton here."

"Hi, I'm Dr. Charles Slovano. I'm a psychologist and have a client named Jack Gardner."

"Jack Gardner?" Denton replied.

"Yes, do you know him?"

"Sure do. What's the problem with Jack?"

"He's a client of mine like I said. Anyway, he was very upset a few moments ago. I sent him out of my office and I think he was heading back to his house. Listen, I think he might be dangerous. Could you have someone just pay him a little visit? I'm worried something bad will happen to himself or those around him."

Denton was suddenly very alarmed. *Hurt those around him?* he thought. *Oh, no.*

"Thanks for the call Dr. Slovano. We'll be sure to have someone drive over there as soon as possible," Denton said.

Denton hung up the phone and went to look for his boss. "Where's Chief Peterson?" he asked another officer.

"He's not in yet," the officer replied. "Isn't expected to come into work until nine o'clock."

Travis Denton decided he would do this himself. He got in his police car and began driving to Jack Gardner's house. *"Dangerous?"* Denton kept repeating as he drove. "Was Jack Gardner really dangerous?" He hadn't even seen it coming. Perhaps Jack wasn't the nice innocent man Denton had taken him for.

Chapter 36

A Treasure in the Sand

Jack Gardner raced back to his Long Island home near the beach. He opened the door and walked upstairs.

Brianne was awake. She was walking around the room getting ready to go to class. "Hey, Jack. Where were you? I was starting to get worried.,

"Do you think you could miss class today?" Jack asked.

"Why? Is something wrong?"

"My grandfather died last night. That's where I've been all morning."

"Oh my God," she gasped.

"Look, I really don't want to talk about it. I can't drop Michael off at my parent's house though. They're in no state to be watching over our baby. Can you stay home today or not?"

"Of course. Whatever you need me to do."

"Just stay up here and watch over Michael for now, all right?" Jack said. Michael was now awake and was making little noises as he turned over in his crib.

"I'm guessing you're staying home from work today too, right?"

"Yes. I'm just going to go downstairs," Jack said. "I need to look for some things. I'll be back up in a couple of minutes."

Jack walked down the stairs and into a guest bedroom he had slept in from time to time. In the back of the room was a closet, a closet that had a lock on it which had to be opened with a key in order to enter. Jack had the only key. No one else had ever been inside this closet to his knowledge, and he wouldn't ever let anyone inside it so long as he had something to do with it.

He made sure to lock the bedroom door before walking over to the closet. He opened up the closet and walked past some clothes that hung in the front. Past them was a shelf, a couple of feet above Jack's head. He pulled over a chair to stand on so that he could pull down whatever it was that he was looking for. The shelves were covered with boxes and files, but Jack only pulled down one box. It was the largest box of them all, but still only about the size of an oversized shoebox. Inside the box was one thing and one thing only. It was a black spiral notebook with no words written on the cover.

He opened up the notebook but did not read anything. It was as though he was just making sure that it was there, that it was safe. He skimmed through the pages, still not reading any of the words written in it, before putting the notebook back in the box. As he did this he heard a knock at the front door. *Probably Dad or Mark,* Jack thought. He left the guest room and walked toward the door as there was another knock.

The person behind the door spoke. It was not who Jack had expected. "Jack? It's Officer Denton. Are you in there?"

Jack slowly backed away from the door.

What the hell do the police want? he thought.

Brianne was walking down the stairs as Jack backed away from the door. "Who's at the door?" she asked.

Jack held up his index finger to his mouth, signaling her to be quiet. "Go upstairs," he whispered. "Don't answer the door."

"Is something wrong?" asked Brianne.

"No, just wait for me in the bedroom. I'll be right up."

Brianne didn't understand but she walked up the stairs anyway and went back into her bedroom.

Jack rushed back into the guest bedroom and picked up his shoebox.

"Jack?" the voice came again. "I just want to ask you some questions." Jack ignored Denton and took the box upstairs. Brianne was sitting on the bed.

"Who was out there?" she asked him.

"Some police officer," he said. "He's still trying to figure out some unsolved answers to the robbery case. I just don't feel like answering any more questions."

"We can't just ignore the police."

"We can for now. He'll come back another time."

"What do you have in your hand?"

"Oh, it's um … something that belonged to my grandfather," Jack lied. "Pictures and stuff. I'd like to go out on the balcony and look at them alone, if you don't mind."

"That's fine. Do whatever you need to do."

Jack walked outside onto the balcony that overlooked the ocean. The ocean was probably a hundred feet below since the house stood atop a steep green grassy hill. There was no way for anyone to walk around to the back of the house, so Jack was not worried about the officer coming around to the back.

He walked up to the railing of the balcony so that he could get the best view of the ocean as possible. To the left a little ways in the distance, Jack could see the beach where he and Brianne had shared momentous occasions together, such as a proposal and marriage.

He opened up the box and pulled out the notebook. He held the notebook in his hands so that it hung over the balcony slightly, but did not open it at first. It seemed as though he was waiting for something. He finally opened up the notebook, bringing it back over the balcony to make sure that he wouldn't drop it over the edge.

He read through each and every page that had writing on them. There were only about ten or fifteen entries all together so it didn't take that long. It was hard for him to read it knowing that it would be the last time. He would destroy the notebook, making sure that no one would ever read it. He would drench it in the sink, making sure that all the ink on every page smeared, making it impossible to read, before disposing of it.

Once he was done reading the very last entry, the most painful of all to read, he put the notebook back into the box. The last entry had made him very jittery. He was holding onto the box tightly, but when he began to turn around to head back into the bedroom, someone called out to him.

"Jack!" Brianne yelled.

The combination of the yell along with Jack's jittery state caused Jack to let go of the box for a moment. He caught it against the top of the balcony railing.

"What?" He gasped, relieved that he had caught the box, but angry that she had almost caused him to drop it.

"Sorry, Jack, I forgot you were out there. I'm going to make us some breakfast. Do you think you could watch Michael until I'm done?"

"Yeah, sure. I'll be there in a moment," said Jack.

Brianne went back inside the room before going down to the kitchen to start breakfast. Jack picked up the box from the railing against which he had been holding it. However, when he picked up the box, he realized that it was upside down. He frantically looked in the box and didn't see a notebook. "Oh, no!" Jack cried out. He looked over the balcony but saw no sign of his notebook. "It must have blown down the hill toward the ocean," he assured himself. "Mother Nature took care of it for me. But I have to be sure."

He went inside the bedroom before going downstairs, forgetting about Michael. He didn't say anything to his wife but ran out of the house and got into his car. He drove down to Dillon's Beach as quickly as he could. He jumped out of the car and rushed onto the powdery sand. He searched up and down the beach but saw no sign of the notebook. He walked past the beach, in the direction of his house, toward the grassy hillside. He went as far as he possibly could, until the ocean took over, and looked up the hill under his house, but there was still no trace of it. Jack sighed with relief. "The ocean took it. It's gone."

He got back into his car and drove home.

Brianne was still eating breakfast when he got back. Jack walked into the kitchen and saw her sitting at the kitchen table. "Nice of you to come back," she said. "You know you left Michael up there all by himself right?"

"Oh, no," Jack gasped. "How could I have forgotten? Is he all right? Is anything wrong?"

"Relax, everything is fine. What is wrong with you today?"

"I don't know. Hasn't exactly been the most pleasant day of my life."

"All right, I'm sorry. Come sit down and eat some breakfast with me."

"I'm not really hungry. I think I'll go upstairs and check on Michael. Make sure everything's all right."

"Yeah, whatever," Brianne replied.

Jack went upstairs and assured himself that Michael was all right. He picked him up out of his crib gently and cradled him in his arms. He brought his son downstairs into the kitchen where Brianne was cleaning up Jack's uneaten breakfast. "Why don't we go down to the beach today?" Jack said to Brianne. "I need some time to clear some of my thoughts."

"What about Michael?"

"He can come with us," Jack said.

"All right, well let's go then," Brianne agreed. "Do we need anything?"

"No, I don't want to swim. Let's just get in the car and get going.

Jack and Brianne got into Jack's Mercedes after securing their son in the child's seat. They drove the short distance to Dillon's Beach.

* * * * * * * * * *

When no one answered at Jack Gardner's house, Travis Denton left with a less than positive attitude. *Where the hell could he be?* Denton thought. He drove around for almost a half hour before calling it quits. He needed time to think. He parked at a local beach: Dillon's Beach. He got out of his car and decided to walk around a little. It certainly wasn't the nicest day of the year. Clouds floated in the sky, blocking much of the sun's light, and a rather cool breeze went along with it. He walked along the beach for a while until he got tired, and climbed up some rocks until he reached a flat surface of rocks that he could comfortably sit on.

He crossed his arms across his chest and held them tight as it was still a bit chilly in the early morning, especially with the strong breeze blowing. Denton looked around and saw a little cave that was created below him which was formed by the large surrounding rocks. He climbed down to the sandy bottom of the cave and saw something on the surface, slightly buried in the sand. He wiped away the sand, and picked up a black notebook. It couldn't have been there long because the pages were still clean and easily readable.

Denton opened up the book, intrigued by names he recognized on every page, but nothing was like the very last pages. "Oh my God!" he gasped only halfway through the journal entry. However, he could not stop reading. It was like a car accident: terrible to watch, but he simply could not stop.

He kept reading until he had reached the end. "Holy shit!" he cried out. He jumped up out of the cave, still holding the notebook, and began to run back down the beach to where his car was. Halfway along the beach he saw the shape of Chief Peterson coming toward him. Denton was out of breath by this point.

"Denton," Chief Peterson called, waving his arms so that Denton would see him.

"Chief Peterson? What are you doing here?"

"I was told you were looking for me. Someone at the station told me I could find you at Gardner's place. Your log at the precinct says you responded to a call about Jack Gardner. I just so happened to have something very interesting to tell you about the Gardner case and some questions for Jack so I thought I would just drive to the Gardner house. Then I saw your car as I drove toward the house. "

"Forget the call," Denton panted. "Look at what I have here." Denton handed over the notebook to Chief Peterson.

"What is this?" Peterson asked.

"I'm not entirely sure. It looks like it belonged to Jack Gardner. It seems to be some kind of journal he kept."

"Did you break into his house and take this or something?" gasped Peterson.

"I found it down there in the sand. In some little cave. I think Gardner might have tried to hide it, or maybe he lost it. It shows what appears to be all the most important times in his life until Melanie Gardner's death."

"Important times? Like what?"

"Well, it describes the day he found the former Mrs. Sanderson cheating on Mr. Sanderson, the first night he met Melanie Stole, a night in which Craig Sanderson's mother had overdosed, conversations he had with Mr. Sanderson, when Craig had found out that his mother had died, when Melanie had cheated on Jack with Craig, a time where Craig had beaten David Cooper, stories of Jack taking Craig into his home, and there were some other entries too," replied Denton. "The only strange thing is that some of the entries are from times where Jack wasn't even present. Sometimes he writes about times that simply involve Craig Sanderson or Melanie."

"How could Jack write about things if he wasn't even present?" Peterson asked.

"I don't know. Maybe Craig told him about certain events that Jack didn't witness. It doesn't seem to matter."

Chief Peterson flipped through the notebook. "Why would he want to bury this?"

Denton took the notebook from Chief Peterson and began turning the pages.

"Answer me," Peterson demanded but Officer Denton wasn't listening.

The officer turned to the last entry in Jack Gardner's journal, the entry that explained it all in detail. "Here you go," Denton said. "You won't believe this."

Chief Peterson quickly took the notebook out of Denton's hands. "You must be kidding," he said in disbelief.

The officer turned to the very last page and began to read.

Chapter 37

The Final Entry

"Are you almost ready?" Jack asked Melanie over the telephone. "We're going to be late. I told you I made reservations."

"All right, all right, Jack. I'm ready now. Come pick me up."

"Finally." Jack got into his car and drove over to Melanie's house to pick her up. On his way to Melanie's house, his telephone rang. "Hello?"

"Hey, Jack, it's Craig." Craig had asked Jack if he wanted to hang out that night because the next day he was leaving to fly to his mother's funeral in Denver. Jack, however, told Craig that he couldn't see him because it was his wedding anniversary. Craig was upset but Jack couldn't worry about that on such an important night. He took her to a fancy French restaurant: Le Rivage. After that, they spent some time atop a hill, overlooking the New York City lights and making love in Jack's car before heading back to Melanie's house.

By the time they got back, night had fallen. It was about eight o' clock and Jack knew that Craig's flight was scheduled only a couple hours later.

"Thanks for a great night Jack," Melanie said as they pulled up to her house.

"The night isn't over yet, my dear," Jack said with a smile. "You'd better believe that much is true."

"Oh," she said excitedly. "You have more planned, do you?"

"Oh, yes. The restaurant and the hill were just appetizers. Trust me. The main event is still to come."

"All right," Melanie said. They walked up to her porch and Melanie opened the door. The couple walked into her house, and walked straight up the stairs to her bedroom. Jack took a seat on the bed and looked around the room. Plastic covers hung down from the walls on each side, covering all inches of the walls like Saran Wrap. The walls of the room had recently been painted, but Melanie was not happy with the overall look of the room. She planned on repainting the ceiling and wanted to protect the walls. However, no one besides Jack knew this little detail.

Melanie came into the room and sat down next to Jack. "I can't wait for our next anniversary," she said. Jack lay back onto the center of the bed, and Melanie followed him, resting her head on his shoulder and cuddling next to him. It wasn't long before they were making love.

"Ouch!" Melanie said. Jack seemed to be much more aggressive than normal and didn't seem very interested in foreplay. He climaxed quickly and immediately rolled off of her.

They laid there for ten more minutes before they heard the doorbell ring.

"Finally," Jack said.

Melanie looked perplexed. "Are you expecting someone?"

"Yes," Jack replied. "Wait here. I'll be right back."

Melanie still looked confused as ever, but she expected it must be some kind of surprise for her. Melanie rested on the bed, anticipating who would be coming to visit her shortly. Moments later she heard the door shut, followed by two sets of footsteps coming up the stairs. She didn't know why, but she suddenly grew very nervous.

Into the room, right behind Jack, came a man Melanie did not recognize. She had never seen him before but had heard about him plenty.

"Hello, Melanie. I'm Mr. Sanderson. You've heard of me I'm sure." Mr. Sanderson wore a long black coat and gloves to match.

"Craig's father, of course," Melanie smiled. "To what do I owe this visit?"

"Well," Mr. Sanderson said, returning her smile. "Revenge."

"Revenge," Melanie said with a laugh. "Revenge for what?" Melanie did not take him seriously and had absolutely no idea what he was talking about.

"I think you know exactly what this revenge is for," Mr. Sanderson said. He spoke in a low, mysterious, and evil tone.

Melanie stood up from the bed, for the first time slightly alarmed. "What is going on, Jack?"

"What is going on?" Mr. Sanderson laughed. "As if you didn't know. This, my dear, is revenge of the sweetest kind." He walked over to her, so closely that she backed up in the bed and sat down against it so that he was standing over her.

"Revenge for what, Jack? What did I do?"

"Don't play stupid," said Mr. Sanderson. "For you know exactly what you did. You broke the sacred laws of marriage, that special bond that is formed when a couple puts on those rings and makes the promise to be truthful to each other always. That kind of person just doesn't deserve to live now, does she?"

Mr. Sanderson grabbed her by the arms, standing her up to her feet and throwing her against the bedroom wall. She resisted, however, trying to squirm free of his hold. But when he wrapped his arms around her head in a chokehold, she could not break free.

"Son, if you would please?" Mr. Sanderson said to Jack as he threw him a black duffle bag.

Jack nodded his head in agreement. Jack opened the duffle bag and pulled out a long rope. Melanie began to cry as she panicked about what was soon to happen to her.

"Relax, my dear," Mr. Sanderson said to her. "This won't hurt a bit. … All right, I lied," Mr. Sanderson said. "It most likely will." Mr. Sanderson let out a rather menacing laugh.

"Jack, I don't know what he's talking about!" Melanie pleaded. "Can you at least tell me what the hell I did?"

"What the hell you did?" replied Mr. Sanderson. "That's not difficult to put a finger on. Let's see. You're about to cause an innocent man to be put to death. The man who was supposed to be my son and Jack's best friend, the man you deemed worthy to break your special bond of marriage with."

"It only happened one time, Jack! And we weren't even married."

"One time?" Jack finally jumped in. "Tie her up," he commanded, and Mr. Sanderson followed his directions. He tied her to the dresser so that her back was pressed up against it.

Jack reached into his back pocket and pulled out several pieces of paper. "One time?" he repeated. "Well, these love notes that he sent you seem to show different. I believe the last one explains your most recent affair … a week ago, at Craig's place."

"But Jack …"

"Quiet!" he interrupted her. "There's no need to explain. I don't want to hear it. Finding these letters gave me all the answers I needed." Jack walked back to the wall and put his hands over his eyes. Melanie could tell Jack wasn't sure about what he was doing.

Melanie's tears were now rolling profusely down her face, and Mr. Sanderson laughed as if to mock her. "I told you there's nothing to cry about, my dear. Just accept your punishment."

Mr. Sanderson pulled out a long knife from his duffle bag. It was an unusual knife, with a long blade, and a spiraling handle. The most unique part was that on both sides of the knife were deep ridges that formed several sharp points.

Melanie let out a shrill. "Oh, my God! What the hell is wrong with you people?"

"There's nothing wrong with *us!*" Mr. Sanderson said. "There's something wrong with foolish girls like yourself who think they can take advantage of men! Think they can go behind their backs! Well, this is one sin you are going to pay for."

"Is it really worth going to jail for?" Melanie pleaded.

Mr. Sanderson let out a loud laugh. "No one you see before you here today is going to jail, my dear. You think we're stupid? We know what we're doing. Did I go to jail after I killed my cheating ex-wife and her boyfriend? Of course not. I disposed of them both in my own way. I took them both out looking eye to eye with them. Jack here wants to do things a little differently, however. You ... I can dispose of you no problem, because honestly ... you make me sick. You make me want to kill you. But Jack ... he can't kill his best friend eye to eye. No, we'll let the state prosecution do that for us."

Melanie just sat there shaking her head with tears streaming down. "This can't be happening," she said. "It just can't."

"Oh, you'd better believe it is," Mr. Sanderson said with a laugh.

"There's no way you will get away with it!" she said. "The police will catch you!"

"No, I don't think so. The police will catch the real criminal—my so-called 'son' Craig Sanderson. You see, he's linked to this crime in more ways than you can imagine. Those plastic covers on the walls, they keep fingerprints nice and fresh don't they?" Mr. Sanderson smiled before continuing. "They won't find the knife because I'm going to take it back to my house and hang it on my wall as a trophy, just like the one I used on my wife. And, well, once they find Craig at the airport with these items ..."

Mr. Sanderson took out what appeared to be Craig's police uniform, ripped on the left sleeve, and a black and white mask. "It will be over. It was nice Craig gave Jack a key to his house. Made it easy to take his police uniform from his closet."

"How could you do this to your own son?" Melanie said.

"My son?" Mr. Sanderson said, shocked. "Craig Sanderson is not my son. A son of mine would not do that to his best friend. No, my son is Jack Gardner, and I would do anything for him. Anyway, enough chit chat, my dear. It's time for the main event." Mr. Sanderson took the knife and walked over to Melanie, kneeling down to her eye level. He looked at the knife, running his finger up and down it as though he was admiring it. "Ah, what a beauty," he whispered. "It's a shame it's going to be dirtied by someone like you."

Jack was still sitting back against the wall. He wasn't watching. He wasn't even sure he wanted this to happen. He bit his nails and closed his eyes. He touched the wall on both sides of himself four times. *Maybe we shouldn't kill her,* he thought. *She's just a young girl. People make mistakes.* He continued to bite his nails as Mr. Sanderson shined his knife. *Maybe I really do love her ... No ... No ... Get those stupid ideas out of your head. You don't love her. She betrayed you just as Mr. Sanderson said. She doesn't deserve to live. In my heart she has betrayed me in a way that can never be forgiven,* Jack kept telling himself. *But the way we plan to take her life, along with her dignity, is so cruel that no one in their right mind would dream of doing it. Then again, with the mixture of love and betrayal, no individual could possibly be in their right mind. It'll make a vicious plot of evil, to rape and kill a young girl, seem like a walk in the park.*

Jack couldn't stop thinking these thoughts as Mr. Sanderson was saying something to Melanie. Jack had not been listening. He wasn't paying attention until he saw Mr. Sanderson raise the knife above his head in a striking motion. Jack looked into Melanie's eyes and saw more fear than he thought humanly possible.

"Wait!" Jack cried out. Mr. Sanderson snapped his head around toward the wall where Jack was standing.

"Wait for what?" Mr. Sanderson said, but Jack did not respond. He looked around the room, searching for something to say. "Is there something wrong, my son?" Still Jack did not respond. Then Jack heard the faint ring of the doorbell.

"Someone's at the door," he blurted.

Mr. Sanderson stood up. "Who is it?"

Jack looked out the bedroom window. The front door was visible from this window, but Jack lied and said he couldn't see who it was.

"I'll go check," Mr. Sanderson said, leaving the room and going downstairs.

"Who is it?" whimpered Melanie.

"Your lover," Jack replied. "Craig." Jack could tell Melanie was frightened to death. Her voice trembled as she spoke.

"Please, Jack," she begged. "Don't do this to me. You *can't* do this to me."

"You're right," Jack admitted. He got down on one knee and began to untie the ropes, until he heard Mr. Sanderson coming back up the stairs. "Hold on, I'll get rid of him," Jack whispered. Melanie still looked as frightened as ever, but she did as Jack suggested. There were still a couple knots to be undone. Mr. Sanderson came back into the room with a smile on his face.

"It's Craig," he said.

"Craig?" Jack questioned, as if he didn't already know.

"Yes. I'll wait here for a moment. He should go away."

As they waited, Jack looked around the room and thought of all of the great times he and Melanie had shared together in that room: all of their talks of the future, how they would have children and live a beautiful life. Mr. Sanderson was talking to Melanie again in a menacing manner, but Jack wasn't listening to what he was saying. Jack started to get angry with Mr. Sanderson. For some reason he actually felt like saying, "Leave her alone!" Maybe he really did love her.

There was another ring of the doorbell. "Why isn't that son of a bitch leaving?" Mr. Sanderson muttered. He put the knife down on the dresser. "I'm going to check on him again. Make sure he doesn't try to get into the house." After Mr. Sanderson walked down the stairs Jack picked up the knife. He walked over to Melanie and cut the ropes with the knife. "Follow me," he said.

"Why can't you just tell him you don't want me dead?" Melanie asked. "Won't he listen to you?"

"No chance. Once he's all excited about it, there's no way he's going to just let you go. Plus, I'm like a son to him. He feels he needs to protect me and teach me. Once he comes up, I'll tell him I'm taking you downstairs to rape you."

"Rape me?" Melanie gulped.

"It was supposed to be part of his plan. Anyway, once we get downstairs, kick me or something and run out the door. Don't call the police. You'll be fine."

Melanie nodded to agree. However, Mr. Sanderson did not come back as quickly as the last time. The whole time he was gone, Jack continued to think about all the times he shared with Melanie in that room. He stroked her hair gently and smelled the unique scented perfume she always wore. He thought about all the future plans they had talked about: their house they would buy, and the kids they would bear. And for a moment he felt as though he truly loved her. *But in all these plans, substitute my face for another's and that is what we have now,* he thought. He looked at the bed. *Substitute me lying in that bed for another man, and that's what we have. Substitute everything I've given her, just for her to run behind my back with my best friend. Yes, substitute him for me. She wanted him more than me!*

At that moment, something came over Jack; something he couldn't explain or control. He grabbed Melanie and wrapped his left arm around her in a hug and squeezed tightly. Melanie let out a gasp. Melanie and Jack were pressed together so tightly that they were separated only by the twelve-inch knife held in Jack's hand, sticking straight into Melanie's heart. Jack pushed the knife deeper into her heart and she let out an even louder gasp. All the air was out of her by then, and although she tried to scream, nothing would come out. Jack stared into her green eyes, holding her helpless body against himself, and saw that they were watering up with the immense pain that was traveling through her body. It wasn't but moments later that Jack could no longer hear her desperate attempts to retrieve air and felt her pulse stop beating.

She was dead.

Tears trickled down Jack's face. *What have I done?* he thought. He stared at Melanie, the bloody mess that was left of her upper half, and he couldn't understand what could have driven him to commit an act such as this. "I thought they said love was the *greatest* mystery of all," he said to himself through tears. "What is so great about this? Why couldn't you have been faithful? Why wasn't I good enough for you?"

Jack picked her up gracefully, cradling her like a baby, and gently placed her in the center of the bed. He kissed her forehead gently before walking away from her, muttering once again, "What have I done?"

Moments later, Mr. Sanderson reentered the room. "Craig left. I guess he … Why Jackie Boy, you didn't wait for me." he said with a smile."

"I know, I … I … I … I don't know what came over me. What have I done?"

"You did exactly what you were supposed to do," Mr. Sanderson assured him. "She deserved every bit of pain that she felt. She stabbed you straight through the heart and now you've repaid the favor. She's been killed, and now it's time to take away her dignity, just as she did to you."

Jack wasn't listening. He was resting his head against the wall, filled with disbelief. How could he have actually taken someone's life away from them; especially a helpless young girl? Mr. Sanderson climbed onto the bed and began ripping apart Melanie's clothes. The knife was still in her, sticking out of her chest, but her breasts were now exposed along with the bottom half of her body. He unbuttoned his pants and pulled them down so that they were around his ankles.

When Jack saw this he turned around and yelled, "No! Don't!"

"What do you mean *don't?* We have to follow through with the plan." He kept going about his business.

"No! You're not touching her. Get the hell off!" Jack walked over to Mr. Sanderson, took the knife out of Melanie's chest, and put it to Mr. Sanderson's chest. "I'm serious."

Mr. Sanderson stared at him for a long moment. "Fine," he said. "This is your call. You deal with it the way you want to."

"Thank you," Jack said. "I'll give your knife back to you later. There's still one thing I need it for."

"All right. Make sure you don't forget the duffle bag. Keep his uniform and the mask inside it, and make the switch. You're sure you can handle this?"

"Craig's expecting me to take him to the airport. All I have to do is make the switch. It shouldn't be that hard," Jack said.

"Good luck, my son," Mr. Sanderson said, and he left the house.

Jack walked over to his wife and stared at her for a long time. He looked at her finger, to the gold wedding ring he had given her as a symbol of his commitment to her. He carefully took it off her finger and placed it on the dresser next to the bed. "Good-bye, Melanie," he whispered with eyes full of tears.

Jack quickly washed his hands and rushed out of the house and quickly drove to Craig's apartment. When he got there, Craig was getting everything ready for his trip. Jack walked in with his key and saw Craig bringing out the black duffle bag that he planned to take with him to his mother's funeral. It was the only bag Craig owned, and Jack was quite aware of that.

"Hey, Jack," he said. "Thanks for coming."

"No problem," Jack responded. "Are you about ready to go?"

"Yeah, let me just get some things out of my room. I'll be back in a minute or two, all right?"

While Craig was in the back bedroom, collecting everything he needed, Jack quickly went back outside of the front door, where he had dropped a black duffle bag; the one Mr. Sanderson had given him at Melanie's house. He picked up the bag and quickly switched the identical black duffle bag Mr. Sanderson had given him with the one Craig planned to take to Colorado. First, Jack threw Mr. Sanderson's duffle bag where Craig's had originally been, and then Jack threw Craig's bag in the trunk of his Mercedes.

When he came back to the apartment, Craig already had his bag, or Mr. Sanderson's bag, around his shoulder. "All right, I'm ready," Craig said.

The two of them got into the car. Craig held onto what he believed to be his bag the whole way to the airport. It was a short drive, no more than fifteen minutes. When they arrived, Craig thanked him for the ride, and they said their goodbyes.

"Take care," Jack said as Craig shut the door and walked away. "I'll miss you," he said under his breath.

Jack quickly sped back to Melanie's house. The mission wasn't over. Jack feared that somehow the police would still be able to link him to this murder. When he got into the house, he ran up the stairs, straight into Melanie's room. He tore down the plastic coverings that were on the walls so that there would be no explanation as to why old fingerprints would appear so new. He took them and put them into his trunk where he would dispose of them later. He had carefully left the knife under the bed and went to retrieve it. Jack looked at the knife. "Mr. Sanderson was right about one thing. This knife is definitely a beauty."

As Jack held the knife, he didn't know if he could find the courage to do what he needed to do. But, he deserved it. He did a terrible thing to a young girl, no matter what she had done to him first. He needed to punish himself, and it didn't hurt that it would secure his innocence as well. After all, who was crazy enough to kill someone and then stab himself?

He lifted the knife in the air and quickly jammed it into his left side. He let out a cry of pain at the first stab. Never before in his life had he experienced physical pain such as this. But he could take it. Three more times he stabbed himself in the exact same spot on his left side. Next, he followed with four stabs in the same place on his right side. By the time he had finished stabbing himself, he couldn't stand. Blood was pouring out of him and dripping out of his mouth. He crawled on his hands and knees to a telephone, dialed the emergency number, and waited for the police to arrive.

The officer closed the journal.

Chapter 38

No, Not My Jack

Mrs. Gardner was still lying on her bed when the doorbell rang. She was hesitant to get out of bed to answer the door. Everyone else in the house had gone back to the hospital, but it was far too painful for Mrs. Gardner to deal with any of the paperwork so she stayed home. Plus Mr. Gardner felt it was best if Mrs. Gardner had the house to herself to be alone with her thoughts. With no one home to answer it, she finally got out of bed and walked down the hall to the front door. After all, she figured it was most likely Jack and she wouldn't mind having him there to comfort her. However, when she opened the door, she received an unexpected surprise. Two police officers stood outside the door, both looking unusually anxious.

"Hello Mrs. Gardner. My name is Officer Peterson. This is Officer Denton."

Mrs. Gardner shook their hands when they offered them.

"Is this important, gentlemen? I'm sorry but I've had a very rough morning."

"I'm afraid it is, ma'am," Officer Peterson said. "Have you seen your son, Jack?"

"Jack? Why?" Mrs. Gardner was alarmed. "Is he okay?"

"Mrs. Gardner, I'm not sure how to say this … But your son … he … well … we think he was involved in a murder."

"Yes, I know. He was almost killed by Craig Sanderson."

"No, ma'am," Officer Peterson said. "He wasn't stabbed by Craig Sanderson."

"I saw the marks. He still has the scars!"

"Yes, but they didn't come from Craig Sanderson. He gave himself those scars, Mrs. Gardner."

"What are you talking about?"

"Mrs. Gardner, were you aware that Jack kept a journal?"

"Yes. He used to write in that thing all the time. Why?"

"Well, somehow we came across it … Mrs. Gardner … in the journal … he … he admits to the murder of Melanie. He explains how he did it."

"What?" Mrs. Gardner gasped. "What are you talking about?"

"Your son killed his wife!"

"My Jack? My Jack would never do that!" Mrs. Gardner looked terrified and in complete disbelief.

"Mrs. Gardner, we don't have much time to talk. Do you know where your son is?"

"Let me see the notebook!" she demanded. "It's probably not even his. Just let me see it! Now!"

"Mrs. Gardner!" Denton said. "We believe your son may be dangerous. We think he might be with his current wife right now. We think she's in serious danger. Please tell me where your son is!"

"Show me the notebook first!" she demanded once more.

"I'm afraid we need to keep that in police custody," Officer Peterson said.

"I don't know where he is," Mrs. Gardner said defensively. "Even if I did, I wouldn't tell you. My Jack would never do something like that. You gentlemen have no idea what you're talking about. I have nothing more to say to you, so if you don't mind, please leave."

The officers didn't say a word but rushed back into their car and drove off.

"Well, Denton," Officer Peterson asked as he drove. "Is there anyone else you can think to ask?"

"There's one person. She'll be sure to know where he is. I'm not sure she will answer her cell phone though. We don't speak often, but it's worth a try."

Mrs. Gardner shut the door and went straight back to her room. She knew her son couldn't have possibly done what those officers claimed he did, but still she had to see. She went straight to the phone and dialed the number she found in the directory—the number for the house of Joseph West.

"Hello," West answered.

"Hi, is this Joseph West?" Mrs. Gardner asked.

"It is. Who is calling?"

"You worked on the Melanie Gardner case, is that correct?"

"I did. Who wants to know?"

"I'm Jack Gardner's mother. I'm not sure if you are familiar with him."

"Of course I remember Jack."

"Yes, well he often talked about how dedicated you were to the case and, I was hoping you might be able to share any of the case information you might have with me."

"That case was already solved. Mr. Sanderson killed that poor girl. What would you possibly want with the files?"

"Meet me somewhere. I'll tell you why I want to see them and you can decide for yourself whether to show me or not. Deal?"

* * * * * * * * * * * *

Whether it was pure curiosity or something deeper, West decided to meet Mrs. Gardner and see what she could possibly want with the files he had collected. He told her to meet him at the café on Market Street, the same café where he had met with Officer Denton on several occasions.

When Mrs. Gardner arrived at the café, she didn't know exactly who to look for. She had forgotten to ask West what he looked like or what he would be wearing to identify him. However, she saw a lanky, slightly gangly man sitting at one of the tables. He had wavy brown hair and was holding files, so Mrs. Gardner figured the chances were that it was Joseph West. Mrs. Gardner walked up to him. "Excuse me, are you?"

"Yes, I am, Mrs. Gardner. Please, have a seat."

Mrs. Gardner sat down on the chair across from him. "You look so much like your son," he said.

"Forgive me if I'm not friendly, but I've had an awful day that just keeps getting worse."

"I am sorry to hear that. What is wrong?" he asked. He once again had coffee by his hand, but did not take a sip of it.

"I can't even say the first thing that happened, and the second I don't care to think about either. But I feel it's the only way you will let me have a look at those papers."

"So, tell me how I can help?" West insisted.

"The police showed up at my door about a half hour ago—an Officer Peterson and Officer Denton. Do you know either of them?"

"Officer Denton. Yeah, I know the guy. He helped me solve the Melanie Gardner case. We became pretty good friends. What did they want?"

Mrs. Gardner hesitated. "They told me that … that my son killed Melanie. That he killed his wife."

Joseph West's eyes lit up. "Jack killed her. But all the evidence … it showed Mr. Sanderson did it."

"Jack didn't kill anyone!" Mrs. Gardner cried. "Please, just let me see the files. Please!"

"Just tell me one more thing," West commanded. "Are they looking for Jack now? Have they found him yet?"

"I told you he didn't do it!" It was as though Mrs. Gardner was trying to convince West, but he wasn't buying it.

"I know. Just tell me if they're looking for him."

"Yes, they are. Happy?"

Joseph West slid the file folder across the table to Mrs. Gardner. She frantically searched through the many papers in the file, but nothing jumped out at her; nothing until she stopped upon coming across the autopsy report of Melanie Gardner. She had never looked at it before, and actually didn't know much about how Melanie died; only that she was stabbed. Mrs. Gardner read that she was stabbed, straight through the heart. She moved on until she came across the police report of that night. She read the description of Jack Gardner's wounds.

As she read about her son, she couldn't believe what she was seeing. "Oh, my God," she gasped, placing a hand over her mouth in horror. While reading the report, she saw that it stated Jack Gardner was stabbed in both sides four times each. "I can't believe it," she said with horror as her voice shook uncontrollably.

"What is it?" West asked impatiently. "Tell me!"

"OCD," was the only word she muttered before getting up from the table and driving back to her house.

West immediately called up Travis Denton and asked if they had found Jack Gardner yet. Denton told him that they had, and to meet him down at Dillon's Beach.

West didn't know how they found Jack, but that didn't matter. He had to get down to Dillon's Beach. He had to see how it ended.

Mrs. Gardner rushed into her car and sped all the way home, tears flowing down her eyes. When she got home she rushed into the garage.

She took the razor blade out of Mr. Gardner's tool belt, and took it into her bedroom. She did not lie on the bed this time. Instead, she stared straight into the mirror at herself. She took the razor blade out and placed the blade on her bicep, before dragging it down her forearm, all the way down to the middle of her wrist.

She looked at herself in the mirror one last time and whispered, "This time, I'm going to be the selfish one."

Chapter 39

One Final Stroll Down Dillon's Beach

Jack Gardner and his wife Brianne were strolling along the beach before the police officers arrived. Brianne had just gotten an unpleasant phone call but didn't want to tell Jack what it was about.

She was holding a baby carrier in which little Michael was sleeping. They went up to the large rocks which led into the cave where they had once made love on a rainy day. They climbed up to the flat area and Brianne set the baby carrier on the rocky ground next to them. She was extra careful to make sure the baby was not in any danger of falling off the ledge, but the flat area was about twenty feet by twenty feet so she wasn't too concerned even though it was fifteen feet in the air.

"Just tell me who called," Jack said. "It wasn't the police was it?"

"All right, fine!" Brianne finally gave in.

"So it was the police?"

"Well, kind of."

"Who was it?" Jack said.

"Travis Denton…my cousin," Brianne replied.

"Your cousin? What the hell do you mean your cousin?"

"My cousin…Travis…didn't you know that? Didn't you see him at the wedding?"

"Yeah, but he was in his police uniform," Jack said. "…I thought he was…he never told me…why didn't you ever tell me you had a cousin who was a police officer?"

"I didn't?" Brianne said. "We really were not very close. I used to see him when we were kids, but our families grew apart. I think our parents argued about many things. We just stopped seeing each other years ago."

"What did he call for?" Jack asked.

"I don't know. He was talking crazy. He said to stay away from you. That you were dangerous or something."

"Dangerous?" Jack was more alarmed than ever. "Why would he think I'm dangerous?"

"I don't know. It's nothing to worry about. I hung up on him and told him I didn't want to talk to him anymore." Brianne was now kneeling down and playing with Michael who had just awakened and was crying for his bottle.

"Oh, all right. Are you sure there's nothing to worry about?" Jack asked.

"Yeah, I told you, he was just talking crazy. He kept saying something about finding some journal. Do you know what he's talking about?"

Jack's eyes grew wide and his knees buckled. He felt his heart beat so loudly he thought it would jump out of his chest, and the inclination to vomit was overwhelming. "You said a *journal?*" Jack asked.

"Yeah. He said he found some journal on the beach. I had no idea what he was even talking about."

Jack began pacing back and forth quickly along the rock ledge, biting his nails intensely.

"Anyway, enough about my cousin," Brianne said. "There's a reason I agreed to come to the beach with you today. I wanted to tell you something."

Jack wasn't listening however. He was still pacing back and forth, not sure whether to come clean to Brianne or not. *She's going to find out anyway,* he thought. *I would rather her hear it from me than from the police.*

"Jack," Brianne said with a smile. "I'm pregnant. We're going to have another child!"

"What?" Jack said, stopping dead in his tracks and turning his head to Brianne. "You're what?"

"It's going to be a girl, Jack. I just know it. I'm going to name her Michelle. Michael and Michelle." Brianne ran over and gave Jack a huge hug.

Jack couldn't believe it. Another one of his children was coming into this world, yet he knew that he was leaving it, at least the civilized world.

"Brianne, I need to talk to you," Jack said.

"What is it?"

"First, I want you to know that I love you." Jack sat down next to Michael and Brianne followed him. They all sat on the rock overlooking the ocean and Jack knew it was the time.

"Brianne, the case I was involved in … it wasn't a robbery case. It was a murder case. My ex- wife was murdered."

"Jack, stop," Brianne said, rubbing Jack's back to comfort him. She could tell that this was clearly a touchy subject with him. "I know all about the case," she admitted.

"What? You do? How?"

"Jack I knew you were married. You never talked about your ex-wife once. Don't you think I wondered what happened to her? Plus my cousin is a police officer. He called and told me about the murder when he found out we had started seeing each other."

"So why didn't you ever tell me that you knew?"

"I could tell you didn't want me to know," Brianne said. "I was just waiting until you wanted to come out and tell me."

As Brianne spoke, Jack saw someone running towards them in the distance. "Who is that?" Jack asked.

"You've got to be kidding," Brianne said. "That's Travis now. I told him not to come here!"

"Brianne, we don't have much time," Jack said with a panicked look on his face. He placed his hands on her shoulders and looked her straight in the eyes. "I want to tell you everything."

"What do you mean? Tell me what?"

"I killed my ex-wife Melanie," Jack exclaimed.

Brianne didn't say anything. She stared at Jack in disbelief. "No," she said. "You didn't! You couldn't have!"

"I made a mistake. I thought I was in love back then. I didn't want to kill her. I was driven by what I thought was love. She was cheating on me. It drove me crazy. I've regretted it every day since it happened. With you I was finally able to move on. Thank you for everything you've given me. You've taught me what love really is."

"What's happening, Jack? Why does it seem like you're saying goodbye to me."

"Your cousin is going to arrest me, Brianne." Jack looked to the distance. Denton was now much closer.

"You have to run, Jack! Right now!" Brianne screamed. "I'll take care of him. Just go!"

"I can't run. That won't solve anything."

"It'll keep our family together. I'll meet up with you somewhere. We can still be happy together."

Jack didn't respond. He simply wrapped his arms around her in a big hug.

Brianne was screaming frantically. "We have a family, Jack! Me, you, Michael, Michelle. We can still have a life together if we run!"

"I love you, Brianne. I don't want that life for you."

"Jack, please!" Brianne begged him one final time, but Jack would not run. Little Michael was now crying loudly, but neither of them could pay attention to him at this point.

Denton was within one hundred yards, and Jack could see an overweight man waddling slowly after them in the far distance. He presumed this was Chief Peterson.

* * * * * * * * * * * *

As Denton ran at full speed towards Brianne and Jack, what he saw frightened him more than ever. He saw Jack Gardner, with his arms tightly around his cousin. They were standing close enough to the edge of the high rock, with only the ocean below them. He saw Brianne pushing Jack away, but Jack would not let her go. He kept pulling her to him and wrapping her up in his arms. "He's going to kill her!" Denton cried out.

He ran as fast as he could towards the base of the rocks, and Jack saw him coming. Just as Jack turned to raise his hands in surrender, right when Denton was in range, the officer pulled out his gun and fired a round right into Jack's chest.

Jack let out an empty gasp for air. The shot threw him backwards and he stumbled off the side of the rock, onto the sandy surface of Dillon's Beach.

"Travis no!" Brianne cried. She ran to the side edge of the rocks and looked below to where Jack laid helpless in the sand, moving back in forth in agony.

Denton ran up the rocks to where Brianne was standing. "Are you all right, Brianne?"

"What the hell have you done?" Brianne screamed at him. She was crying hysterically, with tears pouring down her eyes.

She ran down the side of the rocks to where Jack was lying. "Jack! Please tell me you're okay. Please!" Tears were falling off her cheeks and onto Jack's face as she knelt down beside him and held his head in her hands.

Jack did not speak; he couldn't. The pain was like nothing he ever could have imagined. He looked up from his back, up to the rocks above, and pictured his son Michael. Then Jack realized the pain of leaving him fatherless and Brianne husbandless was far greater than any pain caused by the bullet.

Jack mustered up all the strength he had to speak to Brianne one last time. "Brianne," he whispered coughing up blood.

"Yes, Jack?"

It was extremely difficult for Jack to look Brianne in her watery eyes, but he knew he had to do it. "I love you ... Please don't tell Michael ... I don't want him to know ... Tell him about the man I really was ... The man you knew and loved ..."

Jack's eyes rolled back into his head and his eyelids shut. His head fell back helplessly in Brianne's hands and she let it fall gently into the sand. She placed her head against his chest and let out a scream when there was no longer a beat.

She got up from her knees. By now, Denton was standing right behind her. Chief Peterson had now arrived, out of breath from all of the running, and even Joseph West made his appearance seconds later.

Brianne looked Denton in the eye in disbelief and shook her head. "Why the hell did you shoot him?" she cried hysterically.

"He was going to hurt you," Denton said. "He was about to throw you off the ledge. He's a killer, Brianne!"

"He wasn't going to hurt me!" Brianne cried. "He loved me and I loved him. He was turning himself in!" Brianne ran past the officers and past Joseph West. She ran up the rocks and across them, picking up little Michael and running down sandy Dillon's Beach. She never looked back.

"You did the right thing," Chief Peterson said to Denton as they stood next to Jack's dead body. "Who knows what he would have done to that poor girl?"

Denton nodded, but he didn't know if he was in complete agreement. Maybe he shot too early. Maybe Jack really was going to turn himself in. Maybe he wouldn't have hurt her.

"It's just one of those unfortunate consequences of being a police officer. Take the bad in with the good, Denton," Chief Peterson advised him. "Trust me, there will be plenty of good."

Joseph West had not said much during the whole ordeal. He sat there with his arms folded, not saying a word. It seemed as though since he worked so hard on the case for so long, he just wanted to make sure he was there when every bit of it was solved.

"That whole time, the testimony, all the evidence, everything Jack said, it was all a lie," West said.

The officers simply nodded their heads.

"He never saw any tattoo on a killer's arm," West laughed. "No anything."

"Didn't you say you were going to tell me something, sir?" Denton asked Chief Peterson.

"Ah, yes. Ironically we found out similar information at the same time."

"You knew Jack did it also?" West asked.

"Well, I didn't know for sure. But things weren't looking good for him. In questioning Mr. Sanderson we were able to find some incriminating evidence against him."

"You know what doesn't make any sense?" Denton blurted out, breaking the silence. "When I showed up on the scene, the night of the murder, Jack Gardner had stabbed himself."

"Yeah, so," West finally chimed in.

"Well, when I found him bleeding to death, there was no knife to be seen. He claimed the killer had gone off with it. Yet, it wasn't in the bag that the police found on Craig Sanderson. In the journal he doesn't even explain it. What happened to the knife? Where did Jack Gardner hide it?"

Everyone looked around at each other, but no one had an answer.

An hour later they all traveled to Melanie Gardner's old house to search for the last piece of the puzzle. The house hadn't been put up for sale yet and was relatively untouched since the night of her death.

Under the bed in the guestroom, crammed into a tight area barely visible where the springs met the base, was the unique knife that they had been looking for, with its spiraled handle, its long blade, and its jagged edge. The blood on the knife was dry, but still apparent on its long shaft. It wasn't the blood of just one; however, it was the mix of blood between Melanie and Jack Gardner; the mix of these two people, which caused innocent lives to be slain and relationships to be destroyed.

A note was attached to the knife. It read:

To whoever finds this note,

You may or may not know the history behind this knife. You may not know the story of Melanie Gardner and the terrible events that happened leading up to and causing her death. You may or may not know who killed her and why she died. I'm sure the story will be changed gradually with time, and eventually told as something it is not. Although I'm sure you don't know who I am, please know that I am in no way a murderer. For what I have done was not committed with malice at the individual herself, but rather with remorse that it was a deed that had to be done. I was in no clear state of mind when I committed this act, and I know that I will regret it every day of my life. They say love is the greatest mystery of all, but they do not know. For nothing is great which can cause us to go insane ... insane enough to kill ...

ABOUT THE AUTHOR

Malice and Remorse is Zachary Gard's first novel. As a child, Zach was described as a "mystery man." *Malice and Remorse* shares Zach's creativity with all.

A graduate of California State University–Chico, Zach resides in the Bay Area. He's an accountant and spends free time writing suspense novels.